PRAISE FOR *DAWN GIRL*

"Terrific story about a young female FBI agent who must battle her own demons in search of a monster who is killing young women."

"This was a great novel, it built up to a heart pounding pace that continued to increase in the last quarter of the book."

"Not only was the story line exceptional, it was so descriptive that you could picture what you were reading, as if you were watching it on television or in the movies."

"I truly found this book to be one of the best thrillers I have ever read."

"This is an interesting story about murder and a dysfunctional family. The characters are interesting, believable and well developed."

PRAISE FOR LESLIE WOLFE

"Leslie Wolfe has the talent that is comparable to the likes of a Tom Clancy or a Michael Crichton, or even James Patterson."

"Leslie Wolfe has a wonderful ability to make you feel as if you were right there watching the events unfold in this fast paced and nail-biting thriller."

"Leslie Wolfe knows how to blend advanced technological data with powerfully written human behavior responses and the result is a novel that few will want to put down once the story begins."

DAWN GIRL

BOOKS BY LESLIE WOLFE

TESS WINNETT SERIES

Dawn Girl
The Watson Girl
Glimpse of Death
Taker of Lives
Not Really Dead
Girl With A Rose
Mile High Death
The Girl They Took
The Girl Hunter

STANDALONE TITLES

The Surgeon
The Girl You Killed
Stories Untold
Love, Lies and Murder

DETECTIVE KAY SHARP SERIES

The Girl From Silent Lake
Beneath Blackwater River
The Angel Creek Girls
The Girl on Wildfire Ridge
Missing Girl at Frozen Falls

BAXTER & HOLT SERIES

Las Vegas Girl
Casino Girl
Las Vegas Crime

ALEX HOFFMANN SERIES

Executive
Devil's Move
The Backup Asset
The Ghost Pattern
Operation Sunset

For the complete list of books in all available formats, visit:

Amazon.com/LeslieWolfe

DAWN GIRL

LESLIE WOLFE

ITALICS PUBLISHING

$\mathllap{\textit{II}}$ ITALICS

Italics Publishing Inc.
Edited by Joni Wilson
Cover and interior design by Sam Roman
ISBN: 978-1-945302-60-2

1

READY

She made an effort to open her eyes, compelling her heavy eyelids to obey. She swallowed hard, her throat raw and dry, as she urged the wave of nausea to subside. Dizzy and confused, she struggled to gain awareness. Where was she? She felt numb and shaky, unable to move, as if awakening from a deep sleep or a coma. She tried to move her arms, but couldn't. Something kept her immobilized, but didn't hurt her. Or maybe she couldn't feel the pain, not anymore.

Her eyes started to adjust to the darkness, enough to distinguish the man moving quietly in the room. His silhouette flooded her foggy brain with a wave of memories. She gasped, feeling her throat constrict and burning tears rolling down her swollen cheeks.

Her increased awareness sent waves of adrenaline through her body, and she tried desperately to free herself from her restraints. With each useless effort, she panted harder, gasping for air, forcing it into her lungs. Fear put a strong chokehold on her throat and was gaining ground, as she rattled her restraints helplessly, growing weaker with every second. She felt a wave of darkness engulf her, this time the darkness coming from within her weary brain. She fought against that darkness, and battled her own betraying body.

The noises she made got the man's attention.

"I see you're awake. Excellent," the man said, without turning.

She watched him place a syringe on a small, metallic tray. Its handle clinked, followed by another sound, this time the raspy, telling sound of a file cutting through the neck of a glass vial. Then a pop when the man opened the vial. He grabbed the syringe and loaded the liquid from the vial, then carefully removed any air, pushing the piston until several droplets of fluid came out.

Dizziness overtook her, and she closed her eyes for a second.

"Shit," the man mumbled, then opened a drawer and went through it in a hurry.

She felt the needle poke deeply in her thigh, like it was happening to another person. She felt it, but distantly. She perceived a subdued burning sensation where he pushed the fluid into her muscle, then that went away when he pulled the needle out. She closed her weary eyes again, listless against her restraints.

The man cracked open ammonia salts under her nose, and she bounced back into reality at the speed of a lightning strike, aware, alert, and angry. For a second she fought to free herself, but froze when her eyes focused on the man in front of her.

He held a scalpel, close to her face. In itself, the small, shiny, silver object was capable of bringing formidable healing, as well as immense pain. The difference stood in the hand wielding it. She knew no healing was coming her way; only pain.

"No, no, please…" she pleaded, tears falling freely from her puffy eyes, burning as they rolled down her cheeks. "Please, no. I… I'll do anything."

"I am ready," the man said. He seemed calm, composed, and dispassionate. "Are you ready?"

"No, no, please…" she whimpered.

"Yeah," he said softly, almost whispering, inches away from her face. "Please say no to me. I love that."

She fell quiet, scared out of her mind. This time was different. *He* was different.

2

DAWN

"What if we get caught?" the girl whispered, trailing behind the boy.

They walked briskly on the small residential street engulfed in darkness, keeping to the middle of the road. There were no sidewalks. High-end homes lined up both sides, most likely equipped with sensor floodlights they didn't want to trip.

She tugged at his hand, but he didn't stop. "You never care about these things, Carl, but I do. If we get caught, I'll be grounded, like, forever!"

The boy kept going, his hand firmly clasping hers.

"Carl!" she raised the pitch in her whisper, letting her anxiety show more.

He stopped and turned, facing her. He frowned a little, seeing her anguish, but then smiled and caressed a loose strand of hair rebelling from under her sweatshirt's hood.

"There's no one, Kris. No one's going to see us. See? No lights are on, nothing. Everyone's asleep. Zee-zee-zee. It's five in the morning."

"I know," she sighed, "but—"

He kissed her pouted lips gently, a little boyish hesitation and awkwardness in his move.

"We'll be okay, I promise," he said, then grabbed her hand again. "We're almost there, come on. You'll love it."

A few more steps and the small street ended into the paved parking lot of what was going to be a future development of sorts, maybe a shopping center. From there, they had to cross

Highway 1. They crouched down near the road, waiting for the light traffic to be completely clear. They couldn't afford to be seen, not even from a distance. At the right moment, they crossed the highway, hand in hand, and cut across the field toward the beach. Crossing Ocean Drive was next, then cutting through a few yards of shrubbery and trees to get to the sandy beach.

"Jeez, Carl," Kris protested, stopping in her tracks at the tree line. "Who knows what creatures live here? There could be snakes. Lizards. Gah…"

"There could be, but there aren't," Carl replied, seemingly sure of himself. "Trust me."

She held her breath and lowered her head, then clasped Carl's hand tightly. He turned on the flashlight on his phone and led the way without hesitation. A few seconds later, they reached the beach, and Kris let out a tense, long breath.

The light of the waning gibbous Moon reflected against the calm ocean waves, sending flickers of light everywhere and covering the beach in silver shadows. They were completely alone. The only creatures keeping them company were pale crabs that took bellicose stances when Kris and Carl stomped the sand around them, giggling.

"See? Told you," Carl said, "no one's going to see us out here. We can do whatever we want," he said playfully.

Kris squealed and ran toward the lifeguard tower. In daylight, the tower showed its bright yellow and orange, a splash of joyful colors on the tourist-abundant stretch of sand. At night, the structure appeared gloomy, resembling a menacing creature on tall, insect-like legs.

"It looks like one of those aliens from *War of the Worlds*," Kris said, then promptly started running, waving her arms up in the air, pretending she was flying.

Carl chased Kris, laughing and squealing with her, running in circles around the tower, and weaving footstep patterns between the solid wood posts.

"Phew," Carl said, stopping his chase and taking some distance. "Stinks of piss. Let's get out of here."

"Eww…" Kris replied, following him. "Why do men do that?"

"What? Pee?"

"Everybody pees, genius," Kris replied, still panting from the run. "Peeing where it stinks and bothers people, that's what I meant. Women pee in the bushes. Men should pee in the water if they don't like the bushes."

"Really? That's gross."

"Where do you think fish pee? At least the waves would wash away the pee and it wouldn't stink, to mess up our sunrise."

"Fish pee?" Carl pushed back, incredulous.

"They don't?"

They walked holding hands, putting a few more yards of distance between them and the tower. Then Carl suddenly dropped to the ground, dragging Kris with him. She squealed again, and laughed.

"Let's sit here," he said. "The show's on. Let's see if we get a good one."

The sky was starting to light up toward the east. They watched silently, hand in hand, as the dark shades of blue and gray gradually turned ablaze, mixing in dark reds and orange hues. The horizon line was clear, a sharp edge marking where ocean met sky.

"It's going to be great," Carl said. "No clouds, no haze." He kissed her lips quickly, and then turned his attention back to the celestial lightshow.

"You're a strange boy, Carl."

"Yeah? Why?"

"Other boys would have asked me to sneak out in the middle of the night to make out. With you, it's a sunrise, period. Should I worry?"

Carl smiled widely, then tickled Kris until she begged for mercy between gasps of air and bouts of uncontrollable laughter.

"Stop! Stop it already. I can't breathe!"

"I might want to get on with that make out, you know," Carl laughed.

"Nah, it's getting light. Someone could see us," Kris pushed back, unconvinced. "Someone could come by."

Carl shrugged and turned his attention to the sunrise. He grabbed her hand and held it gently, playing with her fingers.

Almost half the sky had caught fire, challenging the moonlight, and obliterating most of its reflected light against the blissful, serene, ocean waves.

Carl checked the time on his phone.

"A few more minutes until it comes out," he announced, sounding serious, as if predicting a rare and significant event. He took a few pictures of the sky, then suddenly snapped one of Kris.

"Ah... no," she reacted, "give that to me right this second, Carl." She grabbed the phone from his hand and looked at the picture he'd taken. The image showed a young girl with messy, golden brown hair, partially covering a scrunched, tense face with deep ridges on her brow. The snapshot revealed Kris biting her index fingernail, totally absorbed by the process, slobbering her sleeve cuff while at it.

"God-awful," she reacted, then pressed the option to delete.

"No!" Carl said, pulling the phone from her hands. "I like it!"

"There's nothing to like. There," she said, relaxing a little, and arranging her hair briefly with her long, thin fingers. "I'll pose for you." She smiled.

Carl took a few pictures. She looked gorgeous, against the backdrop of fiery skies, pink sand, and turquoise water. He took image after image, as she got into it and made faces, danced, and swirled in front of him, laughing.

The sun's first piercing ray shot out of the sea, just as Kris shrieked, a blood-curdling scream that got Carl to spring to his feet and run to her.

Speechless, Kris pointed a trembling hand at the lifeguard tower. Underneath the tower, between the wooden posts supporting the elevated structure, was the naked body of a young woman. She appeared to be kneeling, as if praying to the rising sun. Her hands were clasped together in front of her in the universal, unmistakable gesture of silent pleading.

Holding their breaths, they approached carefully, curious and yet afraid of what they stood to discover. The growing light of the new morning revealed more details with each step they took. Her back, covered in bruises and small cuts, stained in smudged, dried blood. Her blue eyes wide open, glossed over. A few specks of sand clung to her long, dark lashes. Her beautiful face, immobile, covered in sparkling flecks of sand. Her lips slightly parted, as if to let a last breath escape. Long, blonde hair, wet from sea spray, almost managed to disguise the deep cut in her neck.

No blood dripped from the wound; her heart had stopped beating for some time. Yet she held upright, unyielding in her praying posture, her knees stuck firmly in the sand covered in their footprints, and her eyes fixed on the beautiful sunrise they came to enjoy.

3

CRIME SCENE

Detective Gary Michowsky cussed under his breath, as he pushed open the door of the Palm Beach marked Crown Vic. He bit his lip and tensed his weary muscles, preparing for the sharp pain that was going to shoot through his back the second he put his feet on the ground and tried to get out of the car. If he'd been deemed worthy of one of the new Ford SUVs deployed to police all over the state, maybe he'd have less trouble getting in and out of his vehicle. But no, not him, not yet anyway.

He waited for his partner, Todd Fradella, to get out of the car first. He didn't want a single whiff of his sciatica attack to make scuttlebutt in the squad room. Last thing he needed was a slew of stupid jokes perpetrated by smart-ass detectives and uniformed pricks, targeting his age, his ability to do his job, and most of all his self-esteem. He wasn't that old; only 49. A few months short of the big five-oh. No age reason for the sciatica attack, other than, of course, lifting weights without a belt, thinking he was still 20. The daily proximity of his young partner, Fradella, with his bohemian good looks, his shoulder-length hair, and endless supply of calls from hot chicks, didn't help a bit. He felt compelled to compete, to hold on to whatever youth he still had running though his veins.

Yeah, so for a few days he was screwed, having to work in excruciating pain, despite the painkillers he popped every couple of hours. He couldn't take time off, not with the new case landing in their backyard. The captain would raise at least one of his eyebrows if he even asked.

Fradella hopped out of the cruiser with enviable, youthful agility, and slammed the car door behind him. The shockwave sent a quick, sharp blade of pain to Michowsky's back, a reminder he had to take it easy. He grunted, then discreetly grabbed hold of the door frame with his left hand, using it as leverage to pull himself out of the cruiser. A couple of terrible seconds later, he was on his way to the cordoned area, walking with his back almost straight, even if he moved a little slower than usual.

The lifeguard tower was already surrounded by yellow police line on improvised stakes stuck in the sand. The first respondent team had been fast, doing their jobs at securing the scene. Michowsky stopped at the line, hesitant. Bending to go under the line as he usually did was out of the question. He decided to go around it, seeing that the line didn't extend all the way into the water. He walked as quickly as he could and managed to go around the line just as the coroner's van pulled in, its wheels half-buried into the soft sand.

He reached the lifeguard tower and caught the first clear view of the victim. He almost gasped. The victim's posturing was shocking, making her appear alive. Completely naked, she was kneeled on the sand, slightly bent forward, but her back was straight and her head upright. She was strikingly beautiful, even in death. He shook his head bitterly. Sometimes his job made him sick, disgusted with life, with the monsters of mankind.

"What do we have?" he asked, remaining a few feet away from the body.

A uniformed officer approached, his notepad open in his hand.

"Call came in at 6:48AM. Those two kids over there found her." He pointed at a boy and a girl sitting on the sand next to the cordoned area, hunched closely to each other, their shoulders touching. The girl cried quietly. "Carl Collunga, 16, and Kristen Bowers, also 16. You see that point over there, in the sea oats, marked with evidence tag 7? She threw up over there, the girl, Kristen. A couple of times. She was quite upset."

"I see. Parents notified yet?"

"Oh, yeah," the uniformed officer replied. "They're on their way."

"What did the kids say?" Fradella asked.

"They said they came to watch the sunrise and found the body there. Nothing else."

"Sunrise, huh?" Michowsky snorted.

"Yeah..." the officer laughed. "Some date they had, these two."

"Background on these kids?" Michowsky asked, leaning against one of the wooden posts supporting the tower.

"Well-off families, local, no records, all clear. They snuck out; they're going to get some heat for that when the parents get here."

"I bet. How about her?" Michowsky asked, pointing at the body. "Any ID?"

"There's nothing visible."

"We're not concerned with footprints, I guess," Michowsky muttered, looking at the footprint-covered sand. He watched for a few seconds how the ocean breeze carried specks of sand to and from their crime scene, eroding, altering everything. Nature was the perfect forensic countermeasure, especially there, on the beach. "It's pointless. This bastard is smart... We can't pull any evidence from here. This is a body dump, anyway. There's no blood. But we'll have to dig under the body, just to make sure. Collect some of that sand."

He approached the victim slowly, studying, observing details.

"Ah..." he said, pointing at the girl's hands.

"Yeah," Fradella replied. "I didn't see that either, not at first anyway."

Her hands were bound together with fine, transparent fishing line, almost invisible, holding her palms together in a prayer-like stance. From the line that tied her hands together, another line ran upward, tied against the wooden structure, holding her hands in place, and making sure her posture didn't slip. The son of a bitch had put up a show for them.

Michowsky put on a glove, then touched the fishing line. It was taut and resistant. He pressed a little more, but the hands refused to move. Something else must have kept them in place.

"Let's see if there's more," Michowsky said, squinting to see if other ties supported the body. "Check her head. It's too upright to be natural."

"I'm not touching her until Doc Rizza gets here," Fradella replied.

"Smart choice," Doc Rizza said, appearing behind the yellow line. He approached them, followed closely by his two assistants, carrying the usual piles of gear. "Let's set up here," he added, pointing to an area near the tower.

His first assistant, a young man they all called AJ, set down the stretcher and prepared the body bag, unzipping it. Then he opened a case and handed Doc Rizza the liver temperature probe.

Doc Rizza grabbed the probe, not taking his eyes off the young girl's body. With his gloved hand, he gently examined her fingertips, then invited with a gesture the crime scene technician, Javier Perez, to come and scan her fingerprints. Then the coroner pulled back gently a few strands of her long, blonde hair, exposing a deep incision in the left side of her neck.

Michowsky liked to watch Doc Rizza work. He was old style, respectful and meticulous, taking his time, not constantly obsessing over stats and numbers and reports. He was trustworthy; he cared.

"I got preliminary cause of death for you," Doc Rizza announced.

"Shoot," Michowsky said, ready to take notes.

"I'll go with exsanguination, due to sharp force trauma to the neck. For now. You know the rule. Don't quote me on anything until I finish my report."

"Murder weapon? Any hints?"

"I'll have to take molds... most likely a scalpel. No hesitation marks. He's done this before."

Doc Rizza ran his gloved hand through his thinning hair, wiping the sweat beading on his shiny scalp, then stopped and stared at his hand for a split second. "Smart... really smart..." he muttered. He removed the contaminated glove and threw it in the waste bag, then put on a new, sterile glove.

"She's not in the system," Javier announced, putting the fingerprint scanner away and grabbing the high-resolution camera. "I'll start with the photos."

"Not yet," Doc Rizza replied. "Give us a minute." He searched for additional fishing line ties and found a few more. They were difficult to see in the shade under the tower structure.

Her head was held in place by a line tied below her jaw and another looped around her forehead, hidden in her hair. Her shoulders were suspended as well, with the line loops also covered by carefully positioned strands of hair.

"I would have expected more ligature points," Doc Rizza said, moving away to make room for Javier's camera. "What else do you need? Oh, yeah, time of death." He checked the probe and frowned. "Preliminary TOD is between 12 and 16 hours ago, maybe more."

"Then she was brought here hours after she died," Michowsky said. "This beach is populated until 9:00, even 10:00PM every night."

"Yeah. It opens up the distance to your primary crime scene, sorry about that," Doc Rizza confirmed. "She could have been killed miles away." He turned to Javier. "You done yet? Help me cut her down."

AJ approached on the other side, supporting the girl's body, and Javier handed him the tools he asked for in a quiet, professional voice. He cut the fishing lines one by one, but the body maintained most of its posture.

"Are you sure you got all of them?" Michowsky asked.

"Yeah," Doc Rizza replied. "It's just rigor. Confirms my TOD estimate. Most likely she was brought here with rigor already set."

Michowsky turned away, leaving Doc Rizza and his techs to finish up. He walked around the police line to the two kids huddled together a few yards away and beckoned Fradella to join him.

When they got near, the two teenagers raised their heads and looked at them without saying a word.

"I'm Detective Michowsky, this is Detective Fradella. I understand you two found the body?"

"Y—yes," the kid replied. "I'm Carl, and this is Kris."

"And that's it? You just found the body?" Michowsky asked. "You didn't see anyone, hear anything?"

"We didn't. I swear," the boy replied a little too fast, triggering Michowsky's curiosity. Was he hiding something? Most likely nothing more than some understandable anxiety.

"What were you two doing here, anyway?"

"Watching the sunrise. Nothing else, really," the boy replied. "Who was she?"

"We don't know yet. If you remember anything else, please give me a call." Michowsky extended his business card. Kris reached out to take it.

"Can we please go home now? Please?" she asked in a subdued voice. "We—we didn't tell anyone we were going out. My parents will—"

"Don't worry, they're on their way. We called them already."

Kris started crying. "Why? We didn't do anything!"

"Don't go anywhere, you hear?" Fradella asked.

They walked slowly toward Doc Rizza's van, slowly enough for Michowsky to be comfortable.

"God, I need some coffee," Michowsky said, rubbing his chin forcefully. "I need to zap my brain with something."

"What do you think?"

"About the kids? I think they're more scared of their parents than of the entire situation."

"No, about this case. I've never seen anything like it. Do you think it's a religious freak?"

"It's hard to say. Sure looks like a ritualistic kill to me. All the posturing, how carefully he made sure she was going to stay in place until she was found, and the sick bastard wanted her found. He wanted a show."

"Speaking of shows, we got circus," Fradella said, pointing at two media vans pulling onto the beach. "Who the hell called them?"

From a few yards away, Michowsky and Fradella watched Doc Rizza threaten a bunch of reporters, unyielding until they'd backed their vans away at least 50 more feet. Then Rizza directed a couple of uniforms to put up another police line, pushing the gawkers farther out and cutting their access to the two kids.

"We need to get her ID confirmed, on the double," Michowsky said.

Fradella nodded, jotting something on his pad. "Run missing persons?"

"To start," Michowsky confirmed. "Maybe she's been gone long enough to be in the system. Someone must have missed her."

"Uh-huh," Fradella replied. "Do you think it's the work of a serial killer? I mean, look... the ritual, the posture, the balls on this guy to bring her here, God knows from where."

Fradella, like most young people, immediately jumped to extreme conclusions. Yet this time, Michowsky couldn't find an immediate fault to his logic other than the body count. Only one victim didn't make a serial killer.

"We need three victims to call it a serial. For now, all I know is that we need help. This," he said, extending his hand toward the tower, "this is much more than we normally deal with. I don't think we're equipped to draw the right conclusions here."

"I'd like to at least try. Would make a nice collar for our team."

Yes, he was ambitious, his new partner. He was quite promising too. He was sharp, motivated, and his heart was in the right place. However, sometimes he wished for a more seasoned partner, for someone who'd already burned through the enthusiasm of youth and had matured enough to know which battles were worth dying for.

"And risk finding another girl just like that tomorrow? Or next week? Because we missed a clue? Be reasonable, partner, we need help. There's no shame in that."

"I thought we could—" Fradella frowned, as he continued his argument but was interrupted by one of the reporters.

"Excuse me, detectives," the man yelled, bent over the police line as far as he could without falling.

Irritated, Michowsky walked toward the reporter with big, angry steps, ignoring the jolts of pain he felt in his back. He approached the journalist and got in his face.

"You're in my space," he said quietly, pointing at the yellow line. "Back off."

The reporter immediately took a step back, but still extended the microphone toward Michowsky.

"Detective, do you have the identity of Dawn Girl? Was this a serial killer?"

Michowsky sucked in a deep breath, trying to calm his taut, raw nerves.

"What's your name?"

"Brandt Rusch, Channel Seven."

"Mr. Rusch, I strongly advise you do not put the name Dawn Girl out there. If I see it printed or quoted anywhere—"

"Then what?" Rusch pushed back. "Freedom of the press, remember?"

"Listen, she's more than a label you slap on a news piece to sell your verbal diarrhea. She doesn't deserve that. She's a person, with a name, a family, and loved ones. Don't do that. Please."

"What's to stop me?"

"I can only ask. Nicely."

"Then give me her name," Rusch insisted, his crooked smile taunting Michowsky, driving him crazy.

"We don't have her name, not yet. As soon as we confirm her identity, we will contact next of kin, then we'll be in touch."

"You'll call me?" Rusch laughed. "I'm not that stupid."

"Give me your card and I will call you. I promise. And no talk about no serial killer either. We don't have any evidence of that."

Rusch pursed his lips and shook his head, then shoved his card into Michowsky's palm.

"You owe me," he said and turned to leave, making his way through the growing crowd.

A second later, another reporter took his place, wielding yet another microphone.

"Detective, did I just hear that Dawn Girl was murdered by a serial killer? Can you confirm?"

It was going to be a very long day.

4

ASSIGNMENT

Tess Winnett refilled her coffee from the hallway pot, keeping an eye on the elevator door. She'd been in early enough to drop off her case report on Special Agent in Charge Alan Pearson's desk before his typical arrival time. She knew she'd get called in when SAC Pearson finished reading it, and she just wanted the whole deal to be over and done with.

She heard a chime, and looked at the elevator doors again, as they slid open and let out another load, a few of her fellow agents, analysts, and technicians, chatting lively, ready to start their day. Small talk... another minor thing in life she missed, another minor thing she didn't know how to bring back.

She shrugged off the dark thoughts and refocused on getting her coffee fix. She filled the travel mug to the brim, then started to put the pot back into the machine, careful not to spill.

"You realize you'll never get laid if you keep doing this, right?" A man spoke loudly right behind her, while passing her by, engulfed in a conversation with another coworker.

She startled and her hands jolted, sending coffee everywhere, projecting it upward. It stained her white shirt and gray slacks. It spilled everywhere on the small table, on the coffeemaker, under it, on the paper tissues, in the sugar jar. A generous splash landed on the wall and rolled down to the floor in tiny rivulets. Another one landed on the carpet.

"Goddamn it," Tess muttered. What kind of idiot put the coffee machine on a stupid hallway, forcing her to have her back against traffic?

She took a deep breath, regaining some of her composure. Someone who wasn't afraid of people had put the coffeemaker there, for everyone's convenience. There was nothing wrong with that. People weren't dangerous there, in the middle of the fifth floor of the new FBI building in Miramar, Florida. These people were fine... they were her coworkers. They were safe. She breathed again, deeper, slower, and started cleaning up the mess she'd made.

"Redecorating this morning, Winnett?" an analyst asked, baring two rows of impeccably white and straight teeth, the mark of good breeding and great nurturing.

"Ah, go screw yourself, Donovan," she replied dryly, continuing to dab at the coffee stains on the wall.

"Always a pleasure to speak with you," the analyst replied unperturbed, heading toward the elevators.

She let another long breath escape her lungs. No one had noticed anything out of the ordinary; it was just a coffee spill. It happens all the time, in offices everywhere. These spills are the reason behind industrial carpet treatments with Teflon, making it easy on people like her to clean up their messes. No one noticed a thing, but they were investigators. Eventually they were going to figure it out, if she didn't get a grip.

"Winnett," SAC Pearson's voice made it across half the floor. "In my office, now."

Frustrated, she squeezed the paper towel into a ball and threw it in the trash forcefully, almost tipping the can.

"On my way," she replied, turning to look at SAC Pearson. He stood at his office door, holding her report in one hand and leaning against the doorframe with the other. He looked tense, impatient. She hustled.

"Close the door and sit down," SAC Pearson said. He sounded uncompromising, almost cross.

She obeyed quietly and waited for the drill to start, cringing on the inside and bracing herself.

SAC Pearson flipped through the pages of her report and jotted a few things down on a notepad.

"You closed the healthcare fraud case with a nice arrest. Congratulations," he said, letting out a long breath, as if the acknowledgment of her success caused him physical pain.

She nodded and chose to remain silent.

"You've also logged a record number of complaints for a single case. Four written, formally registered complaints."

She bit her lip and refrained from asking the obvious question. She was sure SAC Pearson would be generous with the details soon enough.

He flipped through his notes, while the frown on his face deepened, furrowing his thick, bushy brow.

"Is it true you chose to visit and question a high-profile witness at 2:00AM?"

She pursed her lips and nodded once, averting her eyes.

"Says here you pounded on his door until he opened it, and by that time, half the neighborhood was awake. What did you need to discuss that couldn't wait until morning? It was a fraud case, Winnett, not a kidnapping."

"At that time," Tess started to reply, then had to stop for a second to clear her throat, irritated by her own hesitation. "Several people had already started shredding evidence. Any minute of delay could have cost us the ability to bring a full array of evidence to support the case."

"Yes, but you didn't know that at that time." Pearson pushed back. "You only found out about the shredding the following day, didn't you?"

"I sort of did know about it, sir. It was the logical thing for them to do, and the third shift security detail had told me that several executives had been working really late."

"So it was your gut telling you to pound on that door in the middle of the night, so the governor could call me the next morning with your name?"

She bowed her head, feeling defeated for a second, then she rebounded. "It's what we use out in the field, sir. And I was proven right."

Her last comment made Pearson frown even more. His jaws clenched, knotted muscles dancing under his clean-shaved skin.

"You also failed to integrate with the local team, Winnett. You were supposed to form a task team together with local authorities and Medicare representatives. Yet you just bolted out on your own, not informing them of your plans, not even bothering to keep them in the loop. This is not how a team works, Winnett."

This time he was waiting for her to reply, holding a frustrated eye contact. She resisted the urge to look away and managed to reply, "Yes, sir."

"When you're out in the field working a case you are representing this institution, and you have to behave in accordance with its standards and policies. We can't have you embarrass the FBI with your actions, nor can we have you singlehandedly deteriorate the relationships between local law enforcement units and the regional bureau. Our ability to solve cases effectively relies on our aptitude to drive teamwork, engagement, and collaboration. It's in our policies, in the code of conduct you took an oath to uphold and respect."

She didn't find anything to say in her defense. The truth would have been an option, but it would've also guaranteed an even angrier response from Pearson. The local law enforcement officers were slow, indolent, and unable to keep up with what she'd tried to do. She'd already wasted more time trying to explain her actions than it was worth. Even if that was the truth, it definitely wasn't something she'd mention to Pearson, not even to defend herself.

"Speaking of code of conduct, Winnett," he resumed, "you're in direct violation, and this time it's documentable."

"With what, sir?" Tess blurted, surprised.

"You gambled while on bureau time."

"I did what?"

"Didn't you place a bet with a local law enforcement lieutenant? You should be able to remember that bet... Says here you lost a hundred bucks."

"Oh, that," she said, then bit her lip again.

"Yes, that. Care to elaborate?"

"Well, I needed the local team to move faster than they were willing to do. To achieve that, I appealed to the man's ego, and it worked. When I placed the bet I wanted to lose, sir."

"You manipulated that lieutenant, that's what you're saying?"

"Um... yes, sir."

"Jeez, Winnett. There's no limit with you. Have you thought about explaining, collaborating, or motivating the local team?"

"Yes, sir, but the bet worked faster. Only took me a minute, and we were pressed for time."

Pearson ran his hand over his face, as if to wipe away tension, maybe tiredness. Maybe exasperation.

"Finally, you made the arrests on your own, not waiting for backup, and not even bothering to tell your team the warrants had come in. That's against procedure for a reason. You knew it, and you broke procedure anyway. Why?"

She hesitated, then took a deep breath and replied, as gently as she could.

"To your earlier point, sir, it was a fraud case, not a kidnapping. The risk was very low."

"I'm not talking about the risk. I'm talking about a local team who's frustrated as hell because they feel robbed of the credit they deserved. I'm talking about you breaking procedure. Again."

"With all due respect, sir, they didn't deserve much credit in this case. The warrants had been issued and faxed to their squad room, and they decided to get breakfast instead. Donuts and coffee. I just didn't want to wait, that's all. I wanted to close the case. They knew where I was going, and they arrived too late. Their choice, sir."

Pearson stood, pushing his chair back forcefully, and started to pace the office. She followed his movements for a while, then gave up, keeping her eyes focused out the window, on the blue sky promising another sunny day.

Then Pearson stopped, standing tall in front of her. She instinctively pushed her chair back, feeling threatened. Then she stood, reading his posture as a hint their meeting was over.

"We're not done yet, Winnett. Sit down."

She complied, but pushed her chair away even more, putting as much distance as possible between Pearson and her, fighting the panic she felt taking control of her brain. She focused on her breathing, which made things more bearable.

Pearson moved back behind his desk and took his seat. She relaxed, letting out a long breath slowly, discreetly.

"You've worked without a partner for months. You're curt, dismissive, hard to work with. People file complaints because you piss them off. You're a lawsuit waiting to happen, regardless of how smart you are. You're perceived as arrogant, disrespectful, and it's going to stop. Today." Pearson took a few gulps of bottled water. "Do you know why procedure requires agents to work in teams, Winnett?"

She nodded. Pearson continued, not expecting her to answer.

"It's better for everyone involved. You're less likely to get complaints. You're less likely to do stupid stuff and get in trouble. Partners help each other, keep each other honest, have—"

"Have each other's back, sir?" she interrupted, her voice rich with bitter, pained undertones. "I'm sure you can agree that's not exactly true. Not all the time."

"Mike's death was not your fault! You were cleared of all wrongdoing."

"That doesn't mean anything, sir. Not to me. He died when I was supposed to have his back. Now his four-year-old son doesn't have a father. So let's just both agree it's best for everyone's health if I work alone, all right?"

"You don't make the rules, Winnett! You don't set terms, I do," Pearson said, raising his voice. "Is that understood?"

"Yes, sir."

"You're young, Winnett," he said, sounding somewhat calmer, but also more threatening. He flipped through a file for a split second. "Only 34. You could still have a good career as an FBI agent, or choose to take an exit, whether willingly or unwillingly." Pearson paused, pensive for a minute. "I'm putting you on notice. All your behavioral issues will stop, right now. Right this minute. You'll be polite, courteous, helpful, colla—"

"You mean politically correct, sir?"

Pearson shook his head in disbelief, swallowing a curse.

"You will not interrupt your colleagues and superiors when they talk. You'll be a model agent, respectful, and praiseworthy. If I get one more friggin' complaint, you're out, Winnett."

"It's fucking, sir."

"Excuse me?"

"If you feel the need to use an expletive, just go for the real deal. Don't fudge it up. It makes you appear weak."

"Christ, Winnett, you're unbelievable! Do you know why you're even here? Why you're not out already?"

"Um... no, sir." She felt a pang of fear twisting her gut. She hadn't realized things were so bad. Her job was all she had. All she had left.

"How long have you been an FBI agent, Winnett? Ten years?"

"Yes, sir, a little over 10 years."

"You gave me and your fellow agents 10 long years of frustration, but also the best case-solving record in this regional bureau. You bring new methods into our work, and the bureau recognizes and appreciates innovation."

"New methods, sir?"

"The, what's it called, um, the outlier detection analysis you used in your healthcare fraud case. I still can't believe it, but Quantico wants to build it into the manual. They want to call it the Winnett method. Can you believe it?"

She smiled, a tiny smile of pride and achievement.

"Ah, wipe that smirk off your face, Winnett! Method or not, you're on notice. I'll assign you a new partner in the next couple of days, someone more tenured, who can teach you a thing or two about professionalism and respect. Until then, I'm assigning you to the murder case in Juno Beach."

"A murder case, sir? This is not typical procedure. Why doesn't local investigate? Is this your way of benching me?"

"Don't you dare quote procedure on me. Do your job, and be thankful you still have one. Dismissed."

5

HISTORY

Tess drove on the sand at snail speed, muttering oaths under her breath. Hordes of people who didn't belong were sure to invade a crime scene, minutes after the police had been called in. Maniacs of all sorts and flavors owned police radios, from newspeople to plain amateurs who got a thrill out of seeing dead bodies. She'd asked someone about it, one of the profilers from Quantico. He'd said that seeing death is, in a weird way, a celebration of one's life, of being alive. It's the reason some couples have sex after attending funerals. A sick world, that's what it was. Yeah.

Reluctant crowds parted, brought to compliance by the red and blue strobes on her car, and she managed to park in parallel with the coroner's van. The body was still there; good. If she hurried a little, she could maybe catch it as it was found, before the coroner loaded it into the van.

She hopped out of her SUV and slammed the door, then approached the police line with a spring in her step, ignoring the soft sand that had already filled her shoes. Two detectives, most likely the first at the scene, approached the line from the other side. She ran her long, thin fingers through her shoulder-length, blonde hair, then pulled out her badge.

"Special Agent Winnett, FBI. You the primary?

"Yeah, Gary Michowsky, in case you forgot, and this is my partner, Todd Fradella," Michowsky replied, shaking her hand firmly. Fradella's handshake was less convinced, and he averted his eyes.

She bent over to cross under the line and made a beeline for the lifeguard tower.

"Can't believe you called the feds, Gary," Fradella said, barely bothering to lower his voice somewhat. "We could have nailed this case. Just you and me."

Great, just great. An ambitious, young detective, guaranteed to challenge her at every junction and most likely to file a complaint or two, just because he won't be able to claim the collar on his damn résumé.

"Trust me on this, Fradella," Michowsky replied, sounding both defeated and frustrated at the same time. She turned and looked at Michowsky again, this time paying more attention. Something was a little off about him. Maybe he was sick or something. As for Fradella, he was fuming.

She rushed when she saw the coroner and his aides ready to move the body.

"Hold it," she yelled, flashing her badge. "Hey, Doc," she greeted Rizza warmly.

"Hey there, yourself," Doc Rizza replied. "Wanna take a gander before we move her?"

"Yeah, thanks."

She circled the body a couple of times, carefully, closing in at each pass, noticing more. Perfectly posed body, expressive posture. No useable footprints, a sandy mess of a dump site, deteriorating by the second in the strong ocean breeze. A sick, smart, bold killer.

"We're just wasting time now," Fradella complained to Michowsky. "Just watch."

"Why is it you never trust my judgment, huh?" Michowsky said. "Why do you always have to bitch and moan about everything?"

"This was our opportunity—"

"Ah... opportunity for what? To see some more girls get killed before we nail this guy?"

Tess refrained from chuckling. That partnership wasn't made in heaven. She turned to Doc Rizza.

"Do we even know it's a guy?"

"I'd venture to say yes, but I can't be sure. I can't determine that here," he gestured toward the many cameramen lined up at the yellow tape.

"Fair enough," she replied. "TOD?"

"Twelve to sixteen hours ago."

"All right, you can move her now, thanks."

She watched Doc Rizza and AJ, his assistant, struggle with the body in full rigor. Doc and AJ made sure the newspeople didn't catch a glimpse of the body, as they loaded it on the stretcher and then zipped the body bag closed.

"So, it's you again," Michowsky said. "It's going to be a treat."

"You two know each other?" Fradella asked.

"Yeah," Tess replied, "unfortunately."

"Theresa and I worked together on a case a few years ago," Michowsky added. "It was memorable."

"It's Tess, not Theresa."

"As a favor, maybe. It's Theresa on your badge," he pushed back. "To be honest, I was hoping the bureau would send someone else."

"Then it's Special Agent Winnett for you," she replied dryly.

It wasn't her fault she didn't build better relationships. She tried. But this guy, for one, made it impossible. This guy decided to hold onto an old grudge, over a mistake that he'd made to begin with. Sometimes she just didn't get people. People were hard to deal with. Was she supposed to let mistakes go by unaddressed, at the risk of jeopardizing the case? Was she supposed to be the humble one now, to try to forge a relationship threatened already by Michowsky's old grudge? She envied people who were natural-born politicians, smooth operators who knew exactly what to say and when, who had charisma, who were immediately deemed successful even if they didn't have any real results.

She didn't have a clue how to mend things with Michowsky. Instead, she shrugged it off and refocused on the case.

"All right, walk me through it."

Michowsky and Fradella looked at each other, then Fradella decided to speak.

"A couple of teenagers found her at dawn. She was posed and tied in place with fishing line. We cut the line before you got here."

"Any usable prints, tire tracks, anything?"

"Nothing. Javier is taking some sand. The lab will sift through it, see if they can find anything."

She looked around one more time, immersed in thought.

"So what do you think?" she asked.

"Aren't you—" Michowsky started, but Fradella interrupted.

"This is obviously a dump site, a secondary crime scene. As soon as the ME has more details, we'll have a confirmed COD, weapon, and TOD. We don't have an ID yet."

"Your alphabet blurb didn't tell me anything useful," Tess replied coolly. "I asked what you think, not what you know."

"Oh," Fradella blurted, then frowned, while his cheeks hued a little. "We thought it might be a ritualistic killing, maybe with some religious connotations. I also thought it might be a serial killer, based on how everything looks."

"Interesting," she said thoughtfully, her eyes wandering in the direction of the two kids, still huddled together. "Have there been any other victims?"

"No, none that we know of," Fradella replied, while Michowsky promptly rolled his eyes.

"I told you," Michowsky said. "Due diligence first, then conclusions. Otherwise you're just as lame as the media."

Fradella pursed his lips and looked away, embarrassed.

"Detective Michowsky, a word, please?" Tess asked, and took his arm before he could say no.

They took a few steps, then she stopped and let go of his arm.

"Not in front of anyone else," she said. Seeing how confused he looked, she continued. "Scolding Fradella. He resents you now, and for good reason."

"I don't need you to tell me how to speak with my partner. You're not exactly an expert, from what I remember."

"Fine. Suit yourself."

She returned to Fradella and resumed the earlier conversation.

"I agree it might be a serial killer, Detective Fradella, even if we don't have other victims identified yet. He dumped her here, when the Everglades are a short drive away. If he would have dropped her in the Glades, no one would have ever found her. He wanted us to find her like this. That's one of the features of serial killers. They make statements with their kills."

"You don't have enough data to say the word serial," Michowsky pushed back. "I hate the sensationalizing of these cases. What happened to five victims before we can call it a serial?"

"They all start somewhere, Gary. Do you mind if we catch him early? And it's three, not five. New guidelines."

He scoffed angrily. "I knew that."

"I know you don't mind if we catch him faster. That's why you called us, right? So what's crawling up your ass then? Ancient history? I can't help what happened, Michowsky. But I can help you now. We can help each other."

Michowsky ran his hand over his buzz-cut hair, visibly frustrated, but didn't reply.

A few yards away, the two teenagers sat on the sand, holding hands, their backs hunched. The girl was crying quietly, and her swollen, red face was proof she'd been crying for a while.

"How long has she been crying?" Tess asked.

"Since we got here, and she hasn't stopped. Threw up a couple of times too," Fradella replied.

"Any idea why?"

"I'm guessing she's afraid she'll get grounded as soon as their parents get here," Michowsky replied, irritated.

"You're guessing," Tess repeated his words slowly, quietly, with a hint of biting sarcasm. "Teenagers these days don't cry for much, and they don't throw up that easily either. She's definitely more rattled than he is, so something's off. And it's not the dead body. They see dead bodies on TV all day long and don't give a damn. May I?" she asked, gesturing toward the two youngsters.

Michowsky shrugged, and Fradella followed her from a distance, probably curious to see what she wanted to do.

Tess approached the two slowly, then crouched in front of them.

"Hey, guys, I'm Special Agent Tess Winnett with the FBI. But you can call me Tess, all right?"

She extended her hand, and the girl took it first, shyly.

"Kris," she said, then sniffled and wiped her face with a soaked sweatshirt sleeve.

"Carl," the boy added.

"I see you're upset," she said, focusing on the girl. "It's understandable, you know. I'd be scared too."

Kris raised her welled-up eyes, tears still rolling on her cheeks. Tess saw fear in those eyes, an unspeakable fear she recognized.

"I'd be terrified," Tess continued, dropping her voice to almost a whisper. "What if something like that happened to me?"

As she spoke, Tess felt some of that unspeakable fear contaminate her, freezing her blood. She breathed, pushing away the eerie, paralyzing feeling.

Kris nodded, keeping her hazel eyes locked with Tess's.

Tess decided to push it further, on a hunch.

"What if the killer saw me, right?" Tess continued, and Kris nodded, only so slightly. "What if he was right there, a few yards away?"

Kris responded with the same almost imperceptible nod.

"No, Kris," Carl whispered, tightening the grip on her hand.

"What if I came within a few feet of such a monster, while he was finishing his kill?" Tess whispered, and Kris nodded again. Then she suddenly turned to the side and threw up spasmodically, dry heaves mixed with sobs, while Tess held her hair and supported her forehead.

"Water," she mouthed to Fradella, and he rushed to get some.

Kris convulsed some more, then accepted the water, rinsed her mouth, and raised her eyes to meet Tess's inquisitive gaze.

"Tell me," Tess asked softly. "Tell me what you saw."

"Nothing, I swear," Carl spoke, choked up. "She wasn't there when we arrived. The girl. We played there. Right there. Oh, God..."

Tess maintained eye contact with Kris, who nodded again. Fresh tears welled up again in the young girl's eyes.

"Then we came here, taking pictures, waiting for the sunrise," Carl added. "Then Kris looked, and she was there. The dead girl."

"Oh, goddamn it," Michowsky muttered, and Carl promptly clammed up. Tess shot him a murderous look.

"The killer came within a few feet of you and you didn't see anything... I understand this must be scary," Tess continued, touching Kris's hand. "But you're alive and healthy and well. He didn't touch you and he never will. You know why? Because we'll catch him. And this? This will be our little secret."

"You promise?" Kris said quietly.

"Yes, I promise. It won't take long until we get the bastard." She stood and beckoned Michowsky to follow her.

As soon as they were out of the kids' earshot, she turned and faced him, angry as hell.

"Do that to me again, and I'll have you on report. Don't ever intimidate a witness into not speaking with us, you hear me?"

"I didn't—"

"You didn't do your job, neither of you," she interrupted, now that Fradella had caught up with them. "You completely botched that interrogation, and you missed critical information. This killer was audacious enough to dump a body in full rigor, 20 yards away from these kids. We're talking about an individual who takes a tremendous amount of risk to make a statement. He's highly sure of himself and ready to kill again on a dime."

"You don't know that," Michowsky replied, no longer trying to hide his anger. "You're assuming."

"What do you think would've happened if the kids would've spotted him dumping the body, during all that time he took to secure it with the fishing line? He would have killed them both, right where they stood."

"No, I meant you're assuming these kids actually told you the truth, that the body wasn't there when they arrived."

"You don't fake that," Tess replied, pointing at the two youngsters. "You assumed, Michowsky, you assumed they were afraid of their parents. You assumed, you didn't press on, and you were wrong. Just like last time," she blurted, instantly regretting that last phrase.

Michowsky's face scrunched up in anger, and his fists closed.

"Someone moving a body in this advanced stage of rigor needs a large SUV, minivan, or truck," Tess continued. "Now that we have the precise time the killer was here, we can pull video from street cameras. Pull all surveillance in the area, see what you can find. I don't think there was a lot of traffic at that time."

"I don't need you to tell me how to do my job," Michowsky snapped.

"Well, apparently you do. Let's just get it done."

Michowsky squinted, his jaws clenched, and his mouth twisted, flanked by two deep ridges.

"You haven't changed a bit, Special Agent Winnett. I heard you're on your last stretch with the bureau. People are saying everyone's fed up with you. With a little luck, who knows? Maybe this will be your last case. The world will have one less bitch with a badge."

She hesitated, taken aback by the harshness of his words. Every one of the words he'd spoken tore her up inside. She managed to reply with a shred of dignity.

"Keep on dreaming, Michowsky. The day's still young."

6

SONYA

Tess followed their car all the way to the precinct and took a few minutes securing a parking permit from the front desk. Then she climbed the stairs to the second floor and found both Michowsky and Fradella huddled around a computer. She stood next to them, unsure what to say. It seemed like everything she said only made things worse with Detective Gary Michowsky, far from what she wanted.

Fradella searched through the missing persons' database, every now and then comparing the faces in there with the picture on his phone.

"There she is," Fradella said, "this is her. Sonya Weaver, 22. Reported missing five days ago, on March 22."

She took a step back, suddenly feeling sick to the stomach while staring into Sonya's beautiful blue eyes. Five days... five days of terrible fear, of torture, of pain. She felt her skin crawl, as a million goosebumps sent frozen shivers to her taut nerves. She shuddered.

What did that monster do to her for five whole days? Tess rubbed the back of her neck furiously, running her left hand from her nape to the side of her neck, under her ear, pressing hard. Five days... they'll find out soon enough, once Doc Rizza wrapped up his examination. Yet she was sure that no matter what they found in the coroner's report, Sonya Weaver had welcomed the blade ending her life.

She shuddered again and took another step back, backing into a desk. She leaned against it and closed her eyes for a second, trying to get her bearings. Against her closed eyelids, nightmarish images formed freely, haunting her. She opened her eyes, still yearning for the solace brought by withdrawal into oneself, another little thing she'd lost forever. Instead, she welcomed the crisp light of day, the only thing that dissipated her nightmares and shattered her fears.

"What's wrong?" Michowsky asked, sounding indifferent.

"Nothing," she lied, "just a migraine. I'll get some coffee. When was she last seen?"

"Um… five days ago, in the evening. She vanished after a night out with friends. They were celebrating. She'd just graduated from college, cum laude," Fradella replied.

"All right," she said, rubbing her nape one more time. "Let's get phone records, social media accounts, financials, the works. When's Doc Rizza going to be done?"

"He just started," Michowsky pushed back. "It's not even noon yet. You're in one hell of a hurry."

"And you aren't?" Tess replied, staring at Michowsky intently. Then she lowered her eyes. "Let's start over, what the hell. We're on the same team."

"Are we?" Michowsky replied coldly. "It doesn't feel like that from where I'm standing."

"We're trying to be, but it's a process," she said, fighting to contain a chuckle. Men and their egos. They just had to have the last word. She silently promised herself she'd shut up, no matter what his last word was going to be.

"Whatever," Michowsky said, somewhat appeased, making it easy for her to change the subject.

"Let's do a Google search for her; see what we can find."

Fradella executed. Many young women named Sonya Weaver had their profiles online. They found the right Facebook profile and started looking at her past postings, pictures, and interests.

"Nah, the public stuff's too general," she commented after screening a few days' worth of postings. "Nothing usable. We need to get access to her entire profile. Let's get her ID confirmed. We need to notify next of kin."

"Yeah, we know that," Michowsky replied dryly, a little irritation tinting his reply.

"Before doing that, I want to speak with the cop listed on her missing person's report. Who handled it?"

"That's one Felipe Garcia, from North Miami," Fradella replied, reading from the screen.

"Thanks. Let's get moving with the ID."

"Already sent her ID to Doc Rizza."

As soon as he spoke his name, the phone on Michowsky's desk came to life with a loud, disrupting ring tone. The display read, "Coroner." Michowsky took the call on speaker.

"Go for Michowsky."

"Need you all downstairs."

Doc Rizza's voice sounded somber and tired.

7

Autopsy

She lay there immobile, lifeless, seemingly serene, against a backdrop of stainless steel and white tile. A white sheet covered her body, leaving only her beautiful face exposed. Her eyes were closed now, probably the coroner's doing. The sand was gone from her hair, leaving it smooth, shiny, spread silk on the cold, barren steel of the examination table.

Tess swallowed hard, a little choked. She stood next to the table, looking at Sonya's serene visage, murmuring senseless words without even noticing. What kind of man would do that? And yet she knew just what kind of man. She'd seen such men before. In her tenure as an investigator, she'd hunted them down, she'd caught them, or she'd killed them. This bastard would be no different.

She'd been an FBI agent for 10 years and had encountered all sorts of psychopaths, hideous human beings whose minds had been overtaken by the darkness of their deviance, and who had acted on their most sadistic, incomprehensible fantasies, leaving trails of bodies for agents like her to put to rest. One by one, Tess had caught the killers she'd pursued, and yet, a part of her failed to understand them. After 10 years… there wasn't much hope she'd ever understand how such minds worked, and, for the most part, she didn't even want to. She didn't want their horror to contaminate her, she didn't want the abyss to look back onto her. She wanted to know and understand just enough to be able to catch the killers before they could kill again.

Her hand almost touched Sonya's hair, but she stopped herself and plunged her hand deeply into her pocket. How little did they know about Sonya... just that she was a young college graduate getting started with her life. As for her killer, they knew nothing about him. No prints, no traces, nothing. But no matter how smart he was, or how careful he'd been, she'd still find him. That was a fact. It was more than a promise; it was reality. It was the pledge of her impeccable service record that even SAC Pearson had to acknowledge. She *will* find him. Soon.

"I do that too, you know," Doc Rizza said softly.

"What?"

"Speak to them," he said, gesturing toward the exam table.

"Ah... do *they* speak to you?"

"Yes, they do, every time. She's told me a lot already, and we haven't even finished our conversation."

"Care to share?"

"Let's wait for Michowsky and Fradella. They should get here in a minute."

"All right, yes, of course," Tess replied, letting her eyes wander, absentmindedly observing things, countless details about Doc Rizza's office. His diplomas, neatly framed, hung above his desk, probably displayed in chronological order. No other framed pictures adorned the cold walls, but near his desk a couple of shelves hosted a few personal items. A small radio, a predigital relic that probably still worked. A few illustrated reference titles on entomology, marine biology, botany, zoology, also predating their respective database versions, no doubt. A coffee mug with a message reading, "Medical examiners are cool too," a typical sample of their trade's dark humor. She hadn't visited in years, but little had changed.

"How do you stay sane, Doc?" Tess asked.

"After doing this?" he replied, finishing up at the sink. The sound of metallic instruments being dropped in a tray resounded loudly in the large room, echoing against the barren, tile-covered walls.

"Yeah..."

The water stopped running, and, for a second, the only thing she could hear was the low hum of the refrigeration compressor.

Doc Rizza straightened his back and wiped his hands on a paper towel, then discarded it in a sensor-activated trash can. Then he ran both his hands against his thinning hair, one after another, as if to persuade the remaining strands to stay in place. He too hadn't changed much in the years since she'd visited his morgue. A little less hair, a few more pounds, a few more wrinkles.

"I think of each laceration and contusion as useful hints to help you guys catch these animals. By the time they reach me, these victims are gone. They don't hurt anymore. They found their peace. I try to think of that."

Tess glanced at him, surprised. He looked troubled, haunted, despite what he was sharing. He continued after a little while, his voice barely audible.

"There are days, though, when my dinners are liquid, if you know what I mean. I get out of here, and I can't see anyone, can't talk to anyone, I just go home and lock myself in there with a bottle of strong liquor, hoping it washes everything away."

"And does it?"

"Nah... just dulls the pain and the anger a little. Makes it bearable, and gives me the strength to come back here another day."

He clasped his hands together, deep in thought.

"I listen to classical music as often as I can," he continued after a little while. "Classical does it for me... it's pure, clean, filled with emotion, with life. And I fly on occasions."

"You're a pilot?"

"A private pilot, yes. Just the bare minimum license to go up there on my own. I rent a small plane every now and then. I take it up there, and I just let that serenity sink in. For an hour at a time, I can imagine the world is a better place, free of such senseless horror."

He stared into nothingness for a while, then asked, "What do you do?"

She thought of the answer she was about to give. Not much she could really share without opening the door to even more questions.

"Oh... I read, mostly. Crime novels, if you can believe it," she chuckled. The sound of her voice echoed eerily in the cold stillness of the room. "Serial killers, police procedurals, old-style investigations, modern detective stories. Thomas Harris is one of my favorites; I have a bunch of theories on the psychology of Dr. Hannibal Lecter."

"Don't you get enough of that on the job?" Doc Rizza's eyebrows shot up, wrinkling his tall forehead.

"I do, and then some. It keeps my mind open to new ideas though. I'm fascinated about how the world of crime suddenly turned deviant, for lack of a better word, some 50 years ago. Before the 1970s, crime was relatively simple. Stabbings, strangulations, gunshot wounds. Clear motivations, like jealousy, greed, or revenge. Clean, almost elegant crime, compared to today. Whodunit was a challenge for the brain, most of the time. Not something that turned your stomach."

Doc Rizza's face lit up.

"I know exactly what you're talking about. One theory says that in the 1970s, with the expansion of television, people started being more aware of these types of crimes, when, in fact, they had existed since the beginning of time. History has its examples, like Jack the Ripper, or even Caligula, two thousand years ago. Another theory says that even psychopaths need inspiration, and with the current entertainment trends, in music, film, and literature, they get all sorts of ideas. But that's not how you stay sane, Winnett, that's how you get better at what you do. Are you dodging my question?"

"Not intentionally, no. I—"

"Sorry it took so long," Michowsky said, preceded by the whoosh of the automatic doors. "We ran into the captain. He wanted an update."

"Okay, let's get started," the doctor replied. All the excitement brought by their earlier conversation was now gone, replaced by an unmistakable expression of sadness mixed with disgust. "This is not the full report. You know better than to expect that before 48 hours. This is preliminary. I wanted to get you a head start."

Michowsky and Fradella pulled out their notepads.

Doc Rizza let out a breath of air before speaking.

"At this time, I can confirm cause of death. She was stabbed, with a scalpel most likely, then the blade was pushed forward, like this." He took a knife to a mannequin and demonstrated. "He didn't slice. This deep stabbing followed by the push-forward cut caused both her jugular and carotid to be completely severed. There were no hesitation marks. She died of exsanguination, very quickly. Arterial blood spray must have been massive. When you find the primary crime scene, you'll see what I mean. That's where the relatively good news stops."

He waited for Michowsky and Fradella to catch up with their notes, then continued.

"As expected, there are no trace elements or fingerprints on her body. By placing her on the beach, he exposed her to sand and ocean spray, and that washed everything off."

"How about her tox screen?" Tess asked.

"We'll get there. Preliminary toxicology report came back a mess of trace amounts of various chemicals. I've sent samples for a full array. We'll know more in 36 to 48 hours."

"I'll see if I can put a rush on that," Tess offered. "Pull some strings."

"I tried my best, but see what you can do. Maybe the feds carry more weight than us locals. Now, let's go back to her actual death. Blood pooling shows she died and was kept postmortem in that praying position, but without her knees touching the ground."

"What the hell do you mean, Doc?" Michowsky asked.

"It means she was suspended in some sort of harness when she was killed."

"Oh, God," she said quietly.

"Then, *after* rigor was fully set, he moved her and posed the body the way we found it."

"That means ligature marks?" Tess asked.

Doc Rizza pulled away the sheet delicately, exposing only her left arm and leg.

"Very minimal. I was expecting more. The absence of deeper ligature marks can only be explained if he used something like this," he said. He clicked a button on a remote and projected an image on the wall-mounted TV. "These harnesses are sold at high-end sex shops. They're lined with artificial fur and, although they restrict movement effectively, they're also soft and don't break or scrape the skin. They could leave friction marks though, if the victim struggles against such bondage for a long time, which is precisely what I found here," he clarified, pointing at her wrist. "Her ankles show the same type of friction and also her neck. Her waist shows less friction, but there is some, enough to let me estimate the type of harness she was restrained with."

He clicked another button, and the image changed to show a sex harness commercially packaged in shiny colors. The packaging depicted an image of a woman suspended from the ceiling. Her wrists were cuffed and pulled forward, her waist and shoulders supported by a thick, leather-looking band lined with fur, and her legs immobilized at the ankles, with the knees half bent. There was a man in the picture, shown approaching the suspended woman from behind while tugging at the harness straps with both hands, to position her as he wanted.

A wave of nausea hit Tess, as she watched the images on the monitor. She took a few deep breaths, pushing the nausea away. Doc Rizza turned an inquisitive eye toward her, but she dismissed his concern with a twitch of her lips and a quick shake of her head.

"This stuff is available in some stores out there," Rizza continued. "Could be this brand or could be a different one. Here's something you could potentially use: these things don't come cheap. They go for hundreds of dollars. This killer has means. Not many sex shops carry them; only the high-end ones. Very few manufacturers and importers too. You might be able to generate a short list of stores and maybe trace a transaction."

He took a sip of tea from a large cup, then grimaced. It was probably cold and stale.

"She was raped, sodomized, and beaten," he continued, "repeatedly, over the entire time he had her. I'll know more when I'm done with the full exam. I didn't find any fluids; no DNA we can use."

"Fingerprints?" Tess croaked, her voice choked. She cleared her throat. "I mean, hers?"

"Her fingerprints match the ones filed on her missing person's. The report was too new for the prints to have been in the system, but they match. There's more."

"Sorry..." Tess whispered. This was the second time she'd interrupted him.

"She was cut, superficially, many times, using a sharp blade, a scalpel, or maybe a box cutter. I counted 153 different cuts, not more than a couple of millimeters deep, on her back and on her thighs, barely deep enough to leave an almost invisible, hairline scar. All cuts were perimortem. Some are almost completely healed."

Tess felt her stomach tie into a knot again.

"These were not life-threatening cuts. These were done to inflict pain and terror. Think 153 paper cuts," the doc clarified. "There are traces of inflammation on some of those cuts that I can't explain yet."

"You're saying—" Michowsky started to ask.

"He's saying torture," Tess replied, before Doc Rizza could speak, but the coroner nodded as she spoke. "This was about torture, physical and psychological, done for days."

"You said she was beaten, Doc," Fradella asked, "but I can't see any bruises on her face, and not many on her body either."

"For some reason, this killer preserved her face almost intact. I did find a bite mark on her lower lip, almost completely healed. Depending on how deep it had originally been, she could have been bitten several days prior to her death. I'm not sure the bite mark is related, but we can't rule it out. As for the rest of her body, the fluoroscope showed signs of deep bruising though, most likely recent, in the last 24 hours prior to death. Trust me, she was beaten."

"It's almost like he was considerate," Fradella said. "Face intact, soft restraints."

"Don't be an idiot, Fradella," Tess snapped, more harshly than she'd wanted. "He raped her for five days, for Chrissake. This is not about being considerate. It's about control. It's about complete power."

Tess saw Fradella look away, clenching his jaws. Now she'd done the very thing she'd told Michowsky not to do and scolded Fradella in public.

"Sorry, Detective Fradella, I didn't mean—"

"It's all right," he replied coldly.

"Anything else?" Michowsky asked.

"Yes. This is also preliminary, like everything else I've told you so far. She has been given shots, repeatedly, both intravenous and intramuscular. This finding, combined with a completely empty gastrointestinal tract, but no signs of dehydration, tells me he was feeding her intravenously."

"Why would he do that?" Fradella asked.

Tess cringed, in anticipation of the coroner's answer.

"To manage her eliminations," he replied. "Her bathroom needs. He probably kept her tied up in a harness the whole time and wanted things as clean as possible."

"Oh," Fradella replied and looked away.

"Yeah. However, that only explains the IV needle marks, not the ones in her buttocks. I took samples and sent them for trace findings. Her tox screen showed many different chemicals, and that could be how she got them in her system, through shots. As soon as I know, you'll know. That's all I have so far."

They were silent for a few seconds. Deep in thought, Tess rubbed the nape of her neck for a few seconds, vigorously, then insisted a little on the left side, right under her ear. Sometimes, she felt the urge to run her hand over that area, to relieve the painful stiffness of sore muscles and stress. Some people accumulate stress in their upper backs, as their postures suffer, reflecting the tension in their weary brains. With her, it was mostly on her left side. Since she'd started working on this case, the almost forgotten soreness in the side of her neck had come back fiercely, pasting a swatch of burning pain that stretched from her cervical spine to the back of her ear, right there on her hairline. Maybe it was the morgue... too cold, too drafty. Maybe it was the AC in her car. A heating pad later should take care of it.

"So let's make sure we got this right, Doc," she said. "This killer was not hesitant, right?"

"Not for a second," Doc Rizza confirmed. "He's skilled with a scalpel and knowledgeable of serums, with access to whatever medication he needs, from IV fluids to whatever else we're going to find on that tox report. My conclusion is he's some sort of medical professional, most likely a doctor, with unrestricted access to meds, which could mean hospital doctor, not walk-in clinic. Hospice could work too. This man has cut human flesh before. There's no doubt."

"Told you," Fradella said, "this has serial killer written all over it."

"It does, I agree," Tess replied quietly. "We'll need to find his other victims. Doc, any chance Sonya is his first victim?"

"It's possible, but not likely."

"Thanks," she replied, getting ready to leave.

The two detectives led the way to the automatic doors, and Tess followed closely. She turned her head to say goodbye, when Doc Rizza called her name.

"Agent Winnett."

"Yes," she replied. The doors closed quietly behind Michowsky and Fradella. She saw them step into the elevator on their way up to the squad room.

"My dinner tonight will be some liquid of sorts," Doc Rizza said, smiling sadly. "What will you do?"

"I don't have time for liquids, Doc. When your work ends, mine begins. I'm going to catch us a killer."

8

MEMORIES

She climbed into the elevator as soon as the doors opened and waited impatiently for them to close. As soon as they did, she let out a long, shattered breath, feeling her eyes burn with tears. A little dizzy, she reached out and touched the elevator wall. Cold to the touch, the metallic panel offered balance and some relief. She turned and watched her image reflected in the smudged mirror. Tense features, haunted eyes threatened by tears, deep ridges around her mouth, on her forehead.

"Get a grip for God's sake... you're a goddamn FBI agent," she whispered to her own reflection. "You're here to fight for them, not cry for them. You're here to kill the mother—"

She stopped mid-word and pursed her lips, angry at herself. Then she pressed the button for the second floor and set the elevator in motion.

"Catch, not kill, what the hell is wrong with you? Catch, not kill," she whispered.

When the doors slid open on the second floor, she looked her normal self, or almost. She strode to Michowsky's desk, where he was seated in front of the computer, with Fradella leaned against the wall and looking over his shoulder.

"We're ready for next of kin?"

"Yes," Michowsky replied, hesitant to peel his gaze off the computer screen.

"What are you looking for?" Tess asked, recognizing the familiar search screen.

"Other victims. Testing your serial killer theory."

"Anything?"

"We just started. You want to do next of kin now?"

"Give me a couple of hours, will you?" Tess asked, already headed for the stairwell. "I need to talk to that missing persons cop. Then we'll do next of kin, all right?"

She didn't wait for their answer; she didn't have to. They probably weren't happy to put off next of kin notification, pushing it closer to the end of day, when traffic got heavy and everything just got harder to do, with everyone being exhausted and irritable. Then there was also the issue of the press, who'd been pounding on them, demanding to know the identity of Dawn Girl. They couldn't release her identity to the press before notifying her family; that was the procedure, and it made sense. But everyone wanted to know who Dawn Girl was. Who was the beautiful, young woman who met her demise in their small, quiet, little beach town? Her presence on the beach, no matter how brief, had burned a disturbing memory in the minds of the peaceful locals. They all wanted answers; they wanted Dawn Girl to be put to rest, and her killer gone—gone from their lives, their neighborhoods, their coffee-time conversations.

Tess plunged her key in the Suburban's ignition and, as soon as the engine started, set the dials on maximum AC. Standard-issue FBI vehicles were black, but that color made little sense in southern Florida. It overheated in the torrid sun, scorching her lungs when she inhaled, and burning her skin when she sat on the leather seats. The vehicle had powerful air conditioning, and within seconds she could breathe normally in the overheated SUV and could touch the steering wheel without wincing.

She caught herself delaying her departure, fumbling with the GPS and the radio settings. She didn't have to think why. She knew already. Next of kin notifications aren't easy for anyone to handle, and it never gets any easier. But for her, after having to tell Rose that her husband, Mike, had died in a shooting, notifications had never been the same.

Mike had been her partner and her mentor as a young federal agent, teaching her all the ropes, how not to get killed, and how not to get discouraged in the ongoing struggle with the red tape of bureau politics. For almost nine years, he'd desperately tried to build some political correctness into her, not much, just enough to keep her out of trouble. His teachings had caught a little, maybe enough to work when she was calm, not a speck more. He'd also showed her how to be a good investigator, how to ask the right questions and go after her instincts, even if they made little logical sense. Over the years, the two of them had built a great working relationship that extended naturally into a solid friendship, including Mike's wife, Rose, and later their son, when he was born. They'd become Tess's family, the three of them. They were her Thanksgiving dinner plans and her Christmas mornings. They were all the family she had.

Then one ill-fated day, they were closing in on a drug ring with terrorist connections. The gangbangers had figured out that raising money for terrorism was easier if they raised seed money and then grew it exponentially through drug operations. Tess and Mike worked on a joint task force with the DEA, and had SWAT backup when they arrived at that house.

They busted through the doors and spread out inside, clearing one room after the next. She heard voices as agents entered the rooms. "Clear!" "Clear!" Then she entered a room where she didn't find anyone, so she moved on, shouting, "clear!"

Then the gunshot came. A single, thunderous gunshot, coming from upstairs, followed by the heavy thump of a body hitting the floor. The rest was a blur in her memory, with occasional shreds of clarity, nothing more. They finished clearing that house soon thereafter, and the shooter was quickly overpowered and taken out in cuffs. A young kid, maybe 19, maybe 16. SWAT and DEA officers were heading out of that damned house, one by one, but Mike wasn't anywhere to be seen.

When she finally went upstairs looking for him, holding her breath and feeling the fist of fear tearing at her gut, she knew already. She didn't have to ask. She found Mike lying lifeless on the stingy carpet, blood still pooling from the bullet hole in his temple.

She remembered screaming, then pushing aside the comforting hand of the SWAT unit commander. Then a blur again, until the moment she rang the bell at Mike's house.

Rose opened the door and at first she smiled, but within a split second her smile froze. Tess stood in that doorway, paralyzed, unable to utter the tiniest sound, but Rose didn't need words; she understood all too well, just by looking at her haunted eyes, her drawn face, her shaking hands. She screamed, an agonizing, endless shriek, then she slapped Tess across the face, hard, leaving red marks on her tearful cheek. Again the hit came and again. Tess stood there, defenseless, not even blinking, not thinking for a second she didn't deserve every single one of those blows. Mike had been her partner, hers to keep safe, hers to watch over, hers to keep alive. She'd failed.

Suddenly Rose had her arms around her neck, sobbing uncontrollably with her face buried in Tess's chest, and that was worse to bear. She wrapped her arms around the tiny, fragile figure, and hugged her tightly, unaware of her own tears flowing, droplets of liquid sorrow entangled in Rose's hair.

That was the last she'd seen her, except the funeral. She didn't dare ring that doorbell, not sure if she'd ever be welcome there again. She blamed herself... why wouldn't Rose blame her too? There was no redemption to be found for Mike's death, and she didn't want to cause his widow any more sorrow. She'd driven by their house a few times, even stopped across the street for a few minutes, making sure they were okay. No... that wasn't all of it. She wished she'd somehow muster the courage to cross that street and comfort her friend at a time of great loss, but couldn't find the words. Couldn't stop her own tears.

A quick honk brought her back to reality. The traffic light had changed a while ago, but she hadn't noticed. She floored it, passing through the intersection just as the light was changing to yellow.

9

MISSING PERSON

She signed in at the front desk of North Miami Police Department. The front desk officer, a young, hesitant man who couldn't have been more than 25 years old, took an entire minute to stare at her badge before offering her a seat and calling her party to join her downstairs.

A few minutes later, another ridiculously young officer invited her into a small conference room, scantily furnished, and more deserving to be called an interrogation room than anything else. This one didn't wear a uniform though; he just packed the standard issue Glock and wore his badge on his belt.

She followed the silent gesture made by the young officer and took a seat, frowning.

"I'm here to see Detective Felipe Garcia, in regards to the Sonya Weaver disappearance."

The young man extended his hand, smiling confidently.

"I'm Detective Garcia, nice to meet you."

"Jeez, Garcia, are you even 15?" Tess reacted, while shaking his hand.

Taken aback, the young man cut the handshake short and blushed a little. He frowned and pulled away. Tess bit her lip, reflecting bitterly on how she knew just what to say to irritate the crap out of every single human being she met.

"What do you need, Agent Winnett?" Garcia took his seat across the table, his welcoming smile evaporated.

"I need to know everything that was done in the Weaver case. Who you talked to, what you found, every single thing."

"Why is the FBI looking into this case? Has a ransom request been received?"

"Why don't you answer my questions first, if you don't mind," Tess replied coldly, irritated by the detective's relaxed demeanor. There was no real sense of urgency in his manner of talking about Sonya's case. That didn't mean he didn't do his job. It was more of a feeling she had, or maybe her expectations were too damn high.

Garcia opened a manila folder and reviewed some notes.

"Sonya Weaver, 22," he recited. "Disappeared on March 22, late at night, after a night out with friends at Club Exhale."

"What kind of club is that?"

"Dance club. One of the hottest nightclubs in the area. I'm surprised you haven't heard of it."

She let his comment pass.

"Walk me through what happened."

"Sonya and two of her friends, Ashely King and Carmen Pozzan, were out partying at the Exhale. Out on the dance floor, mingling, having fun, meeting people, making out."

Tess flashed a glare his way.

"Just quoting from their statements, Agent Winnett, that's all. I'm not the one who's judgmental here," Garcia replied, then shook his head once, a reaction to what he must have thought about her.

"And? What happened next?"

"Sonya simply vanished from the club. No one saw anything, no one remembered anything."

"Video surveillance from the club?"

"Inconclusive. Our techs couldn't find her leaving the club, and all cameras were working that night. But it was dark, and club lights don't help much with video clarity."

"Who reported her missing?"

"Her parents, after the girlfriends went to their home in the dead of the night. But we didn't log the case until the next morning. With young adults, there's always the chance they went away on their own or are passed out somewhere, from too much alcohol or drugs."

"This case was different. Why didn't you make an exception? It wasn't someone who went out and didn't come home on time. It was someone who vanished from a dance floor full of people, for Chrissake," Tess let her anger seep in her voice, too hard to control when faced with the indifference she sensed in the man slouched on the chair in front of her.

Garcia looked irked by her raised tone, almost insulted.

"I *did* make an exception, Agent Winnett. Typically, we don't log such reports for at least 24 hours. That time, I logged it in less than 12."

"Then what?"

"Um… I interviewed the two girls. The only thing that was anything out of the ordinary had happened almost a month before. They were out partying, at the same club, when Sonya hooked up with some guy and left with him, but then later ditched him in the parking lot. Next morning she'd told Ashely the guy was some kind of creep, and that she'd gone home alone."

"When was that?"

He checked the file again.

"On February 28. I don't think it was related. I think it shows she liked to party though."

Tess felt her blood boil. How easy it was to slap a label on someone and make it their fault. She liked to party, hence she wasn't deserving of a full investigation. She liked to party, so whatever happened was her fault.

"Did you follow up on this lead?"

"N—no," he replied. "She didn't go missing until three weeks later. It wasn't really a lead."

"Then what else did you do?"

"The usual. APB, credit card monitoring, press releases, the works. She's too old for an Amber Alert, but short of that we did everything."

"All right, but you, personally, what did you do? How did you investigate her case further?"

He stared at her, not sure how to react. He folded his arms on his chest.

"You know how busy we get. Our caseload—"

"I'll tell you what you did, Detective Garcia. You sat on your ass doing nothing, while she was out there for five days, getting tortured and killed."

10

THE PROMISE

Rush hour had crept in while Tess was visiting with Detective Garcia, and now she had to crawl through traffic at an infuriating pace. Her car wasn't equipped with a siren. It did have emergency lights built into her front grille, rearview mirrors, and sun visors, but she delayed the moment she'd have to engage those. The procedure was clear. She couldn't use the emergency lights in the absence of a real emergency.

Yes, per the procedure manual, conducting an investigation into someone's death was not considered an emergency, nor was the delivery of bad news to a victim's family. It wasn't all good at the FBI, nor was it all logical, but it was the career choice that still made sense for her. She inched along with the horrendous traffic on I-95, remembering the moment she'd decided to become an FBI agent.

She'd been a promising law student, acing her exams all the way through third year. That summer she interned for a big law firm in Fort Lauderdale, received the highest praise from one of the partners, and the invitation to get in touch when she passed her bar exam. She still recalled how thrilled she was that day. She thought she had everything figured out. Later that night, she joined her friends at a bar and shared the story of her achievement. One of her friends had said, "Whoa, you're going to be so loaded! We won't see you anymore, 'cause, you know, these hotshot lawyers work, like, a gazillion hours, but we'll know who to call for money." She recalled all of them laughing, the happy, carefree laughter of invincible youth, but she didn't laugh with them. Was that all she wanted to do with her life? Be busy and loaded? Provide access to justice for whoever could afford it the most? It didn't make sense. Not to her. She wanted her life to make a difference, beyond someone else's bottom line.

She spent the entire night tossing and turning. By the next morning, she knew what she wanted to do with the rest of her life. She had probably chosen the most difficult way a young lawyer could rid herself of student loans, but she hadn't looked back since; hadn't regretted her choice for a second.

She turned onto the Weavers' street, a quiet, upscale suburban setting featuring half-million dollar homes, each engulfed in its own private oasis. She pulled in front of the generous driveway and took a few seconds to run her fingers through her hair. Long, sleek, and a natural ash blonde, it ran shoulder length and was parted in the middle, the simple, unpretentious hairstyle of a busy professional. She walked the distance to the front door, straightening her shirt and jacket, then rang the doorbell, cringing inside.

A middle-aged woman with dark circles around her eyes opened the door without a word.

"Mrs. Weaver? I'm Special Agent Tess Winnett with the FBI. May I come in?"

The woman's face lit up a little, as she showed Tess the way into a nicely furnished living room. Everything was dark, the shades lowered, not allowing much light to come in. She flipped a switch and turned on the ceiling light, two dozen or so candle-shaped lightbulbs in a crystal chandelier.

"Sorry… migraines," Mrs. Weaver apologized.

Tess noted the aged elegance of everything in the room. The furniture, dark, sculpted oak, featured several bookcases filled with books. Armchairs flanked the fireplace with floor lamps next to them, the ideal setting for book lovers who enjoyed reading together. The marble mantle hosted several rare, geological artifacts. An amethyst cathedral and several other large crystals of fascinating colors that Tess couldn't name. It was the peaceful home of affluent intellectuals.

Mr. Weaver appeared from the kitchen, shook her hand quietly, then sat on the sofa next to his wife. The two clasped hands together, holding their breaths.

"You found our little girl?" Mr. Weaver asked.

"I'm afraid I have terrible news, Mr. Weaver. We found Sonya's body earlier today."

"No… no…" Mrs. Weaver whispered between sobs. "Not my baby, no. Please, God, no."

"Are you sure it's her?" Mr. Weaver asked, his chin trembling badly.

"Unfortunately, we are positive."

The man shielded his wife in his arms, nesting her face against his shoulder. She clung to him with agonizing fingers, grabbing and twisting at his shirt.

"Find him, Agent, promise me you'll find him."

Tess nodded, choked.

"Promise me," the man insisted with a trembling voice. He suddenly seemed 10 years older, frail, and broken.

She looked him firmly in the eye as she spoke.

"I promise."

11

MEDIA LUNA

It was already dark when Tess left the Weaver residence. Weary and lightheaded, she climbed into the Suburban and let out a sigh of frustration. Not a single piece of actionable information gathered from Sonya's parents. Nothing. Sonya was a good girl, honors student, recent graduate, nothing worth mentioning, not even a squabble with a neighbor.

She recalled hearing her cell phone buzz a number of times during the conversation with Sonya's parents. She pulled it out and checked the screen. A couple of irritated voicemails from Michowsky, followed by two text messages. One read, "This is Michowsky, we're still waiting for you to do the next of kin." The second message, also from Michowsky, read, "Dawn Girl story broke on local TV at 7. Damn it, Winnett, where the hell are you?"

She sighed again and closed her eyes for a second. Then she texted him back, "Can't talk now. See you in the morning." There'd be hell to pay when they heard she visited the Weavers on her own. Yeah... better handle that one in the morning, after a big cup of coffee.

A pervasive, gnawing sensation in her stomach reminded her she hadn't touched a bite to eat the entire day. She paid a virtual visit to her fridge back home and remembered it was almost empty. Too drained to go shopping for a microwave dinner, she decided in favor of a better, easier option. A few minutes later, she pulled in the side parking lot of a small bar named Media Luna. Crescent Moon wall lamps, backlit with a yellowish light, were the only element of décor on the exterior walls.

Tess entered the dimly lit bar and propped herself up at the counter, on a four-legged stool that had seen better days. The entire place had seen better days. The bar had been smoke free only for the past couple of years, but hadn't been renovated. The walls still bore the patina of heavy smoking and low margins. The original paint, an undecided burgundy or reddish brown, was cracked in places, exposing here and there the white drywall underneath.

The liquor license was pretty much the only framed art on those walls, but there were dozens of pictures affixed with pushpins, all of them taken right there, at the bar. Over the years, the same patrons had grown older, lost some hair, added some pounds, all the usual markings of the merciless passing of time. But some of the same faces stayed loyal over the years, pinned against the wall behind the shiny, stained counter, in a testimony of good times and memorable evenings.

She leaned on her elbows, stuck firmly on the counter, and buried her forehead in her hands. Three stools over, a man had greeted her with a smile and an idiotic pickup line. Then he kept his eyes fixed on the TV screen in the corner, as soon as he'd caught a glimpse of her badge. There was another guy seated toward the far end of the counter, staring despondently into the bottom of his almost-empty glass, mumbling something to himself. Not a whole lot of business for Media Luna that night. No surprise... It was a Wednesday, still too early in the week to start celebrating the approaching weekend.

The bartender looked at her and grinned. She winked and ventured a weak, crooked smile. He continued to rinse some tall glasses, keeping the occasional eye on the TV screen, where the latest news, sports, and weather took turns on the air. Tall and tan, the bartender looked good for his almost 60 years of age. He hadn't shaved his salt-and-pepper beard in a few days, and his wavy, long hair looked more salt than pepper those days, but overall he looked good, in a Kenny Rogers kind of way, or even a younger Willie Nelson. What would have appeared as unkempt for others, just worked out well for that man.

He still wore his Hawaiian shirt with the top three buttons undone, and the tattoo on his chest caught everyone's eye. A tribal design of a tiger with hypnotic, piercing eyes, embedded in a flame motif that expanded and transformed into the tiger's stripes, the tattoo had earned the bartender the nickname by which everyone knew him, but only a few were allowed to call him.

He finished rinsing the glasses, then put one on the counter and started mixing a drink. Tess watched him work, feeling a little more relaxed, a little less haunted by the day's horrors. She reached out to the peanut bowl and almost grabbed a few.

"Don't touch that," the bartender said. "That's the yuckiest thing I got in this whole joint. Everyone's dirty hands have been in there." He took out a brand new pack of peanuts from his pantry, and a clean bowl, and opened it for her. "There."

She didn't reply, just munched absently, while he finished mixing the drink. Then he stuck two fine straws into the murky drink and placed it on a coaster in front of her.

"Just how you like it, kid."

"Thanks much, Cat."

She played with the straws a little, making the small ice cubes rattle against the glass, and pushing the herbs toward the bottom. Then she took a couple of sips, her eyes pinned on the TV screen, where the local news was about to hit.

It didn't air first. A piece about a new sinkhole opening under a home in Tampa took the first slot. It came just after that, against a backdrop of poorly edited, remote shots that didn't show much, and some voice-over commentary, equally bad.

She gestured toward the bartender, and he cranked up the volume on the TV.

"Her body was found early this morning, prompting the public to call her Dawn Girl. Her name hasn't been disclosed yet, pending notifications. While we do not have a confirmed cause of death, it is most likely one of a violent nature, bringing the fear that Juno Beach has a serial killer on the loose."

"Goddamn it," she muttered, making a throat-cut gesture with her right hand, prompting Cat to mute the TV.

"Hey, I was watching that," the man at the end of the counter protested, a little slurred. Cat didn't bother to acknowledge him.

Then he pulled a stool and sat right next to her.

"That you?" he asked quietly. "You working that?"

She stared into the glass for a few seconds.

"Yep," she eventually said, her words heavy, spoken through a shuddered sigh.

Cat looked at the man sitting a few seats to their left and made a gesture with his head, inviting him to leave. The man obeyed promptly, sprang to his feet, and gulped down the remnants of his drink on his way out, then dropped the empty glass on the door end of the counter. The other man though, the one at the far end of the counter, didn't look up, no matter how intently Cat stared at him.

"'Excuse me for a second," he said, then went to the end of the counter. "You need to call a cab," he told the man. "Now."

"You cuttin' me off?"

"Yeah. Come back tomorrow. This one's on me, but you need to leave."

"A' right, a' right, I get it. I'm goin'," he slurred, dragging his footsteps toward the exit. The moment he closed the door behind him, Cat locked it, and turned off the Open sign.

"You don't have to close the joint every time I hit bottom, Cat," she said, feeling tears choking her. She took another couple of sips, emptying her glass. He'd already started to fix her another one, and the familiar smells and sounds pulled her back, drowning her in memories she couldn't erase. The first time she'd landed on Catman's doorstep, on a dark night just like this one, a dark night that had engulfed her entire life, changing it forever. She'd come in there covered in blood, holding on to shreds of her clothing with trembling hands, still panting from the desperate run to save herself. Cat had done the same back then… sent all his customers away, locked the bar, and tended to her for as long as she needed. He was a complete stranger back then. He was a dear friend now.

"Here you go," he said, putting another drink in front of her, this time in a larger glass. "I fixed you a double."

She chuckled bitterly. "Thanks, Cat."

He sat next to her, quietly, waiting. She nibbled at the peanuts every now and then, her brain flooded by a sludge of dark thoughts and painful memories.

"I made a promise today, Cat," she eventually whispered. "I promised her parents I would catch her killer."

"And you will. You always do, right?"

"No… not always. There's one… one who got away. The one who never had a case number. You know who. And I tried, Cat. I still try. I still search for that stupid tattoo, 'cause that's all I can remember. I still dream of the damn thing. A snake, curling up… how can someone only remember that, and nothing else?" She fell quiet for a while, frowning, scrunching her face in despair. "I've looked at thousands of snakes, from thousands of tattoo places. And I got nothing, with all my fancy FBI credentials, and all the databases I can search. For years, I've been looking for a white male with a snake tattoo on his arm. No chance in hell. Nothing, just like with this guy today. We got nothing. No trace elements, no prints, nothing. Just… what he did to her."

"How long has it been?" he asked softly.

"We found her this morning."

"Not her… you."

"Oh…" she replied, and looked away briefly. "Ten years, seven months, and twelve days. Yep, still counting."

"You never reported it?" he asked gently, touching her hand to offer comfort.

"To what end, Cat? I was days away from starting my FBI training. It would have ruined my career. It would have stayed on my record for the rest of my life and for what gain? I didn't need law enforcement help. A few weeks later, I *was* law enforcement, with a gun and a badge, and I still couldn't find him."

She yanked the straws out of her glass and gulped a mouthful of her murky drink. Her hand trembled a little setting the glass down.

"I still have that spare room upstairs, kid. It's yours for as long as you need it."

She squeezed his hand, feeling a tear rolling on her cheek.

"Can't. Not now. I made a promise today and I intend to keep it. You don't know... this bastard's really... we have to catch him, Cat. I *have* to catch him."

"I'm sure you will. If anyone can, you can," he replied, a little more emphasis in his voice. "I'm impressed you work these cases, kid, you know, all things considered."

"With my history, you mean?"

He nodded.

"Yeah... It's not like I only work serial killers or sex crimes. We get cases assigned, all kinds of cases. I just wrapped up a healthcare fraud case, all white collar. But I've worked a few of these bad ones over the years, and none of those threw me off like this one. This one's different, Cat. Somehow this one's different. The worst I've ever seen."

She rubbed her nape repeatedly, absentminded, introspective. Then she rubbed the left side of her neck, right under her ear, until the burning sensation faded away.

"Why?" he asked quietly. "Why is it different? Only you can answer that, kid."

"It's weird, it's almost like... I don't know, really. I go to the ME's office without any idea of what he's going to tell us, but when he gives us his findings I'm..." she paused for a long, loaded beat. "I don't know what the hell I'm talking about, Cat. This case just gets to me, that's all. Triggered all kinds of shit in my mind. But I'll be fine."

She made an effort to restore some of her composure. There was no need to pull Cat into the depths of her own personal abyss.

He picked up on that and sprung to his feet.

"Since you last visited, I added this grill. Now we serve burgers and fries." Then he leaned playfully against the counter. "Want some?"

"Love some!" she replied, feeling a bit of normality return to her life.

He threw a few patties on the grill, and they instantly sizzled. He took a couple of handfuls of frozen fries and dropped them in a deep fryer, then peeled the wrapping off some cheddar cheese, and warmed up the buns. It was so peaceful, so heartwarming to see Cat work. A simple world, contained, safe, where no harm could come her way.

"Have you seen Jim lately?" he asked, without turning his head.

"Oh, God, how I saw that coming," Tess laughed. "He might be Jim to you, but he's still Dr. Navarro to me, you know."

"And?" he pressed on, still focused on his burgers.

"No, not recently." She frowned, unable to find a serious reason why she'd stopped talking to her off-the-books shrink. "He was helping, but..."

Cat turned on his heels and put two large plates with burgers and fries on the counter, then swirled again and produced the mustard, ketchup, and mayo bottles. One more swirl, and they had pickles.

"But?" he pressed on.

"There's only so much he can do, you know. We're keeping it off-books, so no prescription drugs, just talk. I wouldn't want any drugs, anyway. We talked and talked, but part of me will always struggle. He says I have PTSD. I don't need a label; I know what I have. I'm... damaged, and, for the most part, it's beyond fixing. Breathing exercises and talk will only get me so far."

He took a large bite and chewed slowly. She followed suit.

"Yeah, all right, but why stop trying?"

They ate silently, while Tess struggled to answer that simple question. There was no answer, not a logical one, anyway.

"You're right, I shouldn't have," she eventually stated. "I'll finish this case, and then I'll go back. I'm already afraid they'll notice at work, you know, me being weird, bitchy, jumpy."

He nodded, finishing a few fries.

"I'm just, you know, uneasy around people. Dr. Navarro said I've become suspicious of all people, because of... what happened. Maybe he's right, but maybe I'm right to be suspicious too. Do you know how fast they'd kick me to the curb if they knew what was going on? Who do you think wants someone with PTSD carrying a badge and a gun? A federal agent with panic attacks?"

"Maybe you could start trusting people again," Cat said gently. "Not all of them are bad. Some are, but not all."

She looked at him with weary eyes. How could she even try? Where would she start?

"People are bundles of pain and fear, each wearing their own brand of misery," he continued. "Trust me, I know. When they're at the end of their rope, they come here, with their stories. Try to trust a few, see what happens."

"I can't, Cat. I've forgotten how."

"You trust me, don't you?"

"Yes, but you're special," she smiled sadly.

"Maybe at your work you could find some trustworthy people worth your shot."

"They're not exactly happy with me at work these days, and it hurts, because I love my job. But I snap at people, and I'm angry all the time. Then, this case." She pushed her plate aside, unfinished. "Every time I catch one of these freaks, I find a little more closure. Maybe one day I'll have enough closure to feel normal again."

"You'll catch this sick son of a bitch, right?" he asked, smiling widely, and tilting his head.

"Oh, yeah, Cat, I know I will. Don't know how just yet, but I will."

12

THOSE WHO DIE

It wasn't eight o'clock yet when Tess arrived at the squad room, carrying three cups of coffee on a carton in one hand, and a bag of fresh donuts in the other, her peace offering to the team she'd ignored all evening the day before.

"Finally," Michowsky said, springing to his feet and grabbing his jacket. He opened a drawer and took his gun.

"Whoa, not so fast," she said, offering him one of the coffee cups. "It's done already. Let's go to the ME's instead, see what's new."

"What do you mean it's done?" Michowsky asked, putting the cup down untouched.

"Next of kin. Spoke with them last night."

"Without us?" Fradella intervened. "Why the hell did you do that for?"

"Oh, well, North Miami took longer than I thought, then traffic, so I didn't think you'd still want to do it that late. I thought you'd already gone home. I'm sorry," she said, "I really am."

"Don't do that again, all right?" Michowsky said. "We're supposed to be a team. That's what you said."

"Scout's honor," she pledged.

"Is there any honor involved in selling cookies door to door?" Fradella quipped.

"Lots of honor, I swear."

"Okay, let's go downstairs," Michowsky said, still frowning.

They shared the elevator silently, Tess feeling grateful for how easy she'd appeased them for the next-of-kin visit. It didn't hurt if complaints stopped landing on SAC Pearson's desk for a change.

A whoosh and the door opened, letting them feel the chilly air of the morgue. Doc Rizza was on the phone. He waved at them, inviting them to take a seat. Michowsky and Fradella did, but she continued to stand, pacing slowly along the walls.

Behind Doc Rizza's desk, the top diploma framed was his medical degree. The doc had studied in California, at Berkeley. Interesting. Then her eyes wandered lower on that wall, where she saw he'd obtained a second PhD, in clinical psychology, this time from Florida State University. It was definitely worth bouncing some ideas back and forth with Doc Rizza. Then she noticed the blanket and pillow thrown on the sofa. He hadn't gone back home the night before. He lied about his planned liquid dinner and just stayed up and worked.

"Your intervention paid off," Doc Rizza said, ending his phone call. "Tox screen came in this morning at six."

They gathered around him, and he turned on the wall-mounted TV, then went to his laptop and opened an email attachment. He scrolled through it.

"We have confirmation on the full toxicology array, both in her blood and at the many injection sites. She was drugged with several powerful, rare compounds. One was flibanserin, a drug that enhances libido in women."

Tess winced.

"Then we see here low-dose opiates, but also stimulants and pain-threshold-lowering drugs. This one in particular, a variant of methylphenidate, is a central nervous system stimulant."

"Doc, isn't the pain-threshold stuff you mentioned common?" Fradella asked. "Painkillers are everywhere."

"Pain-threshold lowering means they make you feel *more* pain, not less," Doc Rizza replied. "Put that in conjunction with the thin cuts all over her body and you have chemically enhanced torture."

"Oh, God, that's... that's sick."

"And the rest isn't?" Tess reacted, scoffing bitterly.

"Her nostrils had traces of ammonia. She fainted, and he broke vials of ammonia salts under her nose to wake her up. He did, in fact, nourish her intravenously, with 5 percent glucose solution. That's all I have on the tox screen. Still waiting on the trace substance in her inflamed cuts. I'll give you the list of compounds you could trace."

"This is Miami, Doc," Michowsky said. "You can get anything from anywhere."

"Some of this stuff's pretty rare. It could be contraband, of course. You never know."

"The killer knew his way around these drugs. This isn't something you just pick up from a TV show or the Internet," Fradella said.

"Precisely," Doc Rizza replied. "This man has some form of medical training. Moving on."

He tapped on some keys, and the TV displayed a close-up of Sonya's mouth.

"The bite mark. I've analyzed the scar tissue, and it could be older, say anywhere between seven and fifteen days. It's hard to be precise with bite marks, but it definitely predates the abduction; it's most likely unrelated. The bite was strong enough to pierce her skin in two places, but didn't leave much of a scar."

"Could this have been accidental somehow?" Tess asked.

"I can't think of a scenario in which it could, other than maybe she bit her own lip for some reason, but then something made her bite too hard. Possibly a shock of sorts... like running over a pothole while driving. It's possible, not probable though. Same goes for erotic biting. It could happen, but not likely."

"Two weeks, you said?" Michowsky asked.

"About there, yeah. Then… I found minute traces of perfume on her body. Sent it to the trace lab. You might want to work your magic and rush that."

"Uh-huh," Tess acknowledged.

"Next, DNA. No, don't get excited, there is none. I've swabbed everything that could be swabbed and haven't found a single trace. He used condoms and was very careful what to touch. Most likely he used gloves too. One more thing."

"Shoot," Tess replied.

"There are signs of sexual asphyxia. She has been strangled almost to her death a few times, before she was killed."

They stared quietly at Sonya's livid face, shown on the wall screen.

"That's it, that's all I got," Doc Rizza concluded.

"Doc, let's walk through this," Tess said. "We're dealing with an experienced cutter, probably a medical professional, one who knows a whole lot about drugs, who's bold enough to dispose of a body in full rigor yards away from unsuspecting bystanders, and who's got a place remote enough to feel comfortable torturing someone who must have screamed like hell for five days. Am I missing something?"

"N—no, you nailed it."

"If you had to guess, what kind of man are we dealing with?"

"I don't like to guess, you know. I can posit he's relatively young, late 20s or early 30s, affluent, bold. He needs an elaborate form of gratification. He's a clinical psychopath, and I'm willing to bet his MRI shows structural abnormalities in his amygdala."

"Anything else we could use?" Tess asked.

"I'll let you know if I think of anything else."

"All right, Doc, thanks," Michowsky said and turned to leave.

She stayed behind, looking at Sonya's face on the monitor, quietly reflecting on how little separates those who live from those who die.

13

EARLY VICTIMOLOGY

The ride in the elevator was just as quiet as the earlier one, only for different reasons. This time, they were each immersed in their thoughts and a little grimmer than before. Tess made no exception. Libido enhancer? Pain-threshold-lowering drugs? The killer was a psychopath, no doubt, but even for a psychopath, what kind of brain would concoct such an elevated recipe for torture? Before the doors chimed open on the second floor, she had her answer. This narcissistic, sadistic psychopath didn't get off on the sex. He got off on the pain, on the power. That's why he'd been careful not to damage Sonya's face. To him, the victim had to present the image of a pristine creature engulfed in pain and completely under his power. There was no religious ritual involved, like they'd originally thought. There was a ritual all right, but it had nothing to do with religion. It had everything to do with asserting power, *his* absolute power. Sonya was posed in a praying position all right, not to God, but to him. That was the killer's fantasy.

"Let's get busy, guys," Tess said, walking briskly toward Gary's desk, and grabbing her laptop bag on the way. "It's time we found his other victims."

"We searched all evening yesterday, while waiting for you to come back. There's nothing, no one fits this MO," Michowsky replied.

"Where and how exactly did you look?" Tess asked.

"We did database searches for all victims under 30, Caucasian, who were posed in some manner. We found a couple, one on the Gulf Coast near Tampa, and one close to here, in Miami," Fradella replied. "But we discarded both those victims. They weren't related."

"Why?"

"The Tampa one was badly beaten, face bashed in, doesn't fit this guy at all. The other one was shot, but otherwise intact, no beatings, no rape. Again, not a match."

"How far did you search?"

"Statewide is all we have access to," Michowsky replied, frowning.

"Then it's time to up the ante," Tess said, powering up her laptop. "First, I'll put a live alert. We'll be notified the minute another young woman goes missing in the southeast."

"You'll get tens of pings before the day is over," Michowsky said. "Not sure how useful this will be."

"Until we narrow it down, let it ping us," Tess replied. "We don't know what kind of cooling-off period this killer has. He might be out there right now, abducting his next victim."

Michowsky nodded, but looked unconvinced. Fradella came to stand behind her.

"Can I see what you're doing?"

"Yeah," she replied, a little morose.

Having a man stand in such close proximity behind her, where she couldn't see what he was doing, triggered her anxieties, but she decided to force herself to accept his presence. She needed to act normally, and, most of all, be logical. Todd Fradella was a cop, and a nice man too. They were huddled in the middle of a squad room swarming with other cops. No one was going to attack her there, so she decided to make the effort and stifle the voices of panic rising inside when he approached her to look over her shoulder. She focused on the search and noticed she could breathe a little easier. Damn hypervigilance.

"Feds use something called DIVS, or Data Integration and Visualization System. It pulls information from all databases hooked into it, essentially the majority of law enforcement databases everywhere. It provides us with a single search interface. Let's put in some parameters," she added. "Let's go back, um, two years."

"Would that be enough?" Fradella asked.

"Probably not, but we don't have many filters that we're certain about, so we'll be flooded with results. Once we figure out how to narrow down our victimology, then we can go back further in time."

"Huh," Michowsky said, "you're really that certain this guy's a serial killer?"

"What, after all you've seen downstairs, you still aren't?" Tess asked. "What more do you need to see?"

"I'm just thinking we would have heard of it. If we had a serial killer in our backyard we would've known about it."

"What if he's not from here? What if Miami isn't his usual stomping ground?" Fradella asked.

"Precisely," Tess answered. "You have to think globally, or, in this case, nationally. He could have started elsewhere. He could have changed his MO over time, and not been visible to you until now. Let's find out what the data tells us. So, two years' time frame, then... let's say murder victim, case still open, female, Caucasian, adult under 30."

"Why adult?" Fradella asked. "How do you know?"

"Pedophiles are a different animal. They don't get aroused by raping and torturing an adult. Only a child, of tender age most of the time."

"God..." Fradella reacted, his face conveying the utmost disgust.

She hit enter, and the system returned 127 victims.

"Oh, wow," Fradella reacted. "That's a lot of unsolved murder cases."

"We'll apply exclusion filters next and bring it down a little." She leaned back against her chair, thinking. "Most serial killers have a set physiognomy. Their victims are stand-ins for the real target of their rage, typically a woman who rejected them, hurt their ego, or did something they perceived as damaging. Let's build in Sonya's physical characteristics to this search."

DIVS crunched the data with the new parameters and returned 32 possible matches.

"They can't be all his, can they?" Fradella asked.

"Most likely they're not."

She added "found on beach" as a filter, and the database returned zero results. What were they missing? The beach was an important factor; it had to be. The excessive risk he took when he posed Sonya's body on the beach, the boldness of his actions led her to the certainty that the beach, as his body dump location of choice was critical somehow. Maybe even beyond physiognomy.

Displaced rapists went to extremes to abduct, torture, and rape victims who looked almost identical to the object of their rage. Their victims had to have the same hair and eye color, the same height and weight, even an almost identical hairstyle. An investigator, looking at victims' photos, could immediately pinpoint the commonalities. But not all serial killers were displaced rapists. The medical examiner's findings pointed toward a sadistic killer, which spoke more to the anger-excitation model rather than anger-retaliatory. The excitation killer's victims could transcend physical traits, even cross racial lines. But even the anger-excitation killers had scenarios, fantasies that fueled their rage and their arousal, and such a scenario could very well include dumping the body on the beach. Maybe the beach was part of his signature, and Sonya's blue eyes and ash-blonde hair were irrelevant, just coincidental. Maybe that beach meant something... that particular location, or maybe ocean beaches in general. Maybe sand... or water? Maybe his stressor, that traumatic trigger event that leads to escalating, homicidal behaviors in certain psychopaths, had happened on a beach.

She deleted the physiognomy filters and kept the beach filter, then hit enter.

"Hello," she said, more to herself.

The database returned two other victims. They were both found on the beach, facing sunrise, at dawn, posed. One near Atlanta, the other one near Summerville, in South Carolina. They were kept for at least three days, tortured, and raped.

"We've got a pattern, guys. Now we know. Let's get the case files, and put the ME reports in Doc Rizza's hands. He'll help us further develop this killer's signature. Let's move!"

They stood, ready to leave, but Tess suddenly sat back down, and retrieved the parameters screen in the database search function.

"What?" Michowsky asked.

"Databases are precise when it comes to people's age of adulthood. People aren't. People make mistakes sometimes," she clarified.

She deleted the parameter "adult," and replaced with "over fifteen years of age." She hit enter again, and a third victim popped up, a young Asian girl, found on an eastern-facing Lake Michigan beach. She was seventeen years old at the time of her death.

"Now we can talk victimology," she said, sounding confident, but frowned, a little preoccupied.

Had she found all of them? What if the beach thing was new, just a recent step in this murderer's evolution? What had he done with the victims' bodies before he'd become bold enough to pose them in plain sight, only yards away from bystanders? How many others were out there, yet to be found?

14

CASE FILES

Page after page of case-file material was spewing from the color printer, and Fradella put them together with one hand, holding what was left of his pizza slice with the other. Tess swallowed her last mouthful of pizza, half-chewed, then sprung to her feet.

"We need a whiteboard here, right here," she pointed at a spot on the conference room wall. "We need it now. Tell them if they don't have it up in an hour, we'll use the wall instead, and they'll have to repaint."

"Tell whom?" Michowsky asked quietly, ostensibly amused.

"Whoever does these things for you, the facilities people."

Michowsky shot Fradella a quick glance. Fradella sighed, resigned. He wiped his greasy fingers on a paper towel, then ran them against the back side of his jeans, just in case. He grabbed his car keys from a drawer.

"Be right back," he said, disappearing into the stairwell.

"Get a big one," Tess shouted across the squad room, making several people shoot her disapproving looks.

Michowsky took Fradella's place next to the printer.

"How are we doing with this? How many have we got?"

"We have all three case files. We're halfway through printing the second one. By the time Fradella's back, we should be ready."

She leaned against Fradella's desk and grabbed the last slice of pizza, now cold.

"I still feel we're missing something," she said. "Do we have the last 24 hours prior to Sonya's abduction fully mapped? Do we know everything she did, all the people she talked to, every credit card transaction, every minute?"

"N—no, not yet. We started on it and we have some of the data, but not all. We're waiting on phone records and social media passwords."

"Still?"

"Yeah. Paperwork took forever."

She chewed silently for a while, thinking about the filters she'd put in her DIVS search. She only went back two years. But this level of murderous skill, precision, and self-confidence one doesn't build in two years and three victims. It takes longer, no matter how deviant, how angry and motivated the killer was. How many victims did she miss?

Four was enough to establish victimology. Or so she hoped. It would have been easy to redo the search and open up the time frame. Maybe she'd find fifteen victims instead of four. Yet studying fifteen case files would have taken them significantly more time than just four. What if he was getting ready to kill again? What if some poor girl hung in those horrendous harnesses right now, screaming in unspeakable pain, wishing she were already dead? No. She needed to maintain her focus, and study the four victims they already knew about. Only until they found the killer. After catching him, connecting him to any other of his earlier victims would be easier, without the potential risk of jeopardizing more lives. They'd have time after they found him. Now they didn't.

"So, when are you calling in your team?" Michowsky asked. He wiped his mouth with a napkin, then finished his soda and crushed the can before sending it to the recycle bin with a precision shot, 10 feet through the air.

"I'm it. There is no team. I'm all you're going to get."

"I see," he said, frowning. "Well, you got us this far, right?"

Tess searched his face with scrutinizing eyes. She didn't see much confidence written in his facial expression; just a little maybe, and some acceptance. He seemed drained somehow, his features almost fallen, inert.

"What's up with you?" she asked. "You seem down."

He remained quiet and turned his head to the side, watching the printer's rhythmical motions for a few seconds.

"Come on, it can't be all because I don't call 20 more feds right now, can it?"

He scoffed bitterly.

"No, it's not that. It's me."

She waited patiently for him to continue, when he was ready.

"It's my goddamn back. I threw it out a couple of days ago, at the gym. I've been popping pills like breath mints since. And I missed it."

"Missed what?"

"The kids, at the dump site. That was on me and only me. A fuckup like that can throw a case sideways. You had to come in and clean up my mess. I'm glad you did, by the way, but it doesn't make it any easier."

"We all screw up, Michowsky. When I screw up, I'm on a roll, one after another, like beads on a string."

He chuckled lightly, still staring at the carpet. "Fradella doesn't even know. About my back."

She looked at him intently, then smiled.

"But, of course, he doesn't, right? He's so young, and strong, and perfect." She took two steps toward him, and he looked at her, a little irritated.

"News flash, Michowsky. You're not old, and you're not dead either. You're just…" she hesitated, not sure how to put it. "Middle aged. You're approaching midlife crisis. So go wreck a Ferrari and come back all fine."

He scoffed again, this time visibly amused.

"No Ferrari, huh? Then let's just catch this son of a bitch, and take some pride in that. Not much else you can do on a cop's salary."

A chime, and Fradella got off the elevator carrying a large whiteboard.

"I'll get someone to stick some nails in the wall," he said.

"No time for that," Tess replied. "Here, let's just lean it against the wall, on these chairs. That will do it for now."

They put the whiteboard in position and started working. At the bottom of the board, Tess drew a timeline going back two years. She marked the dates when the girls were abducted, killed, and found. Then she added any kind of incident they found in their files, with even a remote chance of being related to the case. For Sonya, she marked the day she'd been at the club with her girlfriends, the day she'd met the so-called creep she later dumped in the parking lot. Tess wondered what the creep had done to earn his moniker. What could he have done, in the few minutes it took them to exit the club and reach the parking lot, to make Sonya send him on his way? Was he creepy, but otherwise okay, as in, he was sent away and got lost, end of story? Or was he the kind of creep who gets even? The kind who stalks the prey who rejected him, and when the time is right, he abducts her?

"Detective Fradella," she said, "you go to clubs, right?"

"Um, sometimes, yes."

"Play this scene out with me, will you? So you pick me up at the club. We dance and make out on the floor. It's great, so great that I decide to let you take me home. We walk out of the club, hand in hand, after we say goodbye to my friends. Then what do we do?"

Fradella smiled, a little uneasy.

"Um, we continue to make out on the way to the car. If you're into me, I'm not going to let you cool off. We kiss and—"

"We kiss, precisely," Tess announced, triumphantly. Then she circled a date two weeks prior to her abduction, a date only eight days after the day she went clubbing with her friends. It was the approximate date Doc Rizza had estimated Sonya's lower lip bite had happened.

"See? That's what made him a creep. He bit her. A smart girl, she walked away. This creep is a definite lead. We can't ignore him."

"That could work, yes," Michowsky said, "but the dates don't work. I don't think Doc Rizza could be off by more than a week on stuff like that."

She pursed her lips, frustrated. It would make more sense if the dates aligned. But they didn't.

"We need to go back and talk to the girlfriends. They have to remember something about the creep."

She shuffled the case file papers from North Miami Missing Persons, where Detective Garcia had documented his interviews and had discarded the creep lead as irrelevant and unrelated. Unfortunately, little else was in the case notes; nothing she could use.

"Okay, let's finish this," she said, pointing at the whiteboard.

Above the timeline, they placed each girl's picture, at the top of the board. Then they pasted a few crime scene photos for each victim, then listed key elements of each case. When finally done, they stepped back and looked at their work.

"I like to work serial killer victimology in a matrixed format," Tess announced, then clarified, seeing how puzzled they looked. "I just build a table and put in there all the commonalities we can find."

She drew a table under the photos and above the timeline and started writing their names, aligning the names with the photos above. She added one more column, and titled it, "?"

"I thought you call them unsubs," Michowsky said. "And what's he doing in the victims' table?"

"I can call him the unsub if you prefer," she replied, correcting the table header. "This is a commonalities matrix. We identify what the victims have in common, then we add what little we know about the unsub, and maybe we can establish where their circles intersected. As we uncover suspects, we could add them to the matrix, and see who's a better match. Clear?"

"Crystal," Fradella replied, tilting his head with a smile of appreciation.

"The first to be found, almost two years ago, was May Lin, Chinese-American from Chicago, 17 years and 10 months old. She was found north of Kenosha, on the east-facing beach of Lake Michigan. Her father, Hiro 'Hank' Lin, is a real estate developer, major bucks." She added a line to the table, and on the first column she wrote, "$$$." Then she put a checkmark under May's name, on the dollar's column. "This is one of the things these victims have in common. They're from rich families. But we also know, per Doc Rizza's impeccable logic, that the unsub is pretty well off himself." She added a checkmark on the unsub's column, on the dollar's line. "The unsub held her for only a day and a half, and what else are we noticing?"

"She wasn't dumped naked," Michowsky said. "The local cops thought someone had covered the body when they found it, but they couldn't establish that. She was covered with a..." he checked his notes, "common, hotel-grade bed sheet. No trace fibers, no wear and tear, nothing. He probably bought it new and unsealed it at the dump site, wearing gloves."

"Yeah, exactly. You know that means remorse, right?" Tess asked. "In theory, at least. Psychopaths don't feel guilt or remorse."

"So is it possible she was his first victim then?" Fradella asked.

Tess shuffled through the case printouts.

"No hesitation marks on the lethal blow or on the other cuts found on her body. We can't assume she was his first victim. No, let's consider this unverifiable for now. All right, victim number two, found 10 months ago. Shanequa Powell, 21, an African-American from Atlanta. She was found, yes, you guessed it, on a stretch of east-facing beach of Lake Lanier, northeast of Atlanta. She'd been gone almost four days when they found her. She majored in economics. Adoptive mother is *the* Carolyn O'Sullivan, bestselling romance novelist. Of course, loaded," Tess added, and checked the dollar's box, "and college grad." She checked the respective box, then took a sip of water from a bottle.

She looked at the table for a minute, wondering what else the victims had in common. The geographical dispersion of the abduction and dump sites limited any common places or events the victims might have frequented. It's relatively easy, when victims are from the same area, to establish where the unsub might have first set eyes on them. A church they all go to, a gym, or a massage parlor. Maybe a grocery store, or a car shop. In their case, however, geography was their enemy. One victim per state, and at the age where they don't travel, don't do much other than school, local friends, and social media. Could this predator have been an online stalker before grabbing them? Definitely a theory worth looking into. She scribbled a note at the side of the board, and circled it. It read, "check the online angle."

"What's that?" Michowsky asked. "You forgot us again, you're working alone. We're not spectators, you know."

"Oh, come on, seriously? I was doing you a favor, writing down all this stuff. Jeez..." Amazing how men bristle out of anything. Everything is threatening their egos. She shrugged it off and continued. "I was thinking he could have stalked them online, that's all. With this spread-out geography. And no, you're not a spectator, so you do the next one, all right?" She handed the marker to Michowsky, who scoffed as he took it.

"We have Emma Taylor, 19, Caucasian. She was from Summerville, South Carolina, the daughter of Jerry Taylor, a dentist. Mother deceased. She was found on Johns Island, facing east. She was kept for five days. What else... yeah, she'd just finished pre-med," he added, checking the college box. "Do we consider her for the dollars line? A dentist is not really that loaded."

"They're well off, so, yes, I'd say check the box," Tess replied. "I see a new pattern. These girls are very smart, disciplined, hard-working overachievers. Look at their age, and they graduated from college already? Pretty darn amazing."

She took the marker from Michowsky's hand and added another line, labeled, "Overachiever."

She checked the boxes for Shanequa and Emma, but added a question mark for May. They didn't know that about her yet. May's case file was particularly thin, skimpy.

"Finally, we have Sonya," she added, writing her information in the table. "Caucasian, 22 years old, graduated from Florida State with a marketing and communications degree. Her father is a restaurant owner, so, yeah, bucks. Maybe not megabucks, like with Mr. Lin or Carolyn O'Sullivan, but definitely affluent."

She stood upright and stretched her back, sore from bending forward to write on the board.

"That makes it easy," Fradella said, "the way you do it. Commonalities are really clear."

"Let's look at discrepancies. The first victim is definitely different. Younger, only kept a day and a half, body dumped covered, not naked," Tess listed, counting on her fingers.

"So what makes May Lin this unsub's victim after all?" Michowsky said. "I don't see it. Is it just the beach factor?"

"The beach factor allowed us to find her in the database," Tess replied. "The beach as the secondary crime scene of choice doesn't make her this unsub's victim. Her autopsy report does; what was done to her. That's why we need to see Doc Rizza again. My guess is this table of commonalities will soon add a few lines."

15

EVIDENCE

Doc Rizza read the medicolegal examination reports quietly, methodically, taking notes at times. He didn't say a word until he finished all three, and even then he only spoke briefly, advising them he was going to reread his own findings on Sonya, to make sure he wasn't forgetting anything.

Tess stood, shifting her weight from one foot to the other, waiting impatiently for the ME to finish. She wanted to rush out there and interview Sonya's friends, to see if her gut was right about the creep. She recalled being told on several occasions, by SAC Pearson and by another supervisor before him, that she tended to rush into doing things without giving them enough thought. That she favored action over collaboration, and that she many times left her team behind, frustrated, eating her dust. Was that a bad thing, though? They'd told her yes, it was a bad thing, and it needed to stop. It destroyed team cohesion, and was more than likely going to lead to errors, to costly mistakes made during the course of lengthier investigations. Yet her case record was perfect. It might have annoyed others, but for her, the method worked just fine.

On the other hand, her on-and-off therapist, Dr. Navarro, had told her she needed to rush into action, because she couldn't bear to stand still and let unchecked memories and feelings invade her mind. Standing there, in the middle of the chilly morgue, and staring into the crime scenes photos scattered on Doc Rizza's table, she fought a wave of loaded memories—memories she wanted deeply buried, never to come out again. It was hard not to let her mind wander in that direction. It was impossible not to identify herself with all those girls. Mostly she hated the thought that she'd always have such memories, such scars to bear and hide. Time could only bring limited relief, and, in her case, time had stood still for years. Time could be a son of a bitch when it wanted to. It could break your heart when you realized you've forgotten how a loved one looked or how they talked, only so soon after they'd left this earth. Or it could decide to forever torture you, not letting you forget the most agonizing moments of your life, condemning you to relive them over and over again, in sleep or in waking. Leaving you a deranged bundle of taut nerves, unable to enjoy life or to accept love, dreading and yearning for people's company at the same time. Slowly, irreversibly turning you into a freak.

"Yeah, I see what you mean," Doc Rizza broke the silence. He took off his thin-rimmed glasses and rubbed the bridge of his nose. "I'm not 100 percent convinced it's the same man, but there are similarities."

"Do you think—" Michowsky started, but Tess interrupted him.

"What do you see?" she asked. It was better to ask open-ended questions. People tend to be more objective and direct that way.

"They were all drugged, that's true. But that's where the similarities stop. May Lin, the first victim, was chemically subdued. She was given some Rohypnol, orally, most likely in a drink. Sadly, this is quite common these days. She was immobilized with some fabric ties, leaving her with friction burns, much different from Sonya's. The lab identified some fibers in May's case. Silk, cotton, polyester, all very common, a few tiny fibers caught in her abrasions. She was raped several times, and no DNA was retrieved. She was killed with a stab wound to the side of her neck. That fits, but nothing else does."

He talked slowly, and normally that drove Tess up the wall, but he was very organized, structuring information really well, and that saved lots of time. She refrained from interrupting him again.

"Victim number two, Shanequa," he continued, "was given codeine, also orally. No injection marks on her either. Her wrists and ankles were bound with cable ties and presented deep lacerations from the sharp edges of the ties. Shanequa was beaten badly, including her face. This element doesn't fit the profile. She was also raped several times, including penetration with objects, and some form of electrocution. Doesn't fit. There were contact burns on her thighs. Shanequa was strangled to death, which, again, doesn't fit."

He closed Shanequa's file and opened Emma Taylor's.

"Number three, Emma, is where we see the most similarities with Sonya. The first time we find IV marks and proof she was fed intravenously. The first time we find pain-threshold-lowering drugs, but she was also given anxiolytics and opiates. Emma was immobilized in a similar harness, leaving very superficial abrasion marks on her skin, but the harness was different. Also she was the first victim to be sodomized. She too was stabbed in the neck, but with a large, serrated blade." He paused for a little while, running his hand through his thinning hair. "And Sonya, we know."

"So?" Tess asked, impatiently.

"I don't know," he replied. "You seem adamant it's the same killer, but can we be sure? Yes, we have several commonalities, but we have more things that are different. Could they be explained by the natural evolution of a serial killer? Typically, we don't see that. We see them repeating the same fantasy, over and over again. This killer, if it's indeed the work of the same man, only repeated the rape, the beach, and the drugs, but not the *same* drugs."

"So you're saying it's not the same man, Doc?" she insisted.

"I'm saying I'm not sure, and you know I can't speculate."

"I agree. We can't be sure," Michowsky added. "It sort of feels like a serial, but that isn't enough. It varies too much; you can't ignore the differences."

"Doc, have you found bite marks on any of the earlier victims?" Tess asked, remembering her only lead in Sonya's case.

"I saw something in Shanequa's file, a mention from the ME that it could have been a bite on her lower lip, but she was so badly beaten he couldn't be sure."

"Ah… how about Emma Taylor?"

"Let's see…" he mumbled, sifting through the many pages of her medicolegal report. "Emma's face wasn't damaged, and, no, there isn't a bite mark on her lower lip. Um… there's one on her left ear though." He took off his glasses again. "I don't know… bites are common in sexual crimes. We find them quite often, unfortunately. In sexual sadism, biting is an expression of frustration."

"I know you can't speculate… most MEs hate speculations, but if you had to make a call, what would it be? Is this a serial killer's work, or are we looking at multiple, unrelated murderers?"

"I'd eliminate the first victim, May Lin. Her age is wrong, her profile doesn't match, there were almost no drugs, not any requiring medical proficiency anyway. She wasn't dumped naked… really, there's nothing to cling to, other than that beach. As for the second victim, it's a toss."

"How about superficial cuts? Any of the vics had those?" Michowsky asked.

"Only Emma, and not very many. Just a few, most of them almost completely healed by the time she died. On her lower back, buttocks, and thighs."

"I see," Michowsky replied. "So that won't even count."

"Really?" Tess blurted. "You guys really can't see the pattern here?"

"I can," Fradella replied. "I still think it's the same guy."

"I don't, sorry," Michowsky added. "It was a long shot to begin with."

"I could, potentially, see it," Doc Rizza added, "but he's changing MOs too damn much. Nobody does that."

Tess frowned and clasped her hands, feeling a wave of anger rising inside her like the tide. She took in a deep breath; right or wrong, Doc Rizza had a point. Who does that? What kind of anger-excitation killer does that?

And then she knew. The idea came like the metaphorical light bulb, illuminating all details and bringing sense and logic where there had been none.

"I know what he's doing, guys," she said excitedly. "He's experimenting."

Doc Rizza's eyebrows shot up high, wrinkling his forehead. Michowsky's lip twitched in disbelief.

"Huh? For what purpose?" Michowsky asked.

"Remember we just discussed how all sexual sadists, all serial killers have their own fantasy, or recipe if you prefer, that they follow with little variation to get the satisfaction they're craving?"

"Yeah," Michowsky replied, "and?"

Doc Rizza frowned, focused.

"And what if I was wrong when I categorized him as an anger-excitation killer? What if he's retaliatory?"

"Not sure I follow," Fradella said.

"What if he's rehearsing for the final event, the torture, rape, and murder of the woman who's the object of his rage? What if he's perfecting the method in which he can inflict the longest, worst possible pain and terror? What if he wants to find out just how he can get the most satisfaction? I think it's the same guy, and he's experimenting. That's why the number of drugs is increasing, and so is the number of cuts, and the number of days he's torturing them. That's why his cooling-off period is shorter every time."

No one spoke for a few seconds, leaving silence to be disrupted only by the low hum of the refrigeration unit.

"I guess it could work, your scenario," Doc Rizza replied, rubbing his forehead. "Do you think he's getting ready for his final kill? If he does that, he could disappear forever."

Tess paced the morgue nervously, agitated. She needed to make a decision.

"I think I should call Quantico."

16

CALL FOR HELP

Tess finished typing her high-level report, iterating the main points of the investigation for SAC Pearson, as concisely as she could put it. Of course, she could have also called Pearson instead of writing him a report, but she avoided that like the plague. Recently, her interactions with her supervisor had been nothing short of frustrating, and she didn't want any more of that.

She lifted her eyes briefly from the laptop's screen and saw Fradella and Michowsky sitting two desks over, immersed in mapping Sonya's last 24 hours before her disappearance. They still had holes in that timeline, and phone records were not available yet.

Tess read the report again, then hit send. At the end of a very well-structured memo, in her opinion at least, there was a request for assistance from one of Quantico's expert profilers. She hoped an expert in serial killer behavior could shed some light on the numerous unknowns in their case. Was the unsub a retaliatory or an excitation rapist? Based on such varied victimology, who could possibly be the object of his rage? What other motivations could he have for jumping across racial boundaries, physiognomies, and state lines? Where in the world could someone, no matter how affluent, torture women for days on end, in different states, without getting caught? Without raising any suspicion? Where and how did he pick his victims?

Her phone rang, with a custom ring she'd associated with her boss's extension, the quacking of a duck. It was her humorous way of expressing the frustration she felt each time the man called. She cringed, but picked it up immediately, under the curious glances thrown by several squad room cops.

"This is Winnett,"

"Winnett, SAC Pearson here."

"Sir."

"I read your report. First of all, I'm amazed to see you're actually asking for help. The I'm-good-on-my-own, don't-need-a-team Winnett finally comes to her senses. Congratulations."

"Um… thank you, sir."

"You're welcome. Now, as for the profiler, before we waste incredibly scarce and valuable resources, let me tell you I don't see the serial killer you're describing."

"Sir, I put it in the report as well as I could. You have the beach element, naked body dumps, drug use, method of restraint, and method of killing."

"What about victimology? They're all over the place. One's Asian, another's black—"

"If you look past the physical appearances, you'll see most of them are young, smart, college grad overachievers," she said, swallowing a long sigh.

He must have skimmed over her report if he missed all this data. He was an irritating, politically absorbed boss, but he was a good investigator; no way he'd miss the patterns. Unless he'd completely ignored her report.

"Uh-huh, I see what you mean, but still. The Asian victim is definitely not a match."

"Let's say we exclude that one, we still have three. And three is enough to classify him as a serial killer."

"I'd exclude the second victim too, the black girl, Shanequa Powell. Different MO altogether. Do you know how many women are raped and killed every year in our country? Over a thousand cases a year, Winnett, you know that. Most of them have drugs and alcohol involvement."

"I know, sir, but—"

"Don't fall into the trap of serializing random cases out there, because it's an easy trap to fall into. You can only dump a body in so many places, you know. These women have little, if anything, in common other than the beach as a secondary crime scene."

"That could be enough," Tess insisted.

"That's a pretty strong correlation, I'll give you that, but I think only two victims remain, the last two. Emma Taylor and Sonya Weaver. Those were both ocean beaches too."

"I don't think it matters, the type of beach, I mean."

"Ocean versus lake?"

"Yes, I don't think it matters. I think it's about the concept for him. That east-facing beach at sunrise means something to him."

"You have no basis for that, Winnett. You're speculating; you're guessing even."

She bit her lip, thinking. He was right, and she hated to admit it. It was just her gut telling her that a freshwater beach had the same symbolic value for the unsub as an ocean beach.

"All right, let's say you're right," she conceded. "So we're down to two victims, but we're still good to classify this unsub as a serial killer, per the official FBI definition, right?"

He didn't reply immediately and she didn't press on.

"If you want to call it a serial, Winnett, I'll have to send in a team. We can't have you work the case on your own."

She stomped her foot angrily and hoped he didn't hear it.

"Don't take my case, sir, please. I need a win, and I can nail this bastard. I know I can."

"Winnett, it's procedure. How many serial killer cases have you worked? More than a dozen, right?"

"Twenty-one, actually, since I started."

"So you know the drill. And even if you have a team, when you catch your killer, you still win. What makes you think you can only win alone? You didn't have this problem working with Mike."

"Um… it's not that. In this case, I have a strong sense we need to hurry. I'd rather work alone on this one. Please. I'm faster when I'm alone. But I'd appreciate an analyst, if that's on the table. I also need faster lab turnaround times and faster warrant processing. We're crawling here in Palm Beach County."

Her last comment gained her a couple of glares from the cops within earshot. Great.

Pearson scoffed.

"I'll see what I can do. With Quantico though, you might be out of luck. The profiling team is deployed on a terrorism case. They—"

"Yeah, I know, terrorism trumps serial killers."

"Good, I'm glad you get it. I'll assign you a partner in the next few days, and that's not up for debate."

She couldn't bring herself to reply.

"Winnett?" he asked. "You *will* make it work with your new partner. Are we understood?"

"Yes, sir," she said quietly.

"Have you been raking in any more complaints?"

"Not that I know of. No."

"Keep it that way."

He hung up, without saying goodbye or anything. Asshole.

She slammed the phone down on the desk, wishing she could afford to stomp it under her feet and break it into a million little pieces. Then she rushed to the cafeteria, where she poured herself a large cup of coffee, borrowing someone's empty mug without asking for permission. She took a couple of mouthfuls of what must have been a strong contender for America's worst swill and contained a pressing urge to spend valuable time obsessing over who her new partner was going to be. No one could ever replace Mike… no one should even be allowed to try.

Then she opened her laptop and started looking for flights.

17

MISUNDERSTANDINGS

"Going somewhere?" Michowsky asked coldly.

He was grim, tense. He stood in front of Tess's desk, his lips curled up in a grimace, not a smile. His entire being emanated contempt, or at least a healthy dose of aggravation. Tess wanted to ask, but the squad room could prove to be the wrong place for such questions. Anyone's guess... maybe he got a bad phone call, or his pain meds had stopped working. Maybe Mrs. Michowsky had a problem with him and bit his head off instead of morning sex. Maybe his midlife crisis had caught up with him again.

"Yeah," she replied, ignoring his frigid tone. "I think it's time we interviewed the other victims' families. Chicago is the first stop. I need your full name and date of birth to book the flight."

"I'm a Palm Beach County cop, Winnett. There's no budget for out-of-state travel. You're at it alone, just how you like it."

He turned on his heels and walked away.

"Hey," she shouted at his back, "what the hell is that supposed to mean?"

He returned and leaned over her desk, slamming his hands down on the scratched, weathered surface, hard enough to make the whole thing rattle.

"You have to ask? Jeez, Winnett!"

What the hell did she do this time? She refrained from snapping at him, and swallowed the first words that came to her mind.

"Yes, I do have to ask," she replied. "Something upset you and I have no idea what."

"Something?" he snapped, then scoffed. "Not something, you!"

Her eyebrows shot up.

"What did I do?"

"You really don't know, do you? Or you think us so stupid, that you can't believe we actually can understand a few words in English when we hear them loud and clear, huh? What was it... 'We're crawling here at Palm Beach'?"

"Oh..." she said quietly, wishing she could kick herself.

That was her absolute specialty. Stepping on people's toes, hurting them by accident, insulting them when she never had the intention. When it came to people, she was the bull in everyone's china shop. While on the call with SAC Pearson, she'd been so focused on the conversation that she didn't even notice who was around her to hear her words. She didn't think people would understand if they heard only her half of the exchange.

"I—I didn't mean it, Gary," she said in way of an apology. "It was a conversation with my boss, and he wanted to know what kind of help I—um, we need. Please believe it's nothing personal."

"You pissed off a lot of good cops today, Winnett. I thought I might have been wrong about you, but, no, when you're not careful, the stuck-up bitch comes out. It's not a pretty sight."

"Noted," she said firmly, feeling fed up with it. "Now let's focus on our next steps. That is, if you still want to work this case."

"It didn't last long, did it?" Michowsky asked, his lip curled up in a crooked smile.

"What?"

"Your remorse."

She sighed, a long, shuttered breath of frustration and dismay.

"I apologized and I explained. You refused to accept either. What do you want me to do, book us some group therapy?"

Michowsky shook his head, keeping his eyes focused on the floor. Then he looked at her almost defiantly.

"All right, Special Agent Winnett, what do you want to do next?"

She felt the intonation in his words, when he spoke her title and name, as slaps to her face. They were intended as such; Michowsky made it very clear he was distancing from her and wanted his distance, the minimal involvement required to work the case and nothing more. She swallowed a mouthful of cusswords and managed to stay calm. Men and their goddamned egos.

"I will visit the victims' families starting tomorrow morning. My first stop is Chicago. If you change your mind and want to come along, please let me know."

"Why? You need someone you can blame flight delays on?"

"Oh, come on, Michowsky, cut it out already!"

Neither of them spoke for a few seconds, the silence between them interrupted by stifled chuckles from other cops witnessing their exchange.

"Why Chicago?" Michowsky finally spoke, somewhat pacified. "I thought we discarded May Lin as a first victim."

"You discarded her, and so has my boss, but I, for one, haven't. As far as I'm concerned, she's still the first we should be looking at."

"It's actually entertaining to watch you operate, Winnett," Michowsky said. "You pretend to consult with us, pretend to have conversations and collaborate, but in fact you just do whatever the fuck you want, don't you?"

"Well, I'm happy you see it that way," she replied, her voice riddled with biting sarcasm. "Then I'll just tell you I want Sonya Weaver's ex-boyfriend brought in for questioning, and you won't argue, because you already know it's pointless!"

"Well, what do you know? We slow, stupid Palm Beach County cops didn't think of that on our own... good thing the almighty Special Agent Winnett has come to save our lame asses, right?"

She stood abruptly, bewildered. What the hell was wrong with him? How many times did she need to apologize? Her jaw dropped, and she stood there unable to articulate a response, struggling between the words she really wanted to say, and the certainty that she shouldn't further escalate their ridiculous conflict. Another complaint was all it took to push SAC Pearson over the edge.

"Boyfriend's in Interview One. Fradella's been grilling him for an hour," Michowsky said, shaking his head. "You're welcome."

She sat back on the battle-scarred chair and looked Michowsky in the eye.

"Listen, I didn't mean to piss you off, or anyone else for that matter," she explained. "When I said on the phone that Palm Beach was crawling, I said that in the context of warrants being issued, which is county justice, and lab tests being completed, which is not you either. Or anyone else here. Honestly, if you wouldn't be in such a goddamned hurry to feel insulted, you'd use that detective brain of yours to derive that all I said was meant to help us, not offend anyone. Well, maybe except for county justice and the lab, but they weren't here, now were they?"

He looked at her without saying a word, but the tension in his facial features seemed to slowly dissipate, replaced by sadness and weariness.

"Can we just bury the hatchet, Michowsky?" she asked "We're both better than this."

He ran his hand through his buzz-cut hair.

"One condition," he said, "that you tell me why you want to interrogate the ex-boyfriend, when you so strongly believe it's a serial killer murdering these girls. Is the ex a real suspect?"

"He could be," she replied thoughtfully, "in the scenario that all the other prior murders were rehearsals, experimentations for the perfect kill, and that Sonya was the killer's object of rage. Although I doubt that, I have to cover all my bases; but I really want to know what he saw in the recent times they've been together. Maybe she was being stalked, and he noticed it. Maybe he can give us something, anything we can use."

Michowsky made an inviting gesture with his hand, and Tess followed him to Interview Room One. Through the one-sided mirror, they watched Fradella interview the ex-boyfriend for a while, asking all the routine questions, and receiving more or less vanilla answers, as bland and useless as they could get.

She checked her notes to refresh her memory. The ex-boyfriend, Anthony Gibbons, was a few years older than Sonya; he'd just turned 26. He sat on the uncomfortable, metallic chair in the interview room, like he was seated on a fine leather recliner. He leaned back and had crossed his legs man-style, bringing his left ankle on top of his right knee and keeping his left hand casually thrown over his left shin. He was comfortable, attractive, and aggressively sexy in a young Tom Cruise kind of way, and arrogant, of course. Seeing in the file photo how beautiful Sonya was, the two must have made a striking couple.

She could smell the money on him, in his attitude, his posture, his facial expression. Detective Todd Fradella wasn't in control of the interview; Anthony Gibbons was. But, of course, Tess was planning to keep that observation to herself. No more china shops.

"I want to go in," she told Michowsky.

"Knock yourself out. But be careful. This guy's loaded. I'm surprised there isn't an army of hotshot lawyers here with him already."

She entered the interview room and nodded briefly in Todd's direction. Then she flashed her badge quickly, mainly just for show, in Gibbons's face.

"Special Agent Winnett, FBI," she said coldly.

She pulled the spare chair from the corner of the room, its legs screeching across the concrete floor, and sat across the table, staring Gibbons down. He held her gaze, unperturbed.

"So, just how emasculated did you feel when she dumped you, Anthony? Or is it Tony?"

That threw him off just a little. For a split second, she saw a flicker of fear, but then he recomposed, crazy fast.

"What? No... she didn't dump me. Even if she did, I don't really care. There's plenty of—"

"Just stop before saying the word pussy, all right? It pisses me off."

"Whoa... I was going to say opportunity, but hey," he said, smirking arrogantly.

Damn. The guy was cool under pressure. Tess decided to change tactics.

"Then what really happened? Why did you two break up?"

He shifted in his seat, just slightly.

"It wasn't working out. We were arguing all the time. She was so damn cerebral; it drove me crazy. I wanted to have fun... life is short, right? She'd turn down a night out for a good book, or for some stupid conference she'd watch over the Internet."

"You two fought?"

"Like adult intellectuals. None of us was throwing things or scratching the other one's eyes out, if that's what you're asking. We had arguments, conflicts of principle."

"You wanted to party all the time, huh? What do you do for a living?"

"I'm an entrepreneur. I start businesses, then I sell them. For loads."

"I see. Where did you two like to hang out?"

"That's just it. I'd have to drag her out, most of the time. She occasionally liked to dance, so it would be one of those hip clubs in Miami Beach, but mostly she wanted something more low key, like dining out and then a walk on the beach, some boring crap like that."

"What did you want to do?"

"Clubs. I love the action," he replied, and as he spoke his face lit up and a smile broke through.

Ah... he liked to showcase himself in the middle of hordes of hot women, all stripping him naked with their eyes. A narcissist in the making, if not already there. But a killer? Tess didn't get that vibe.

"Tell me how you broke up. Who initiated the separation, and who was left behind, crying?"

"No one, really. Some five or six weeks ago we got into an argument again, then I told her it wasn't working out for me. She said it wasn't for her either, and we went our own ways from there. The following day I went by to pick up my stuff and brought hers, what she had left at my place. Every now and then we'd cross paths, we'd say hi, no hard feelings. I started dating other people, and so did she."

"So all peaceful and nice, huh?"

"Yeah."

"How long have you been together?"

"Um, maybe six months or so?"

"I see."

He wasn't lying, that was clear. His body language supported every word he said. He was relaxed, calm, although annoyingly arrogant, but that's not illegal. His story matched Sonya's actions. Only a week or two after the breakup, she was out clubbing with her girlfriends and making out with the creep. Strange how every story ended up in that focal point, starring the creep, her strongest lead.

Did Sonya go out after that night with the creep, three weeks ago, before the night she was abducted? Between February 28 and March 22, what did she do? Where did she go? When were the damn financials going to come in? She needed to see if she'd gone out after that night, and where. With whom. Maybe there was a paper trail to that creep or to something. Someone.

"When you were going out with Sonya, did you notice anyone following you?" Tess asked, getting ready to end the interview.

"Like who?"

"Anyone being weird around her, anyone hitting on her and not taking no for an answer, someone like that?"

"No... I haven't noticed anyone, and she never mentioned anything either." He rubbed his square chin thoughtfully, then he continued, his voice tinted with sadness. "We weren't a fit, but I cared for Sonya. At first, when you had me brought here, and when I saw you're FBI, I thought maybe someone had made a ransom call, or you have more information in her disappearance. But now... she's Dawn Girl, isn't she? I've seen the news coverage. That was Sonya?"

"The name hasn't been released to the media yet," Tess replied. "I'm very sorry for your loss."

18

GIRLFRIENDS

Tess left the interview room and closed the door behind her. She went straight into the observation room, where Michowsky took a small stool near the one-sided mirror, watching. Her half-empty coffee mug was right where she'd left it, on the small table near that mirror, its content colder and staler by about 30 minutes. In that particular case, not much of a loss; that coffee didn't have any taste to begin with. Impervious, she guzzled almost all of it, thirstily.

"We're letting him go, I presume," Michowsky asked.

"Yeah. He's not involved." She read some notes in the file. "I see here his alibi checked out for the time Sonya went missing, and I didn't hear anything today worth further looking into."

Michowsky knocked twice on the one-sided mirror using his wedding band, the sharp, metallic sound loud enough to get his partner's attention. Tess watched how Fradella thanked Tony Gibbons and escorted him out.

"We need to speak to the girlfriends, ASAP. I think there's value in pursuing the creep angle. How soon can we do it? Can we do it now?"

"You want both of them together? Or one at a time?"

"Both together is fine."

"All right," he said, a wicked little smile tugging at his lip. "You're all set. Interview Two."

"They're here?" Tess asked, surprised. "Detective Michowsky, I'm impressed!"

"We're not completely useless, us county cops," he quipped, with a hint of the earlier disappointment. "We sometimes even think for ourselves."

"Ah... you had to bring it up again," Tess laughed. On an impulse, she patted him on the arm, in a gesture of gratitude and camaraderie. Then she froze and withdrew. The long forgotten familiarity of the gesture, the physical contact with another human being, albeit furtive and inconsequential, all that normality she had lost more than 10 years before, had reappeared for a second, then vanished again. She wasn't ready for it. Not yet.

She cleared her throat, suddenly dry and choked for some reason, and took the last gulp of coffee she had left. She abandoned the empty mug on a small service table, in passing to the observation room adjacent to Interview Two. Michowsky followed her and closed the door behind them.

"These are, um," he checked the file, "Ashely King, 23, note the weird spelling with the "e" before the "l," and Carmen Pozzan, 22. They were with Sonya at the club, the night she met the individual we call the creep. Ashely is the blonde."

"*She* called," Tess intervened. "Sonya called him the creep, not us. Frame of reference is important."

"Yeah, you're right."

"Hey, I need one more favor, and it's big."

"Shoot," Michowsky replied, frowning a little.

"Get those slow-as-molasses people from county justice to step on it with the damn paperwork," she asked, barely containing a smile. If he'd brought it up again, so could she. "We need Sonya's financial records today. As soon as they come in, please ask Fradella to go over them with the fine comb and all that."

"What are you looking for?"

"Uh... just a hunch at this point. But we still have to look at them, right?"

"Winnett, what the hell?" he insisted.

"What?"

"Share, for Chrissake."

"All right, okay. I'm thinking, what if the creep was so creepy she didn't even dare to get out of the house after that night? For a while? What if he scared her so badly, or whatever happened was so dreadful she couldn't even tell her friends? If that's what went on, her spending patterns would show it. We're talking about a young girl with means, remember? They shop, they have 10-dollar, iced cappuccinos every day, they eat out, buy cosmetics and jewelry at least once a week, and last, but not least, they go clubbing with friends. Let's see if her spending patterns before February 28 changed after she met the creep. He might have left his mark."

"Okay. It's definitely worth looking into. You got some insight, you know?"

"Yeah… I've been told."

"Can I throw in your name with the judge, to speed things up?"

"Mine is more or less worthless these days, unfortunately. Use SAC Pearson's, he's my boss. He's still solid currency."

"You got it," Michowsky replied, then hustled out of the room.

Tess half-sat on the three-legged stool in front of the one-way mirror and studied the two young women. A shred of bitter sadness clouded her mind a little, as she took in the details of their appearance. The two girls were beautiful, dazzling young creatures, a pleasure to look at. Young and full of life, of optimism, of that invincibility that crowns youthful existences until the first disaster of their lives reminds them of their frailty, of their innate vulnerability, and forever shrouds them in fear. She used to be like that, just like them. Maybe not as beautiful, but fresh and joyful and unharmed. Maybe not as rich, well, not even close. Buried in student loans and barely making ends meet, yet she had felt invincible, like she was going to be young and carefree forever. Until one night, one dark night more than 10 years ago.

Tess shook her head vigorously, pushing the unwanted memory back to the dark, haunted abyss it had emerged from. She turned her full attention back to the girls. They were somewhat tense, probably uncomfortable to be waiting in a police interrogation room. Interview room, the cops called it, but that didn't fool anyone.

Ashely wore low-cut skinny jeans and a skimpy top, revealing her belly button and a strip of flat, tan abdomen. Long earrings were sometimes visible behind curtains of long, sleek, shiny blonde hair. Her makeup was a little too much for that time of day, but nevertheless classy, not trashy. Just a tad of eyeliner and some discreet eye shadow, pink lipstick, and a hint of blush. She was the one sitting, her shoulders forward, tense, frowning, clasping her hands.

Carmen had that fiery, passionate Latin vibe seeping through every pore of her perfect skin. She held her head up straight, and her long, wavy, dark hair tied in a loose ponytail revealed a beautiful face. Dressed in fancy shorts and a silk, sleeveless blouse, she paced the room nervously, occasionally tugging at the hemline of her shorts. She was probably sorry she didn't wear something longer, more fitting for cold, intimidating police interview rooms. Pacing back and forth, Carmen had the proud bearing of a caged lioness; no matter if captive, still noble.

Tess took a sticky note and scribbled a message for Michowsky to find when he returned. She wrote, "Notice how all the players have means well above average? $$$ is a small, exclusive world." She pasted the sticky in the middle of the one-sided mirror, then went into the interview room to speak with the two girls.

"Good afternoon," Tess said, as she entered the room. Ashely sprung to her feet, and Carmen approached from behind the table. "I'm Special Agent Tess Winnett. Please feel free to call me Tess."

She took a seat, inviting the two girls to follow suit. The girls obeyed, averting Tess's eyes.

"Thanks for coming in today; it's really helpful," she continued. "Why don't you tell me in detail what went on the night of February 28, when you went clubbing with Sonya?"

The girls look at each other.

"We already spoke with a detective, after she'd gone missing," Ashely finally said, her voice unsure, hesitant.

"I know you did, a Detective Garcia, right?"

They nodded.

"Please humor me... I'm FBI. Different methods, you know." Tess spoke lightly with a small smile, encouraging them to ease up a little. "I'd rather hear the story firsthand, than read through Garcia's notes."

"Ah, I see," Ashely said, relaxing her shoulders just a tiny bit. "We went clubbing that night, just the three of us, at the Exhale. She'd broken up with Tony, and—"

"Was she upset?" Tess asked. "After her breakup?"

The girls looked at each other for a split second, then Carmen replied.

"Nah. She was fine. She'd always called Tony her collectible item. She knew it wasn't going to last. No real passion on either side." The two girls giggled quietly.

"Collectible?"

"You know, someone who's like, you know, a fancy scarf, nice to wear on your arm when you go out, but shallow and irrelevant. Not long-term material."

"Was he cheating on her?"

They looked at each other again and both shrugged, almost exactly at the same time.

"She didn't think so, but that wasn't going to last either. Boy toys like Tony always cheat in the end."

"Was he mad? About the breakup?"

"I don't think so," Ashely replied. "He seemed cool with it. He had plenty of girls lined up."

"Yeah, he did," Carmen added.

"All right, so tell me about the night you guys went out the time before last. The 28th, last month."

"We wanted to dance, have a little fun, maybe meet some interesting guys. I was between boyfriends too," Carmen shared.

"How about you?" Tess asked, looking at Ashely.

"I sort of had someone, but he was out of town on business that night and didn't join us. Perfect opportunity to go out with the girls, right?"

"Right... so what happened? Who did you meet?"

"We got there early, because we wanted a table, and we got one. It really sucks at these clubs when you want to catch your breath but can't sit down anywhere. And you're on heels too," Ashely chuckled, a quick, almost stifled tension chuckle.

Tess looked at her for a couple of seconds, practically staring. A table at one of those joints was a grand a night, minimum. They don't seat you at a table unless you get a bottle of booze; obviously, that bottle normally sells for about $950 or more. Not only the girls had cash, they also drew the attention of the entire club by sitting at that table. It was like they'd worn a sign reading, "Look at me, I'm loaded." That, plus they had plenty of booze on their hands.

"What did you drink?"

"Champagne. We didn't want that much liquor. It was just the three of us," Ashely replied.

"Then what happened?"

"We got on the dance floor. The music is awesome there, you know," Carmen said, making a dancing gesture with both her hands and swinging her shoulders. "Two songs into it, this guy appears out of nowhere, and starts hitting on Sonya."

"Hitting, how?"

"Dancing in front of her, smiling at her—"

"Making eye contact, you know," Ashely added. "He was good looking, that guy. She's always so quick to score attention from interesting men."

"Why?" Tess asked innocently.

"Have you even *looked* at her picture? She's gorgeous!" Carmen replied.

"Do you envy her for her looks?"

"Why the—um, why would I do that? I'm pretty gorgeous myself!" Carmen replied, visibly surprised.

"Yes, you are," Tess admitted, unable to contain a smile. "So tell me about that guy, the one hitting on Sonya. Was she into him?"

"Yes, she was. He was hot," Ashely said with a dreamy smile.

"Describe him for me," Tess asked.

"He had blond hair and blue eyes, but he wasn't like a Ken, you know."

"Ken who?"

"You know, Barbie's boyfriend," Ashely said, not containing her disappointment with Tess's limited knowledge of such things.

"I see. In what way wasn't he a Ken?"

"He was attractive, but masculine, even if he had light hair and blue eyes. He was well built, with strong arms."

To handle the weight of a collapsed girl or a body in full rigor, Tess thought. But that thought meant she'd jumped to conclusions, and she refocused. Lots of men have strong arms and don't handle bodies in their spare time.

"What was he wearing?"

Ashely looked lost for a second, but Carmen chimed in.

"He wore a light, white, sport coat, over a cream-colored shirt, top two buttons undone. And jeans, I think. Very sexy. Expensive stuff too. He smelled really good."

"So they danced together? This man and Sonya?"

"Yes, they did," Ashely replied. "Song after song, getting their moves in sync, you know, the works. Then he made his move; it was kinda cool. Too bad Sonya said he was a creep, you know."

"What move?"

The girls quickly glanced at each other.

"Um, these days the clubs don't play slow music anymore, you know," Carmen said, with a hint of sadness.

"They want to make you sweat and drink and spend more," Ashely stated the obvious, her perfectly waxed eyebrows sketching a frown.

"So, after a few songs, this guy got tired of waiting for a slow song. He took Sonya in his arms and started dancing like it was a slow song, but it wasn't. In the middle of the dance floor, they just swayed to their own rhythm. It was awesome… people made a circle around them."

"Then what happened?"

"The obvious, hello," Carmen said, and scoffed. "They left together, that's what happened. Sonya said good night, while he held her hand. She had bedroom eyes."

"Yeah, she did," Ashely confirmed. "He *was* hot."

"Was that the norm with Sonya? To take home guys she just met?"

"No!" Ashely replied. "She'd never—"

"She isn't like that," Carmen interrupted. "This guy was different. He was steaming hot. I don't know how else to explain it. His pheromones must have been skyrocketing or something. It was like he was covered in liquid sexiness. You just wanted to take him to bed, right there, right then. He was, like, wow, totally fuckable."

"Carmen!" Ashely reacted.

"Sorry…" she whispered.

"Then what happened?"

"Then we stayed on for a while longer, danced some more, not a worry in our heads," Ashely said. She spoke with sadness in her voice, the first time Tess had noticed it since they'd arrived.

"The next morning we called Sonya to ask her how it was, you know, their hot night," Carmen added.

"Both of you called?"

"Oh, yeah. For juicy stuff like that, you conference," Carmen replied, all serious. "But she was home alone, sounding upset. She told us she'd dumped him in the parking lot because he was a creep. End of story."

"You let her get away without giving you more details?" Tess insisted.

"We asked and asked, but she wouldn't say. She kept saying she wasn't feeling that well."

"Then she avoided us for a few days," Ashely added.

"No, she didn't," Carmen reacted. "She wasn't well, that's all."

"We could have helped. You know, get her a massage therapist, a chef to fix her favorite, anything she would have wanted."

What the hell ever happened to just making your friend a cup of tea and rubbing her shoulders or ordering in some pizza? The rich live in a different world, but they kill and they die just like the rest of us.

Tess remained quiet for a while, thinking. What could have happened that night, in the club's parking lot? Was that man a real suspect? Or someone who just didn't sound so appealing to Sonya, once they were out of the glamorous lights and sounds of the Miami Beach music scene? Did he do anything to her to creep her out? Or did she just change her mind, being that she never took home men she just met and didn't want to confess her cowardice to her girlfriends?

"On that next morning call, what did she sound like?"

The girls looked at each other again.

"She sounded a little tired—" Ashely started, but Carmen interrupted.

"She slurred a little. We assumed she drank a few more after she got home. We thought she was hung over," Ashely said. "What happened to her? Did you find her?"

"Since that day, has she gone out clubbing with you again?" Tess asked, ignoring Ashely's question.

"N—no," Carmen replied, frowning and fidgeting. "Not until three weeks later, the night she disappeared." The girls exchanged worried glances.

"We went out for ice cream one day and shopping too," Ashely remembered.

"But not clubbing. Not until then."

"Did you two go? Did you invite her and she said no?" Tess probed further, hoping she'd catch a glimpse of what had happened that night, at least by way of its effects.

"No," Carmen replied. "The stars just didn't line up. Ashely had a final, then I had bad cramps the weekend before last. Then we went, and Sonya… vanished."

"Would you agree to work with a sketch artist, to draw a likeness of the man Sonya left with that night in February?"

"I don't remember much," Carmen said, wiping a tear from the corner of her eye.

"Me neither. Just his hair," Ashely whispered, shuddering.

"It could be a starting point. The artist knows what he's doing, he'll walk you through it. I'll get that set up and be in touch as soon as possible."

"Okay, we'll do it. But we need to know what happened to her," Carmen insisted. "Please tell us."

Tess took in a deep breath.

"I'm afraid I have bad news. We found Sonya's body on the beach yesterday."

19

LUNCH

Tess went back to the observation room adjacent to Interview Two, as soon as the two young women left. Michowsky was there, flipping through his notes, visibly looking for something. He raised his eyes from the notebook and met her frustrated gaze.

"So that's that," Tess said, dropping the file folder she carried onto the table, or better said, slamming it. "We've made a ton of progress all day today. We got almost nothing more than we had this morning."

"Got your note on the money," he said, showing her the sticky. "You're right, the richer they are, the smaller their world. Made me wonder about something. Two of the victims' families we ruled as well off, not wealthy. The dentist and the—"

"The restaurant owner, yes, Sonya's dad," Tess cut over him, and regretted it when she saw him sigh with frustration. "Go on."

"I made a couple of calls and guess what? The dentist is also the heir of a large furniture business he runs by proxy, InStyle Furniture. I'm sure you heard of them. Half a billion dollars' market cap."

"Yeah, I know them. How about the Weavers?"

"Mrs. Weaver, who we assumed a homemaker, has made herself a fortune day trading, then stopped just short of the 1990s recession, when she got pregnant. Her net worth is over a hundred mil."

"What do you know? The small world we're looking at just got a whole lot smaller. That's some great instincts you got, Detective."

"Yeah… I've been told," he paraphrased her from their earlier conversation, and they both laughed.

"Where's Fradella?"

"Chasing the Weaver financials. Why?"

"Then it's just you and me then. Let's grab a burger and talk through some scenarios."

"You're on," Michowsky said, getting off his stool a little slower than he wanted. "Let me grab my keys."

"I'll drive. I know just the place."

She matched her steps with his, slowing down, remembering his back hurt. She saw his face light up just a touch when he saw her car, parked very close to the entrance. He must have been in a world of pain.

"We can release Sonya's identity now," she said, as soon as they hit the road. "Agree?"

"Yeah… there's someone who needs to hear it first, that's all."

"Who?"

"A reporter, more or less an asshole, but he made good on his promise to me. Brandt Rusch, you might have heard of him. I owe him one." Michowsky pulled out a business card, then typed fast on his phone, probably sending the reporter an email.

She pulled into the side parking lot of Media Luna, and cut the engine off.

"A bar, mid-afternoon? You're full of surprises, Special Agent Winnett," Michowsky said.

"Their burgers and fries are awesome here. Wouldn't go anywhere else."

They entered and sat at the counter. It was still early; only two or three endurance drinkers soaked their miseries, scattered around the quiet barroom. No music played at that time; probably the bartender enjoyed some silence before the rush hour began, in about two hours' time.

Cat lifted his eyes from his mixers and threw a quick smile their way. She nodded briefly, and winked, a wink only Cat saw. She saw him open the container where he stored his fresh herbs and start mixing her favorite. She smiled to herself, a smile fueled by the heartwarming feeling of home she had every time she came to Media Luna.

Then her smile opened up widely, almost turning to laughter, when she heard Michowsky approach Cat.

"Um, hey, I heard you make great burgers here, can we have a couple? And some fries please."

"Right away," Cat replied, shooting Tess a quick glance and a crooked grin. "Something to drink?"

"Yeah... I'll have a beer, Bud Light." Michowsky turned to Tess, inviting her to order her drink, but she gestured the offer away, and resumed taking in the feeling of safety, of comfort she felt. Cat's bar was the one place on earth where her memories were subdued and her demons tame.

Cat brought her drink, with two thin straws, just how she liked it. Thin straws were better for mojitos; she didn't choke with the herbs. Michowsky's eyes opened wide, seeing her accept her drink with a smile of gratitude.

"They know you here, I see," he said.

"Yeah, you could say that."

"Cocktails while on the fed clock? I confess I didn't see it coming."

"It's nothing, just—"

"How do you like your burger?" Cat asked Michowsky.

Cat wasn't smiling anymore. He looked like he was about to pull the shotgun he stowed under his tacky counter and shove it up Michowsky's nose, if he asked one more inappropriate question. Tess stifled a chuckle, turning her head sideways and burying her smile in her hands, leaving just her entertained glance to tell Cat everything was okay.

"Medium, no onions, no pickles. Thanks."

"It'll be a couple of minutes."

"That's fine," Michowsky replied, then turned toward Tess. "They also know how you like your burgers, don't they?"

"Yeah... they do."

She pulled her tablet out of her bag, and started looking at Sonya's Facebook profile again. She flipped through her most recent public postings, going backwards until mid-February. She looked at the photos carefully, trying to absorb a little more about who Sonya Weaver had been. There was a picture of her with Tony Gibbons, looking like they were the king and queen of America. She was dressed in a cocktail gown, a silver sequined creation that clung to her shape, and he wore an impeccable tux. The caption read, "At the Gibbons Fundraising Gala."

She showed the image to Michowsky. He whistled quietly.

That was the last image Sonya had posted of her ex-boyfriend, dated February 16. Afterwards, she'd posted something at least two to three times a day, and share a few of her friends' postings. She liked puppies... a lot. The fluffy, fuzz-ball ones. She also liked inspirational quotes and life hacks. A perfectly normal, young woman.

"Do we have her login yet? Maybe there's more in her private messages."

"Not yet," Michowsky replied. "Warrant's still pending."

"Here you go," Cat said, putting two large plates in front of them. Then he did a couple of more runs, to get them mayo, ketchup, and mustard, then cutlery and napkins.

She resumed browsing Sonya's Facebook timeline, counting the postings each day.

"These burgers are really good," Michowsky said, chewing with enthusiasm.

"Hey, did you notice Sonya didn't post anything after February 28 for almost three days?"

"Um, no. Eat your burger, it's getting cold."

"Yeah..." Tess replied, then took a few fries and chewed them slowly, savoring them. "It drives me crazy I don't know what the hell happened in that parking lot on the 28th. She was upset, enough to stop posting for three whole days, and that's serious for these kids. Then she started posting again, but no enthusiasm, no pictures either, for the most part. No more selfies since that day."

"Uh-huh," Michowsky acknowledged with his mouth full.

"Then there's this entry, right here," Tess pointed at the screen, "where she wrote, 'I can't stop enjoying life because of a single rainy day.' That was dated March 18."

"Do you think she's talking about the creep?"

"I think this is the moment she decided to not let a single bad experience change who she was and went back to her old ways. Four days later, the three of them were back in the same club."

She took a big bite of her burger and chewed it methodically, thinking.

"Too bad the damn bite mark doesn't line up with that February 28 date. It would have made such perfect sense, if that guy creeped her out because he bit her lip in the parking lot. Otherwise, who bit her? And where?"

"Un-huh," Michowsky replied, "but Doc Rizza—"

"Yeah, I know what he said. Let's ask Fradella to look at the surveillance videos for that night."

"They were inconclusive."

"Not the abduction night, the creep night. The 28th. Have him pore over those videos in detail, see what we can find. I still think this man is our strongest lead, and I can't trust what Detective Garcia did, if anything, as part of the missing person's investigation."

She took a few fries and chewed on them with her eyes half closed. They were perfect; flavored, crispy, not too salty.

Then her phone chimed. She groaned, wiped her fingers on the napkin and checked her messages. The newest one read, "This is Bob from the front desk. There's a Supervisory Special Agent Bill McKenzie here to see you." She texted back, "On my way, ETA 10 minutes," then took a few more fries from her plate.

"We have to run. The profiler's waiting."

20

PROFILER

They found Bill McKenzie already installed in the conference room, crouched in front of the whiteboard. Facilities still hadn't nailed that board to the wall, and Tess muttered a few adjectives in frustration. How long did it actually take to drive two nails into a wall? Did they really have to work crouched, bent over, stepping over one another? It was ridiculous, embarrassing.

McKenzie stood tall to his full six feet and five inches and nodded a greeting. They had crossed paths before, Tess and him, and it hadn't always been the best experience, but he did help her get her man. She would have preferred a different profiler if she had a choice. McKenzie could be stubborn, uptight, and dismissive. Stiff, arrogant sometimes. But he was also bright, perceptive, dedicated, and willing to go the extra mile to test a theory, so all in all, not that bad.

"SSA Bill McKenzie, meet Gary Michowsky," Tess introduced them.

"Agent Michowsky," McKenzie greeted him, while shaking his hand warmly.

"It's Detective. I'm Palm Beach County," Michowsky explained with a crooked smile.

"Agent Winnett, do you prefer we wait for your partner to join us before we begin?"

"Huh," she scoffed, "that will probably be a long wait. I don't have one. Not on this case," she added quickly, seeing

McKenzie's eyebrows shoot up in surprise. Damn procedure manual.

She took a seat at the conference table, and Michowsky sat across from her. McKenzie paced slowly in front of them, close to the whiteboard.

"All right then," McKenzie said. "I see why you called us in, Agent Winnett. You do have strong pattern indicators between these murders. Let's start with first impressions. He's organized and highly methodical. His intelligence is well above average, and he's extremely calm under pressure. This man is fearless and, by the nature of his crimes, a pure psychopath."

"We figured out most of that on our own," Tess said, her words driving frown lines on McKenzie's forehead. "I struggle with his motivation and classification. Is he an anger-retaliatory or an anger-excitation killer? Can there exist a hybrid between these two classes of murderers?"

"A hybrid? Why would you think this unsub's a hybrid?" McKenzie asked. "In my years as a behavioral analyst, I've almost never encountered the need to classify an unsub as a hybrid. The demarcation lines aren't carved in stone, though."

"Look at the victimology, how he crosses physiognomy, even racial lines. At the same time, what he does to these girls keeps evolving. My theory is that he's experimenting, searching for the perfect retaliatory recipe, and, until then, his victims are just lab rats, nothing else. A means to his horrific end."

"Could be. And?"

"That would point toward an anger-retaliatory classification. But when you examine what the unsub does to his victims, the repeated, elaborate rapes, the beatings, the skin cuts, all that points to a typical sexual sadist, which falls under the anger-excitation classification."

McKenzie rubbed his chin thoughtfully, walking slowly in front of the whiteboard, studying the victim profiles.

"I see what you mean," he said. "Let's talk through victimology, one victim at a time. You're saying May Lin is his first?"

Tess lowered her eyes. McKenzie intimidated her, and she hated that. Especially when he asked the right questions, and she didn't know if she had the right answers.

"Well... I ran a search going back only two years. These are the unsolved cases that matched the parameters. May Lin is the earliest in the series, but there could be more victims before her."

"Why didn't you open up the timeframe?"

"I thought it would be better for us to remain focused on a manageable number of victims. Enough to give us clear victimology, but not an overwhelming number."

"Have you looked, out of curiosity, to see how many more candidates would have been returned?"

"Y—yes," Tess replied quietly, shooting Michowsky a sheepish glance across the table. She hadn't shared that bit of information with him, and his disappointed glare showed just how he felt about that. "There are two more cases, but they have even less in common with these four. Both victimology and MOs are quite different."

"I can see why you chose to narrow your focus, Agent Winnett. However, as a matter of process, we never keep blinders on. It's easier to catch a killer if we know who his first victim was. Most of them start locally, with a victim they stumble on during their daily routine."

"I believe we have more insight to gain if we focus on his mature, more experienced killings. With this particular unsub and his constantly evolving methods, I think it helps us crystallize victimology."

"Okay," McKenzie conceded. "May Lin hardly belongs on this board. I'm not sure if she was killed by the same unsub as the other three victims. I've never encountered a serial killer who increases the age of the victims, who starts with underage girls and moves to adult women. Displacement killers stay within set victim parameters, like age and physical features. Lust killers drop victim age, drawing more pleasure from the younger, more vulnerable, purer victim. So, I don't think—"

"Give me a second," Tess said. She sprung to her feet and snatched May Lin's photo off the wallboard. She opened the door, and stuck her head out. "Guys," she said, raising her voice to be heard across the squad room, "can you please come over here? We need a minute of your time."

A woman in her 40s came into the conference room first.

"How old is she?" Tess asked, holding May's photo for her to see.

"Um, hard to say. Twenty-one, maybe?"

"Thanks. How about you? What do you think?"

"Twenty-four, but I'm not sure." That assessment came from the captain.

"Twenty, not more. Look at her eyes. Not a shred of laugh lines at the corner of her eyes. She's young," an admin added.

"Thanks, everyone, that's it," Tess said, then she turned her attention to McKenzie. "See what I mean? He made a mistake. May Lin looked older than she was. It's a known fact that Caucasians have difficulties reading Asian facial expressions and assessing their correct age. That's my theory."

"That's an interesting theory then," McKenzie replied, "because it could tie up with the differences we see in MO for this victim."

"What do you mean?" Michowsky asked, speaking his first words since their work session had started.

"He only held her for a day and a half, not four or five. He dumped her body wrapped in a clean sheet. He was apparently remorseful, which doesn't jibe with his psychopathic nature. He made a mistake, and when he realized, he killed her quickly, painlessly, and dumped her body respectfully. He's probably never going to touch another Asian girl again."

"So you think that's why he—" Tess said, but McKenzie cut her off.

"I think there's more to it. I think this particular victim tells us something about the unsub's psychology. I believe he identified himself with this victim. The sheet he covered her in was a light blue color, pristine, brand new. Blue is a color for boys though. Might be coincidental, but it's something I noticed. He didn't pose her like he did the others. He just laid her down to rest. I think the stressor, the trigger event that made him start killing has something to do with his childhood, or his status as a child. I think what we read as remorse was something else. He felt deeply connected with the child victim."

Tess nodded quietly.

"After May Lin, it took him eight months until he took another girl," Tess said, "Shanequa Powell."

"With Shanequa, he was angry and frustrated. His guilt over May Lin had prevented him from fulfilling his needs sooner. He was angry and he took it out on his new victim. Shanequa was beaten badly. He was at his angriest with her."

"Makes sense," Tess agreed. "Thank you for this insight. Some folks don't believe May Lin and Shanequa Powell belong in this series, my boss included."

"You can never be 100 percent sure," McKenzie replied. "Typically, if you have enough common points and you can formulate a theory that makes sense, then it's a safer bet to keep the victims in the investigation, instead of ruling them out. You can always rule them out later, but you can't afford to overlook any critical details."

"Yup. Let's talk motivation, please. What do you see?" Tess asked.

"This unsub is definitely hedonistic, seeking both thrill and lust. He's not an impotent, who takes his underperformance-fueled rage out on women. Per the ME's report, he's able to function quite well in that department. To him it's about control, it's about power, it's about experimentation with power. He's a power-assertive killer. That's what gives him satisfaction. Look at the drugs he's played with. He's seeking the ultimate thrill, or, per Agent Winnett's theory, the perfect recipe for retaliation against a woman who he believes has done him wrong."

"You're also describing a hybrid," Tess said, a little confused.

"I realize that. If your theory is correct and he's seeking retaliation then, yes, we have a hybrid. A rare occurrence, but it can happen, at least in principle."

"Is he accelerating?" Tess asked.

"And fast," McKenzie replied. "The cooling-off period between his abductions has decreased dramatically. We could potentially expect him to abduct a new victim any day now."

Silence engulfed the small conference room. McKenzie walked toward the back of the room, headed for the coffeemaker. In passing, he came by Tess, accidentally touching her shoulder. She jolted, shot him a brief glance, then looked away.

"Excuse me," McKenzie said quietly.

Damn it, Tess thought. Out of all places and all situations to react badly to someone's accidental touch, she had to do it with an FBI profiler present, the type of professional who could see through her like he was a walking X-ray machine.

McKenzie grabbed a bottled water from the mini fridge and came back to the front of the room. This time, he approached her carefully, making sure he didn't startle her again. He brushed against the wall, allowing her enough space, while Tess watched his every move. He gave her space, and was careful not to touch her again, but he hadn't chosen Michowsky's side of the table to make his way to the front of the room. He walked by her on purpose. He was studying her. *Oh, God.*

She felt her heart race, pounding against her chest like a caged, terrified animal. A jolt of adrenaline sent shots of panic throughout her body, and she froze, trying not to pant. She focused on her breathing, taking slow, long breaths in, holding them for a second or two, and exhaling just as slowly.

"Agent Winnett?" McKenzie asked.

"Yes?"

"I was asking, what's your theory about these drugs? How do you think he's gaining access to them?"

When the hell did he ask that, and how come she hadn't heard him ask it the first time?

She cleared her dry, constricted throat before speaking.

"We think he's a medical professional with access to a readily available, varied stock of medical drugs. He could be working in a hospital, or a long-term care facility. Because he seems very comfortable from a financial point of view, I think he's a doctor. Possibly a surgeon, considering his precision with a scalpel."

"What if he's not?" McKenzie asked. "You noted these victims are all wealthy, and that he might be wealthy too."

"He's got money to burn, and he seems to be moving freely from state to state, where he spends time torturing and killing. He doesn't seem to be tied to any one place," Tess replied.

"That's another concern, by the way," McKenzie said. "Except for Ted Bundy, the vast majority of serial killers stuck to one geographical area. How do you reconcile your theory that he's a hospital doctor, with this type of freedom to roam about?"

She shrugged involuntarily.

"Even doctors have vacations. Maybe that's how he spends his."

"I disagree," McKenzie replied. "These types of killings need preparation. He's spending much more time in the respective areas than the four or five days he keeps his victims. He hunts, and the pleasure of the hunt is one of the rewards for the hedonistic lust-thrill killer. He'd never cut his hunt short; he's savoring it. While he's out there, sizing up potential victims, his fantasies reward him with the promise of an exceptional kill. Your unsub doesn't work, or if he does, he has lots of flexibility."

Tess lowered her head. She hated being wrong, but that's why she'd called McKenzie, to make sure she didn't make errors in her assessments.

"As for medical knowledge, there are documented cases of self-taught serial killers with impressive skill level," McKenzie added. "He could also be a med school graduate, but not an employed doctor."

"How about the drugs, then?" Michowsky asked. "How is he gaining access to those?"

"You can get anything online these days or at the corner of the right street," McKenzie replied. "As you know, there are entire channels of distribution bringing medical drugs from Mexico, for people who don't have access to the expensive equivalents in the US drugstores."

McKenzie drank some water, then continued.

"I can't formulate an opinion on what his stressor might have been; it's too soon and I don't have enough information."

"Do you think he evolved from a rapist?" Tess asked.

"Most likely yes. It could be worth looking at older incidents, but geography will be your enemy in this case. Until you can pinpoint his location, you can't realistically do any of that."

"How about this creep incident?" Tess asked. "It keeps coming back to me as the one lead we might have. Would this unsub frequent clubs?"

"Most serial killers are charming, fascinating, charismatic individuals. They're not all reclusive. Yes, he could be hunting in clubs. I don't like the timeline though."

"What do you mean?" Michowsky asked.

"If the unsub were the creep, too much time passed between the day he eyed the last victim, Sonya Weaver, and the day he abducted her. It could happen, being he's so calm and methodical, but I don't think so."

"Do you think he bit Sonya?" Tess asked.

"Again, the timeline doesn't work. Your ME said two weeks, maximum."

She let out a long sigh.

"I'm visiting the families, starting tomorrow morning," she said. "I'll check to see if May Lin frequented clubs, despite her age. That's another missing commonality we see in her case. Wish me luck."

"You'll catch him," McKenzie said. "I'm not worried. All I can give you now is a partial profile, but we'll stay in touch."

"Ready when you are, SSA McKenzie," Michowsky said, ready to take notes.

"Our unsub is late 20s to mid-30s, most likely Caucasian and wealthy. He's single, probably has fleeting relationships, nothing steady. His intelligence is above average, and he could be charismatic and well-spoken. He travels out of state frequently, for longer periods of time. He drives at least one large SUV with tinted windows, or a truck with a bed cover. He has access to locations where he can torture and kill unheard, undisturbed. He has started as a rapist, or as an abusing sexual partner. He's a paraphilic, predisposed to fetishism. He cuts his victims to torture them, not as a form of picquerism. He's a sexual sadist, and a calm, organized, and methodical predator."

McKenzie smiled slightly in Tess's direction, and added, "And yes, he could be a rare retaliatory-excitation hybrid. When we catch him, we will definitely study him in detail."

Michowsky glanced quickly at his watch, then stood, a little clumsily, leaning against the conference table for support. His back probably hurt bad after so much time spent sitting.

"Thank you, SSA McKenzie," Michowsky said, "I'll distribute the profile. It was a pleasure meeting you."

Michowsky walked out of the room, and Tess extended her hand, eager to evade McKenzie's scrutinizing gaze.

"Thanks for coming in, I appreciate it," she said, looking McKenzie in the eye for a second, then averting her eyes. "I know how busy you guys are."

He shook her hand warmly, holding it for longer than she expected.

"Take it easy, Winnett, you look like shit."

"Huh," she laughed sarcastically, "men these days are such gentlemen."

"You don't have to live with it, you know," he said, speaking with kindness in his voice.

"With what?" Tess frowned.

"PTSD."

"I—I don't know what you're talking about," she replied, a little too fast, feeling her heart pounding in her chest and pulling her hand away.

"Don't be an idiot, Winnett. If I couldn't recognize hypervigilance when I see it, I wouldn't belong doing what I do for a living."

Tess lowered her head, unable to say anything. What was there left to say? McKenzie would probably report her; the first word in his job title was supervisory. He had the duty to report any agents seemingly unfit to do their job. Then they'd put her through countless assessments, to find an excuse to fire her. Then they would, expressing countless hypocritical regrets. End of story.

"Tess, I'm here for you, for whatever you need. PTSD is hard to live with, but it can be managed, made easier," McKenzie said, speaking with the same kindness.

"You… won't report me?"

"Not if you get help," he said, seeking her eyes with a comforting look. "Call me, all right?"

"Yes, I will," she eventually said, then watched his tall figure walk away with a steady gait and equal footsteps.

She closed the conference room door and leaned against it, letting her heart beat as fast as it wanted, while she breathed heavily, ignoring the tears pooling in her eyes.

21

ONE MORE CHINA SHOP

Tess lost track of time for a while, leaning against that closed door and battling her demons, but not slaying that many. Then she returned to reality, as her breathing normalized and her heart rate dropped to standard levels. She checked the time; only a few minutes had passed, in what seemed like ages.

A quick tap on the door, and Fradella barged in. Sweat beads covered his forehead. The day had proven to be a scorcher.

"Oh, so you're done already?" he asked, sounding disappointed.

"Done?"

"With the profiler."

"Yeah, he just left," Tess replied. "We have notes we can share."

"Oh, that's fantastic," he blurted angrily.

"What's wrong?"

"Would it have killed you to call me when he got here? Or am I good only to run your warrants and screen your video surveillance, huh?"

"I honestly didn't think you'd care about it," she said, taken aback. Again, she'd pissed someone off without even knowing. Her absolute specialty.

"Yeah, and why should I care? It's only the opportunity of a lifetime, to sit in a profiling session while experts discuss a case. My case!"

"I'm sorry I didn't think about it. But now I know, and I'll make sure to include you in anything even remotely interesting. How's that?"

"Don't patronize me, Agent Winnett. I'm not that dumb."

"I wasn't, honestly," she replied, just as Michowsky entered the room.

"I've released the profile, for whatever good it's going to do," Michowsky said. "It's not like these cops are going to approach loaded men going about their business in Miami, and ask them what? 'Do you torture women in your spare time?' I don't think we have enough, profile or no profile. Not yet."

"You're right," Tess replied. "We need to tighten the noose. Todd, can you please run these drugs and see where someone could buy them? Try online, black markets, street corners. Talk to informants on the streets of Miami Beach. See where all the channels for these drugs intersect. Maybe we get lucky."

"Ah, here we go again. Here goes Todd Fradella, gofer for Agent Tess Winnett, FBI."

"What the hell is wrong with you?" Michowsky asked. "That's your job!"

"Yeah…" Fradella replied bitterly. "Funny how I end up with the crappiest part of whatever the job is. In about 15 years, I'll get really good at running errands. Maybe I'll get promoted to senior gofer, who knows. That's if I'm lucky, and I kiss—"

"Detective Fradella, that's enough," Michowsky said, raising his voice.

Silence was heavy, palpable after the heated exchange. Fradella stared angrily at Michowsky, who was more surprised than frustrated.

She understood Fradella more than she cared to admit. The younger generations were more ambitious, more rushed than their parents had ever been. The world revolved at a much faster rate, and if they didn't fight with their claws to get ahead, mediocrity swallowed them forever. She felt the same burning ambition to succeed, to learn, to better herself in every aspect of her work. And, yes, she hadn't thought of him; she completely forgot all about him and saw the profiling session as her own opportunity to learn, not his. Truth be told, she remembered Fradella existed when it served her purpose, not his. Guilty as charged. Somehow, she'd become so tense, she barely noticed other people existed. She didn't used to be like that.

"I meant what I said earlier, you know," Tess said. "I'll involve you in anything worthwhile and give you the chance to learn a few tricks."

He didn't reply, but lowered his angry gaze, directing it at the carpet.

"How about we start now?" Tess asked. "We need to find the killer's earlier victims. The first would be great. But we don't know where to look, and it's a needle in a nationwide haystack. Want to give it a try?" She offered him her laptop, and he smiled while taking it, his deep frown dissipating like clouds after a storm. She smiled, involuntarily.

"You saw me work earlier; you know the screens. I'll log in, and then I'll let you run these searches."

"Cool," he said, rubbing his hands and pulling a chair in front of the laptop. "What are we looking for?"

"I don't know, Todd, why don't you tell me?" she encouraged him.

"Rape victims could be in the hundreds of thousands, nationwide and going back several years," he said thoughtfully. "We have no real way of filtering them."

"Let's try something else," Tess offered. "What if he started by beating up a girlfriend or two before he went pro? Where would we find that?"

"Hospital records, maybe even the media, or social media. He's rich, right? People gossip. They love any kind of dirt about fat cats, and they milk it for all it's got."

Tess made an encouraging gesture with her hand. Fradella started typing, under Michowsky's astounded look. It was going to be a long night.

22

PRECONCEPTION

Tess struggled to free herself but couldn't. Panic rose to her throat, choking her, and a whimper came out instead of a scream. Her legs were bound and she couldn't move them, she couldn't run. Her head was pressed hard on its right side into the ground, and from that angle she couldn't see his face. She fought, trying to turn her head and catch a glimpse of him, but failed. She felt the weight of the man's arm, pressing her head down, while his right hand held her left wrist in a powerful grip. She somehow freed her right arm from underneath her body and flailed at him, hoping she'd scratch his face and get some DNA under her fingernails. But the man caught her free wrist and pinned it against the floor with steeled force. She couldn't move anymore, crushed under his weight. In front of her eyes, the silhouette of the tattooed snake on the man's left biceps moved with his skin, taut against his muscles as he tightened his grip. The snake seemed alive, ready to pounce. She tried to scream and made a last, desperate attempt to free herself.

The sound of her own voice woke her, even though the scream in her nightmare came out stifled, a raspy, strangled interjection. She tried to get out of bed, but her legs were entangled in the flat sheet. She disentangled herself, almost panicky, then rose quickly and grabbed the offending sheet, rolled into a ball, and tossed it onto the bathroom floor.

"Damn it," she muttered between splashes of cold water she threw on her face. "Damn it to fucking hell."

She went back to the bedroom, where she reached behind her nightstand and grabbed her holstered gun, Velcroed against the back panel. Her house had many such Velcro patches, where she could put her weapon close enough for her to grab, but out of sight. Discreet, so her very rare visitors wouldn't notice she didn't even dare to use the restroom unarmed.

Hypervigilance, the lifelong sentence survivors have to bear. Always alert, never relaxed. Always expecting the worst scenario, always preparing, always fearful. Insulting people with suspicions and apparent callousness, ignoring friendships, hurting and pushing everyone away. Trapped in a whirlwind of countless bad memories, swirling inside her head, forcing her to relive them forever. Never forgetting. At the whim of anxiety and panic attacks, triggered by almost anything. Someone's voice inflexions, or a certain word. A smell, a feeling, a sound, a goddamned tangled flat sheet. While her weary brain couldn't abandon its alertness, her life passed her by.

It had gone on for long enough.

She needed to get her life back, before it was too late.

Not all hypervigilance was bad though. Her acute senses made her a perceptive, talented investigator, able to feel if the person in front of her lied or had something to hide. Her own personal experience helped her build rapport with victims, gaining her easy access to critical information. She knew what questions to ask, and, more important, how to ask them. Her biggest weakness was also her biggest strength, giving her the edge that had helped her achieve a perfect record as an FBI agent. How ironic.

She still needed to get a grip. She needed to build up the courage to trust someone enough to let that someone help her. She'd let Cat... so it *could* be done, but for her, it was close to impossible. Nevertheless, it had to be done. Soon.

She started her coffeemaker, holstered gun in her hand, then went to the shower. She pasted the holster against a

Velcro patch hidden behind the laundry hamper and let the hot water rinse away the night terror, while she repeated to herself that she was safe now, and everything was going to be all right. Of course, the fact that she'd never found the man who attacked her didn't help. He was still out there, but she kept looking. Maybe one day... or maybe never.

A few hours later, crammed in an aisle seat within earshot of the rear lavatory, Tess buckled up for her flight to Chicago. She ignored the flight attendant's instructions and opened her laptop. After all, safety belts had worked the same way for more than 50 years.

She read her email first, where Fradella had delivered access credentials for all the victims' social media and email accounts. Finally. She started with May Lin's accounts, getting ready for the conversation with her parents.

May's Facebook account showed moderate activity, somewhat less than what was normal for a young girl her age. Her interests varied. Movies, clothes, prices for all sorts of items, from wearable electronics, to shoes, to jewelry. A few young men, some Asian but a few Caucasians too, appeared in some of the photos, casual friends by the looks of it, rather than lovers. Tess went backwards on her timeline until she came across postings with images from a pool party. May had written, "That's it, I'm done. Yay!" A slew of friends had congratulated her, but Tess didn't know for what. When she finally saw what it was, she had to read the posting twice. She'd graduated from college, cum laude, with a business management major. At only 17 years and 10 months!

How the hell did they miss that? They'd all missed it, Chicago PD and Palm Beach too. Argh... the power of preconception, doing damage any chance it got. No one thought to check for a college degree in a teenager's case. School was such a generic term.

She typed a quick message to Bill McKenzie and copied Michowsky and Fradella on it. She wrote, "Bill, May Lin was a college grad, at just shy of 18. This confirms victimology, as young, wealthy, college-grad overachievers. It's no longer coincidental. I think that's how he made his mistake, the unsub. Just like we didn't think to look for a degree because we knew May's age, it's possible he didn't think to check her age, because he probably knew about the degree. Adds a different perspective. Thanks… for everything."

Tess flashed her badge at the flight attendant who insisted she stow her laptop, and the young woman vanished without another word. The job had its perks.

The factoid about May Lin's degree opened another list of unanswered questions. The girls had attended different schools in different cities and had different majors. Where would the unsub find them, and how? There wasn't a single trace of him anywhere near May Lin's cyber sphere. Maybe if she figured out what the schools had in common, she'd find his hunting grounds. Or maybe it didn't matter, and she was chasing wild geese. Maybe he hunted at clubs, where college grads go to celebrate. Where young women are more willing to talk to charming, charismatic strangers than anywhere else.

23

TYPICAL TEENAGER

It was still early morning when Tess landed at O'Hare, bringing her the ultimate enjoyment of driving through Chicago's infamous, rush-hour traffic. After waiting in a long line to get a rental car, and dealing with countless highway tolls that further suffocated the already crawling traffic, she finally pulled up in front of the Lin residence.

The Lins lived in a somber, expensive-looking home near Burnham Park. Three stories high, the townhome had the elegance of Boston's brownstones and the generous size of Midwestern dwellings. She stopped before climbing the few steps that led to the front door, admiring the building and wondering why Mr. Lin, a successful real estate developer, who had the choice of living wherever and however he pleased, would have chosen to live in a condominium. What was it about sharing walls and facilities with others that fascinated people? Some people, not everyone. Definitely not Tess.

She rang the bell, and Mr. Lin opened the door himself. He invited her to the family room and offered her tea. She accepted gracefully and waited for a few minutes, savoring the peaceful, almost somber silence of the room. Tall windows didn't let too much light inside the room, covered by sheers and deep burgundy sash draperies with gold tassels, having nothing but the gloomy, Chicago sky to draw light from. A thick, rich, oriental rug covered most of the floor, absorbing any hint of footstep noise. The room was wood-paneled, artistically decorated with matching furniture in dark hardwood and leather seating. An ageless setting, devoid of electronics, meant for people to interact free of modern life distractions. Here and there, Chinese décor elements brought personality to the setting. Latticed dividers marking the reading room, silk paintings on the walls, and fine alabaster sculptures adorning the fireplace mantle.

Mrs. Lin served tea with impeccable ceremony, making Tess worry she didn't know how to behave. She decided to watch what the others did and follow suit. As soon as Mrs. Lin finished setting up the tea and filled everyone's cups, Tess extended her hand.

"Thank you for seeing me," she said, after introducing herself. "I know it must be hard for you."

After offering her a weak hand with ice-cold fingers, Mrs. Lin sat on the couch across from Tess, right next to her husband. Their son entered the room last and took an armchair.

"This is our son, Han," Mrs. Lin introduced him. "He's 20. He's all we have left. Our daughter would have been nineteen and two months today," she continued, her words tainted by tears.

"What can we do for you, Agent Winnett?" Mr. Lin asked, frowning. "It's been six months since anyone talked to us about May. Last thing they told us was that they didn't have enough to catch the monster who took our little girl. I'm afraid they never will."

She looked at the man with empathetic eyes. His back was hunched and his shoulders tense. Dark circles surrounded his eyes, and when he spoke his daughter's name his voice trailed off, sunken in the unspeakable pain of losing one's child. He wasn't very tall, and neither was his wife. His son was taller than the both of them and looked somehow Americanized, as if his physical features had somehow been altered by the immersion in the American culture.

"Talk to me about May, please. What was her life like? How did she spend the last few weeks before she died?"

The parents looked at each other, while the brother stared at the floor.

"She was a good girl," Mrs. Lin spoke, so quietly Tess had to make an effort to hear what she said. "Studied a lot. She was eager to be done with school so she could start living her life. She'd just finished her college degree, and she wasn't even eighteen yet. Did you know that?"

Tess nodded.

"How does someone do that?"

"She was precocious and very smart," Mr. Lin said. "She worked hard. She started doing two years in one since she was in seventh grade. I offered to move her to another school, one for gifted children, but she wanted to stay where she was, with her friends, and finish school as soon as she could. She wanted to come work with me, in the family business," he added, his voice trailing off, choked. "She made her father proud."

"That must have been hard, doing two years in one," Tess said. "How did her friends react to May leaving them behind like that?"

The parents looked at each other again, and Han briefly lifted his gaze from the carpet, only to lower his eyes back again a second later.

"Everyone loved my little May," her mother replied. "Her friends didn't mind her being ahead, and she always made new friends too."

"They used her homework, notebooks, and test preps," Han added. "It was like having a preview into the next school year. I used it too, in my last two years of high school. It was cool."

His father shot him a disapproving look, then turned his attention to Tess.

"Why?" Tess asked. "What was cool about it?"

"It saved everyone a lot of time on homework."

There wasn't a single hint of Chinese accent in the boy's English, not even the distinguishable melody, the inflections the Chinese put in their English phrases. He sounded as Chicago as they came.

"Interesting," Tess replied, almost smiling. "How did you pay her back?"

"It wasn't like that," Han replied. "May didn't expect anything in return. She just worked her way through school as fast as she could, and the rest of us were in luck."

"How about her social life? What did she do for fun?"

"There wasn't much time for that," her mother replied quickly, "with a double school workload."

"She was hungry for life, my little girl," Mr. Lin added. "But study always came first."

Tess looked at Han inquisitively. No way does a teenager give up all the fun in her life, no matter how desperate she was to be rid of school. Han continued to gaze at the floor and remained quiet.

"We took her to our social events when she wanted to come," Mrs. Lin said. "We wanted to give her the skills to succeed in society."

"What kind of events?"

"The annual real estate investors' conference is one I can think of. It lasts three days, and every evening it has cocktail parties and fancy dinners for major investors and their families," Mrs. Lin replied. "It's a very elegant event. May was thrilled to go. She was starting to have an interest in getting evening gowns, makeup, jewelry." She paused for a little while, clasping her hands nervously in her lap. "She was a typical American teenager, our little girl. No Chinese cultural values took to her, no matter how hard I tried."

"Who was the reception for?"

"Only top developers and investors," Mrs. Lin replied. "People who'd invested at least ten million dollars in the development of Chicago. White glove, exclusive. We attend every year." She stood, her tiny figure seemingly fragile. "Let me show you," she added, as she pulled a photo album from one of the bookcases. "Here it is, the last photo we took with her, as a family."

Tess looked at the photo, studying every detail. It was a group image, probably other investors with their families were in it, about 20 people or so. All tuxes and evening attire, sparkling diamonds and classy looks, wide smiles exposing perfect teeth. The Lin family took a small space among the others, huddled together to the side, the parents behind their children. Han and May, taller than their parents, had crouched at their feet, the four of them forming a charming ensemble.

"May I?" Tess gestured with her phone.

Mrs. Lin held the image up for Tess, as she took a couple of pictures.

"Thank you," Tess said quietly. "How about her social life outside of family events? Did she go out? With friends, on dates?"

"No, she was too young," Mr. Lin replied quickly. Han resumed looking at the floor and seemed somewhat embarrassed, fidgeting in place. This time, the mother stared at the carpet as well.

"Han, if we don't know the truth, we'll never catch her killer," Tess said. "You know that, don't you?"

Han shot Tess a quick, guilty glance, then cleared his throat before speaking.

"Um, she did go out sometimes, when Father was out of town on business."

Mr. Lin sprung to his feet, pacing angrily. "Han!"

Without words, Tess urged him to let the boy finish. Mr. Lin lowered his eyes, but continued to stand and pace.

"Where?" Tess asked. "Where did she go? Did she have a boyfriend?"

"No, no boyfriend. She went to the mall with the girls and to clubs sometimes."

"By herself?"

"No, with her friends."

"How did she get in?" Tess asked.

Han clammed up and shrugged.

"Han, this is important," Tess pleaded. "There will be no consequence to you or your family, no matter what you tell me, all right? I promise."

Mr. Lin stared at his son, his intent gaze an angry, incredulous, disappointed look that promised a world of trouble for young Han Lin. He wasn't helping.

"Han? Please," Tess insisted one more time.

"Fake ID," he eventually whispered, his eyes riveted to the floor again.

Mrs. Lin started crying softly.

"May I please see her room?" Tess asked.

"The police have been through there already," Mr. Lin replied dryly.

"I'm not the police, Mr. Lin. We have different methods."

Mrs. Lin stood and took to the stairs, her tear-filled look a silent invitation. Tess followed her and soon entered May's bedroom. It looked as if the girl was out somewhere, soon to return. The bedroom was kept probably just the way she'd left it, almost 18 months ago.

"Show me," Tess asked, looking Han straight in the eye.

He hesitated, then kneeled on the floor near the immense window. He rolled back the rug and exposed more of the shiny hardwood floor, then ran his long, thin fingers along the edges of the wood strips, until one clacked quietly. He grabbed it and pulled it out with ease, exposing a small bundle underneath. He extracted it and handed it to Tess.

"Thanks," she said, opening the embroidered handkerchief holding the items together. There it was, May's fake ID, so well executed Tess couldn't tell it was fake. An expensive job, using her real picture and a fake name, and making her about 22 years old when she'd disappeared. With it, a wad of cash and a couple of condoms.

"Oh, no," the mother wailed. "How could you do this, Han?"

"I didn't do anything," he replied. "I don't even have one of these for myself. She got it on her own."

"But you knew about it," Mr. Lin said loudly, in a threatening tone. "And said nothing!" Then Mr. Lin spoke something in Chinese, a rapid fire of anger-filled sounds that refueled Mrs. Lin's sobs.

Tess put the fake ID on the desk and started looking through the room. It was exquisitely decorated, like the rest of the house, in a classy, yet youthful style. Her parents had tried to give her a space to call her own, and she'd pasted posters of One Direction, Bruno Mars, and several sports cars on top of the silk-laden wallpaper.

The bedroom came with a walk-in closet, where her clothing was neatly arranged. Tess fingered through the clothes hangers, seeing mostly jeans, jackets, shirts, and blouses, nothing really out of the ordinary. A couple of cocktail gowns were covered in plastic protectors, and Tess recognized the dress she'd worn at the investors' gala. She took a step back and looked again, this time searching for asymmetries and imperfections in the way the clothes were arranged. She saw something, a silk blouse that seemed too thick on its hanger. She removed it carefully and found underneath it a second garment, a little black dress, a sequined tube that must have barely covered May's buttocks. She continued her search and uncovered several items more, a shredded pair of jeans shorts that must have showed a lot of skin, tank tops, and short skirts, all dance-club worthy pieces of clothing.

Then she moved on to May's lingerie drawers, where she didn't waste any time and reached out to the back, where she found lace panties and bras. Hidden at the back of the scarves drawer, a small pouch held her makeup kit, and another was a treasure trove of jewelry. Yep, May had been the typical teenager, living a life her parents knew nothing about.

Tess stood in the bedroom's doorway, thanking May's family for their help. She looked at the Lins, huddled up together, wounded, unable to comprehend why their daughter had lived such a secretive life.

She wished she had more time to spend in Chicago, to interview May's girlfriends, and check out the clubs she'd frequented, but she had a plane to catch.

24

A Night Out

She lifted her arms in the air, looking at the myriad lights spinning and flashing above her head, and let the loud music take control of her body. She moved effortlessly; the rhythm carried her away, and the fancy, laser-enriched light show was worth every dime. She drew arabesques through the air with her thin, manicured fingers, running them through her hair, then letting the wavy, silken strands fall back on her shoulders. Her hips punctuated every statement the music made in the latest club remixes of the year's megahits. Miami's music scene was sizzling, glorifying its torrid night life and hot women, and attracting tourists at least as effectively as its famous beaches.

The rhythm changed somewhat, as the MC faded into another latest hit, and her thoughts moved away from the charm of Miami's attractions and into savoring her newly acquired freedom. She was an adult. Finally, yeah! She felt her heart swell, as she remembered her coming-of-drinking-age improvised ceremony she shared with her best friend Tiffany, when they'd both cut their fake IDs and scattered the pieces through the open window of their speeding Beemer. Nice! She'd grown sick and tired of being afraid she'd get busted every time she went out. What stupid laws, made by stupid people... So you could work, or join the Army and get yourself killed at 18, but you had to wait until 21 to have a drink? How fucked up was that? Well, that was all over now. Let the party begin.

She signaled her girlfriend she needed a break. Tiffany, lost in her moves and making sustained eye contact with some guy, pouted a little, but then turned and walked away. She followed her closely, as she left the dance floor. They made their way with difficulty through throngs of young people, sweating their energy off on the glitter-covered marble. Tiffany wasn't hesitant to push her way through and beelined it to their booth. Walking a couple of feet behind her, she envied Tiffany's perfect, little waist and long, sleek legs for a second, then shrugged the envy away. She wasn't so bad herself. She was taller, and her light brown hair shimmered like silk under the club lights, bouncing on her back in large waves as she walked on her four-inch heels with a spring in her step.

She barely contained a smile when she noticed the impression she'd made on a bunch of guys, who leaned against the bar counter looking for a hookup, sizing girls up, drinks in hand. Yeah, she was hot.

They finally sat at their small table, and she let out a sigh of relief, thankful they'd come in early enough to catch one of the very few booths available.

"Whew, this is so cool," she yelled over the small table, but Tiffany gestured she couldn't hear her. She gestured, "never mind," and wanted to check her messages, while a bartender swung by with tall, frosty glasses filled with chilled champagne.

She opened her tiny purse and went through it in a hurry, but her phone wasn't anywhere. She checked the time on Tiffany's phone and frowned. Drew was never late. She wondered what happened. Her boyfriend must have had a good reason to be late, or the flat tire he'd called her about must have taken forever to fix. Strange… He'd bragged he could switch a flat in under five minutes, like it was something that would make a girl fall head over heels. Yeah, right. Who cared, when a tow truck could come and fix it in no time?

She must have left her stupid phone in her stupid car, and, with Drew being so late, she had to go out and get it. She yelled a few unintelligible words to Tiffany, waving her car keys, and Tiffany nodded. Then she started making her way to the entrance, pushing and elbowing through hordes of sweaty, alcohol-infused dancers waving glow sticks to the beat.

She finally made it to the entrance hallway, where the crowd wasn't as thick, and she could breathe better and walk faster. A young, attractive man locked his fascinating, blue eyes with hers, and she hesitated a good, long second before looking away. If Drew hadn't been in the picture, she would have liked to get to know that guy. He looked familiar somehow and totally hot. She tried to remember, but couldn't place him. Two more steps, and she'd forgotten all about him, flattered by someone else's appreciative glance.

Then she felt someone grab her arm. She turned and saw the man she'd just looked at, holding her arm and smiling, his hypnotizing blue eyes drilled into hers. She pulled away angrily, but didn't manage to free herself. She felt a small prick in the side of her arm and yelled at the stranger.

"Hey," she shouted, barely able to hear herself over the blaring music.

The man didn't react and didn't let go of her arm. She felt his fingers like steel claws dig into her flesh, unforgiving. He still smiled, looking at her, as her knees grew weak, and, instead of pulling away, she started leaning into him for support. A wave of panic rose to her throat as she realized she'd been drugged. Dizzy and nauseous, she tried to grapple at passersby, reaching and clutching at their clothes, at furniture, at the walls. Then she felt him grab her shoulders firmly, supporting her, and felt the hot, humid air of the Miami night against her face. They were outside.

"My girlfriend's had a few too many," she heard the man tell someone. "She needs a bit of fresh air. Excuse me."

She tried to scream, but only a choked whimper made it through her numb throat. Then heavy darkness engulfed her and pulled her into oblivion.

25

EMPTY NEST

Tess had arrived in Atlanta the night before, but willed herself to visit Carolyn O'Sullivan the next morning. Somehow, having the FBI ring the doorbell at 10:00PM made things worse for everyone. SAC Pearson would be proud of her newly found consideration. If only he knew how hard it had been for her to add the slightest delay to her fact-finding mission.

She pulled in front of a tall, wrought-iron gate, and lowered her window to press the buzzer on the access pad. Before she could reach the button, she heard a voice coming from the small box. A camera whirred, training on her face.

"Yes, can I help you?"

"Special Agent Tess Winnett, FBI, to see Carolyn O'Sullivan. I have an appointment."

No one replied, but the gate opened quietly, rolling to the side. She drove through and pulled in front of the main entrance.

Now that was wealthy living. The residence was a massive, two-story, white colonial, at least ten thousand feet. It was built on a slightly sloped stretch of perfectly green grass, in a landscaped garden worthy of a king's palace. Carolyn's romance novels must have been selling like hotcakes.

The main door opened before she could reach the door knocker. Well, of course.

A uniformed housekeeper held the door for her, then showed her into a stunning living room.

"Can I get you anything? Coffee? Tea?"

"I'm fine, thanks."

"I'll get Miss O'Sullivan for you."

She disappeared quietly, leaving Tess to admire the setting. Large, luminous windows let in the Atlanta sun through sparkling white sheers. The furniture was modern, in shades of white and light gray, on accented area rugs thrown casually here and there, bringing swatches of color to a magnificent setting.

The far wall was set up as an ego wall, displaying Carolyn's best-selling titles, awards she had won, and photos of her with several famous people. Tess gave into her innate curiosity and went over to study everything closely.

"That one, right there, is at the Oscars, two years ago," Carolyn said, startling Tess. "Oh, I'm sorry, I didn't mean—"

"No, it's all right," Tess replied, repressing a frown of frustration with her own jumpiness, and shook the hand Carolyn offered. "It's a pleasure to meet you. Back in the day when I had time to read, I was a fan."

Carolyn smiled gracefully and invited Tess to take a seat next to her on a massive white leather sofa. She was a stunning appearance. She must have been in her late 50s, but she looked amazing. Her hair was styled back, revealing her tall, smooth forehead. She wore a cream-colored pants and jacket suit with a darker cream, silk blouse, just a shade darker, for accent. Diamond studs and a ring completed the elegant attire. Carolyn O'Sullivan had class.

"This is about Shanequa, I presume?"

"Yes... but first, let me ask you, ahem, you're—"

"White?" Carolyn asked, with a smile. "Yeah, I get that a lot when it comes to Shanequa. She was adopted. She was the daughter of my late husband's war buddy. When Fred Powell died, it was the natural thing to do. Then my husband died too, only a few years later. Then Shanequa..."

"I am very sorry for your loss," Tess said.

"Not only did her death leave this huge house empty and silent, but my heart too. I feel I failed Fred's confidence, and my husband's. They entrusted me with the well-being of Fred's only child, and I—"

Carolyn stopped mid-phrase, too emotional to continue. She patted the corners of her eyes with a tissue, then took a deep breath, stifling her tears.

"She was everything I had left." She reached out and took Tess's hand with both hers. "Please tell me you found her killer."

Tess lowered her eyes for a split second, then looked at Carolyn confidently.

"Not yet, but we have new information, and we *will* get him, I promise."

"Good," Carolyn replied, still sniffling quietly. "Tell me how can I help."

Tess hesitated for a second. She'd perused Shanequa's social media accounts the night before and didn't find anything useful. No permanent male presence in her photos, so she wasn't in a stable relationship. Not a lot of party photos either. She wondered how much information Carolyn had from the police, how much she knew about what had happened to her adoptive daughter. She decided to tread carefully.

"Tell me about Shanequa," Tess asked. "What was she like?"

"She was intelligent and hard-working, almost shy. She'd never got used to any of this," Carolyn said, gesturing vaguely, "although it was going to be all hers one day. She grew up in a challenging situation. Her mother passed away when she was only four, then Fred struggled to make ends meet for so long."

The housekeeper appeared with a tray with iced tea in tall crystal glasses. Tess accepted a glass and took a sip. It was delicious.

"Don't think we didn't offer to help," Carolyn added. "Fred was a stubborn man, like most men are. Too proud. He worked himself into the ground, that's what he did." She sipped some tea, then placed the glass back on the tray without making a sound. "Shanequa had mourned a lot of people by the time she turned 18, poor girl. Then it was just her and me. After a while, she immersed herself in her studies, and I in my writing. She made me proud. She earned her degree in economics before she turned 21."

"Was she romantically involved with anyone?"

"Huh," Carolyn reacted with a sad chuckle. "No, I would have known. I know romance. I write it for a living. Shanequa hadn't met the love of her life yet."

"How about dates? Casual boyfriends?"

"There were some young men, but—" she hesitated, seemingly uneasy. "It's hard to know what men are after, even without this," she said, repeating her vague gesture. "But Shanequa was smart. If she sensed a man was after money, she rejected him immediately. With her hard life she had growing up, she was a little paranoid, distrusting."

Tess knew exactly how that felt.

"How about girlfriends? Did she go out anywhere with them? To clubs maybe?"

"She had a couple of good friends, nice, smart, hard-working girls, and they did go out on occasions. *I* pushed her to go out and live a little; it wasn't the other way around."

"Any place in particular where she liked to go?"

"I don't think so. They tried different places, I remember her telling me."

Tess frowned. She didn't have anything after their conversation. No new data, no workable clues. Just like with the Lins, she'd probably need to spend time with the girlfriends, figuring out what places they frequented, then poring over countless hours of video surveillance looking for that one face Atlanta, Chicago, and Miami had in common. A killer, hunting for his prey.

Facial scanning software was long past due, although insider rumors had it the FBI was working with a software firm to develop something that could scan through hours of video in just minutes and compare faces. It wasn't going to be available soon enough for her case though.

So far, her only gain from visiting the families was that she got to know the victims a little better. She knew who they were, how they lived, what they cared about. They weren't just police reports and crime scene photos anymore. That was important. She was going to visit with Emma's family next. Her flight to Charleston, South Carolina was in two hours.

"If you remember anything, please call me," Tess said, offering her business card. "This is my mobile number."

"Do you think that's where she—"

A chime interrupted Carolyn; it was Tess's phone, alerting her she had a new message. It was from Michowsky, and it read, "Come back ASAP. New missing persons filing just in. Fits the damn profile to the letter."

26

MISSING

Tess made it to Palm Beach County Sheriff's Office by mid-afternoon, covered in dust, sweat, and airplane grime. She climbed the stairs two at a time and entered the almost-empty squad room, looking for Michowsky and Fradella. They weren't anywhere to be seen, but a uniformed cop lifted his eyes from a report he was typing.

"Where are they?"

The cop pointed his finger at the conference room, then resumed his work on the report.

She entered the conference room without knocking and stopped the conversation that was taking place in there.

"Finally," Michowsky greeted her and moved away from the whiteboard.

She noticed they'd finally hung the whiteboard on the wall, and a second, smaller one, right next to the first, where they had pinned details about the new missing-person case.

At first, she studied May Lin's face, patiently, carefully, as if she'd never seen her before. She wanted to capture all the new information gathered from her visit and make it work somehow, give some results. Then she remembered something. She pulled out her phone and retrieved an image, then handed it to one of the uniformed cops who leaned against the wall doing nothing.

"Please have this printed letter size, full color, and bring it back."

The cop shifted his weight from one foot to the other, uncomfortable and undecided.

"What, now?"

"Yes, now."

He left the room scoffing, without closing the door. Tess was still revisiting May Lin's notes on the board when he came back with the print. It was the photo of May Lin's family at the investors' gala, and Tess pasted it on the board with two pieces of tape.

Then she studied Shanequa with new eyes, remembering what her adoptive mother had shared. Not going out much, working hard, had lost a lot of people. She tried to see those details in the way Shanequa looked before her abduction. Then she looked at the crime scene photos again and found herself grinding her teeth.

Finally, she moved on to the second wallboard, where they'd pasted the photo of a beautiful and confident young woman. In the photo, she wore a thin-strapped, red dress, matching the color of her lipstick. She had smiling green eyes and wavy brown hair, shoulder length, worn casually styled, parted on the right. "Julie Reynolds, 21," Michowsky had written in black marker, right above her photo. Missing since 10:30PM the night before. Already 16 hours since she'd been gone.

Tess frowned and clenched her jaws, trying not to think of what Julie was going through right at that moment, how she must have felt. She knew it too well. Unwanted memories invaded her brain and clouded her vision. Sixteen hours already... sixteen hours of torture, of screams no one heard, of wishing she were dead. How the hell did that happen?

She muttered curses under her breath, reading the rest of the notes and blaming herself for being away in Atlanta when Julie had gone missing. Maybe if she'd been there, they would have found Julie already.

"Talk to me," she asked Michowsky between clenched jaws. "What the hell happened?"

"She went missing last night, guess where? Club Exhale, no less. That's one hell of a coincidence. She went out with friends. Apparently, her boyfriend, Drew DeVos, was late in joining her and a girlfriend of hers, Tiffany. At some point, waiting for Drew, Julie said she was going to the car to retrieve her forgotten phone. That's the last time anyone saw her."

"Background?" she asked.

"Graduated from Stanford law a month ago. Father, Douglas Reynolds, is a big-shot lawyer, with offices in four states. Stepmother, Diane, homemaker and, rumor has it, a bit of an alcoholic. Boyfriend, Drew DeVos, 22, engineering student; he's the one who arrived late at the club last night."

Michowsky scratched the back of his head, running his hand through his buzz-cut hair, and paced back and forth in front of the wallboard.

"It fits," he added. "Too well, if you were to ask me."

"He never took two girls in the same city before," Fradella said. "The unsub… why is he changing his game now?"

"We don't know that he is," Tess replied, her eyes still pinned on Julie's photo. "So far, we have discovered victims in various locations, but we don't know that those victims were *all* his victims, do we? He could have killed more than four women, and we don't know where. He's too experienced, too skilled and organized to be a beginner, so he might have killed in Miami before."

Fradella didn't reply, just grunted almost imperceptibly.

"All right," Tess said, "let's get organized. Detective Fradella, please figure out Julie's last 24 hours, minute by minute. Make calls, pull financials. I've cleared it with my office and we can access financials without delay, since this is an active kidnapping case. Call this number for anything you need; this is the analyst they've assigned to the case to help us with data pulls. His name is Donovan," she added, and handed him a scribbled sticky note.

"Got it," Fradella replied and disappeared.

"You and you," she continued, pointing at the two uniformed cops still hanging out in the room. "Go to Exhale and screen the surveillance videos. Find Julie in the crowds, and watch every move she makes. Don't leave until you pinpoint the exact time she left the club and with whom."

One of the officers pursed his lips, and the other one grumbled. She ignored them both and turned to Michowsky.

"Michowsky, you and I need to speak with her friends and family. We're leaving now."

"Start with the family?"

"Nope, with Tiffany. She was there last night; the family wasn't."

As she turned to grab her bag, she caught a comment from one of the uniformed officers still in the room.

"We know how to do our job," the man grumbled in a low voice, intended only for his partner to hear. "It's not like we need to take any orders from this fed bitch."

She felt a wave of anger rise inside her like a tidal wave. It wasn't because they'd insulted her; she couldn't care less. It was because those cops had time for egotistical, territorial bullshit like that, while a young woman screamed for help in the grasp of a killer.

"I heard that, you know," she said coldly. "You want to find this girl while she's still alive? Or you want to go home early and book a therapy session, so you can bitch and moan about me, and how I ruined your perfect little day?"

The two men hustled toward the door without responding, encouraged by Michowsky's fierce look and head shake, ordering them gone.

"I'll get the car pulled out," she told Michowsky. "Call Tiffany and tell her we're on our way."

27

THE CREEP

Tess almost ran across the squad room, heading for the stairs, car keys in one hand and laptop bag in the other. As she turned into the hallway, the elevator doors squealed open and two young women stepped out. Recognizing them, Tess froze in her tracks. She'd completely forgotten about the sketch artist session she was supposed to book.

"Agent Winnett," they greeted her, offering their hands.

"Ashely, Carmen, thanks for coming in. Let me—" she hesitated, not sure where to ask them to wait. "Just give me a second, will you?"

"Sure," Ashely replied.

Tess checked both interview rooms and no luck. They were already booked, one with a grieving family, and another one with a twitching meth head. Out of options, she decided for the conference room, although she hated exposing witnesses to case information, no matter how minimal. Maybe they wouldn't notice the boards. Yeah… like that could happen.

She invited the two young women to take a seat.

"Water, coffee, anything?" she asked, in a hurry.

"No, thank you, we're good," Carmen replied, after exchanging a quick glance with Ashely.

"All right, hang in here for a few minutes, I'll go find the artist."

She walked back and forth between offices, looking for the artist and couldn't find him. Out of options, she grabbed a phone and called the front desk.

"Hey, Bob, has the sketch artist arrived yet?"

"Haven't seen him today," Bob replied.

"When he shows up, please have him come upstairs to the conference room, okay? I have to run out. The witnesses are in there."

She hung up and went back to the conference room, where the two young women stood, getting ready to leave.

"I see you found him," Carmen said.

"Found who?" Tess asked, raising her eyebrows.

"The creep. Right there," Carmen replied, pointing at May Lin's investors' gala picture. "This guy, the tall one."

On the second row, behind May Lin's family, a tall, blond man stood with an arrogant yet charismatic smile. A memorable face, full of self-confidence, and radiating power, the type of power that lets people know he's intolerant, impatient, fierce. His hair, rebellious, looked tousled, in a permanent just-out-of-bed style that showed a tall forehead and bold eyebrows. Attractive, young, and fit the profile. A strange feeling tugged at her gut when she looked at the man's face; anxiety, adrenaline, excitement, fear? It felt like she was staring into the face of a large predator, a tiger about to pounce, and her gut was telling her to run. *Makes no sense*, she thought. *I catch killers; I don't run from them. You'll be no different, Mr. Creep.*

"Are you sure it's him?" Tess asked, her voice a little raspy for some reason.

"Yeah," Ashely replied. "Positive."

"Definitely," Carmen added. "He's the creep who left with Sonya that night, on the 28th."

"See? He doesn't look like a creep at all, does he?" Ashely asked. "I liked the guy."

Tess studied that face a little longer. If she'd run into this man, would her instincts tell her to be careful? Would any alarm bells go off? She couldn't tell. The image was too small for her to be sure. The photo had been enlarged and was a little blurry, but it was good enough for her purpose. She yanked the photo off the whiteboard, then thanked the two young women and showed them to the elevator.

Then she went back into the squad room, where she'd seen Fradella in passing. He was seated in front of his computer, pulling Julie's credit card history. She put the photo on the scratched, stained desk, and circled the creep's face with a marker.

"Fradella, drop everything and identify this man, please. This was taken at the real estate investors' gala in Chicago almost two years ago. This man is the creep."

"I see May Lin in the picture," Fradella replied, seeming confused, "not Sonya."

"Well, that's exactly it," she said excitedly. "The creep in Sonya's recent past stood inches away from May Lin just weeks before *she* disappeared. This makes it our strongest lead, and we need to move fast."

"What if you're wrong?" Fradella asked.

She frowned, a little irritated. She should have been on her way already.

"We don't have another lead. This man could be the key to finding Julie alive. We've connected him with two of the four victims we know about."

"What if someone else took her? What if this is nothing more than a coincidence, this… creep?"

She pursed her lips, unsure what to say. "Sometimes you have to go with your gut," she said eventually, trying to save time.

"And if you're wrong? Are you prepared to have Julie's death be on you? On a gut call?"

"Listen," Tess replied, "let's be pragmatic here. Identifying this man won't take you all that long. An hour, maybe two, tops. Why don't we stop talking about it and just get it done, huh? Then you can resume working on Julie's last 24."

He slammed the photo onto the scanner, sending rattling vibrations into the battered desk.

"Yes, ma'am," he confirmed sarcastically.

"Don't scan, I have the digital," Tess added, ignoring his attitude. "As soon as you have an ID, send a better photo and his details to my phone, will you?"

He nodded, frowning and averting his eyes.

"Then, when I come back," she added, "we'll run a search and see how many missing persons were last seen at Club Exhale since it opened for business. My gut tells me there are more."

28

VANISHED

Tiffany lived in one of those high-rise condos on Ocean Drive, the pride of Miami Beach, no doubt with the help of parental sponsoring. The elevator, running smoothly and perfectly silent, took less than 40 seconds to unload Tess and Gary on the 22nd floor.

The young girl waited for them with the door ajar, courtesy of the doorman, who had announced them on their way up. Tess knocked, and Tiffany was quick to open the door wide.

"Come in," she said, then led them into a luminous, oceanfront, living room. They introduced themselves and shook hands, while Tess admired Tiffany's attire, one of those soft fabric, beach gowns that flutter and float around one's curves, without revealing much, yet looking that good only on someone with a perfect beach bod.

Tiffany parked chilled cans of sparkling water in front of them, on the small glass coffee table, using coasters with the Exhale emblem.

"So, you were regulars?" Tess asked, pointing at the coasters.

"Um, no, not really," she replied, then blushed a little.

"Are you legal in there?"

"Um, what? Oh, yeah, I turned 21 a month ago," she smiled nervously. "We were celebrating that actually. Julie was the last one in our group to turn legal, just a few days ago. So this was our first Friday night as legal patrons," she chirped on casually, then doubled back on herself. "Um, I mean, like out first night in a club, like, ever," she added quickly, looking Tess sheepishly in the eye.

"Yeah... right," Tess replied. "Tell me what happened."

"We arrived a little early to get us a table," she said, switching to casual mode again. "Around nine or so. We danced for a little while, just the two of us, because Drew was running late."

"Why? What happened?" Michowsky asked.

"He had a flat tire on his way in. We didn't worry much; he's technical, you know. He could fix that himself. So we went ahead by ourselves. We danced, then we took a break and went back to the table, when Julie saw she forgot her cellphone in her car."

"Did anyone hit on you? On Julie?"

"Um, not really... You know, we always get attention from guys when we go out, it's not like... you know."

"But no one in particular?" Michowsky insisted.

"No, no one in particular."

"Then what happened?" Tess asked.

"Julie left to get her phone, and she was gone a while. I thought she'd run into Drew coming in, and they were together somewhere, dancing. I was pissed off as hell, because I thought they'd just left me there by myself, and it sucks sitting alone at a table in a club, right? But then Drew appeared, without Julie, and I freaked out. We both did."

"Then what did you do?"

"We went looking for her. We looked everywhere. I checked all the bathrooms, then we went together in the parking lot, where she'd parked her car when we arrived. Drew opened it, and the phone was still in there. She never even made it to the car..." Tiffany's voice trailed off, as she started crying. "Oh, my God, Julie..."

Tess touched her shoulder in what attempted to be a comforting gesture, but Tiffany didn't react. She continued sobbing, as if she was just realizing the implications of Julie's disappearance.

"There was this girl," she spoke between sobs, "on TV, just a few days ago. They called her Dawn Girl."

Tess and Gary exchanged quick, worried glances.

"Do you think he's got Julie?"

"Who?" Tess asked quietly, although she already knew the answer.

"Dawn Girl's killer," she whispered, afraid to even hear herself speak.

"We don't know that," Tess replied, and Michowsky shot her a surprised glance. "We shouldn't jump to conclusions though. Lots of people go missing every day, for lots of reasons. A ransom call could come in any minute, or Julie could walk in here, embarrassed she took off with some hot guy for a night of steaming passion."

"Not her," Tiffany said, looking Tess firmly in the eye. "She wasn't like that… she wasn't trashy. She's with Drew, and she would have never left with another guy. She loves Drew."

"Good to know," Tess said in a pacifying tone. "But still there's no reason to jump to any conclusions, right?"

Tiffany nodded and wiped her tears with the back of her hands.

"Tell me, last night, when you went looking for her, did you ask the door bouncers if they'd seen her?" Michowsky asked.

"Of course we did, and no, they said no."

She couldn't have vanished like that, from inside the club. Someone must have seen something.

"Tiffany, did you look at CCTV video feeds last night? Did anyone show that to you?" Tess asked gently.

"Yes. When we couldn't find her anywhere, we asked for help from the bouncers. At first they didn't want to help, but later on, when the club closed, Drew and I were by the door, making sure we looked at everyone's faces as they left."

"That's actually very smart," Tess acknowledged. "Well done."

"That's when they took us seriously, when the club emptied and she wasn't anywhere."

"Michowsky, did you see the surveillance video this morning?" Tess asked, intrigued.

"It's dark, grainy, and flashy from the strobes. You can't see anything on most feeds."

"I wonder if those two guys we sent there found anything yet. Can you hook us up? On my laptop, to see the feeds?"

"I guess… let me see," Michowsky offered, and took her laptop.

Tess used the time to stretch her legs a little and walked around the room. White walls with scattered pictures hanging in geometrical arrangements, all framed in black for powerful contrast. Light furniture, casual, almost like patio furniture, seeding the idea of leisure living, of vacation in one's head. Light draperies, light moods on the faces of the people photographed on the walls, light living. Not a worry in this world.

"What's your major?" Tess asked, out of the blue.

"Law," Tiffany replied. "Why?"

"Just wondering how you two met, that's all."

"We grew up together. Our dads are both lawyers, partners in a major law firm. Reynolds and Rohr, you might have heard of it."

She had. She doubted there was a single Miami resident who *hadn't* heard of it.

"How hard was it for Julie to finish law school early?"

"For her? Not that hard. She's super smart."

"Why did she want to finish early? Do you know? What motivated her?"

"She likes money and wanted to start earning her own," Tiffany said, blushing a little. "I'm not like that… I wanted to have some fun while in school. She was just focused, that's all. Anxious to finish what she calls unpaid work." She chuckled lightly. "She wanted to bill someone for all those research hours."

"Here you go," Michowsky said, turning Tess's laptop around. "All feeds are there."

"What time was it when Drew arrived?"

"It was 10:30 or so."

"So if we say Julie left to get her phone at about 10:00PM, would that ring true?" Tess asked.

"Even a little later, maybe 10:15."

"Which one was your table?" Tess asked, turning the screen toward Tiffany.

"This one," she replied, pointing at an empty table, barely visible in the grainy darkness.

The time code read, 10:01:17. Tess fast-forwarded that feed until she saw the two girls coming to take their seats at the table.

"Here you are," she mumbled, and Tiffany nodded.

"Yeah, that's us."

The quality of the video feed was awful. Flashing club lights and strobes, overall darkness, and low-resolution, crappy equipment made for the triple threat of almost unusable video. Nevertheless, she continued to watch the feed, until Julie stood and left the table, exiting the camera's field. She noted the time code, 10:14:29.

"Let's see in which feed we see her entering, when she leaves this one."

They checked a few other feeds and finally found Julie, walking between hordes of people in a hallway, alone, and apparently all right. Then she fell off that camera, at time code 10:16:44.

No matter how hard they tried, they couldn't find her anywhere else, on any other video feed. They even watched the entrance feed, where patrons were seen from behind, leaving the club. She wasn't anywhere among them, not by herself, nor in a group.

At precisely 10:16:44PM the night before, Julie Reynolds had vanished from the middle of a dance club full of people.

29

INITIATIVE

The elevator in Tiffany's high rise descended just as fast and as silently as it had gone up, almost making Tess a little lightheaded. She pondered over the results of their visit with Tiffany. She now had a better understanding of how the unsub operated. A terrible predator, hunting at the center of the herd, not at the periphery, which proved boldness, a boldness beyond anything she'd even encountered before. This unsub went for specific victims, not for victims of opportunity, and he had a way to snatch them without a sound, without anyone noticing, without leaving the tiniest trace.

Why didn't he snatch Julie at the car? Probably because he had no idea she was going to her car. He must have thought she was going to the restrooms. Or maybe he was so confident, so skilled and experienced in his manner of abduction, that he was more comfortable hidden in the noisy, agitated crowd than outside in the quiet parking lot.

"Where do you want to go next?" Michowsky asked. "Parents?"

"No," Tess replied thoughtfully. "Let's see Drew DeVos first. He's a few minutes away, on Indian Creek."

They rode quietly in the car for a few minutes, while Tess mulled over a question she couldn't answer yet. Was the unsub stalking the girls? Or was he an impulse abductor, who saw someone he liked and just went for it? Then how would victimology work? Julie fit the profile: young, rich, overachiever college graduate. He'd have to know all this about his victims before snatching them, which meant he stalked, he researched, he prepared for the hunt. Or did he? What if he got all that information some other way?

"Do you think we're going to get her in time?" Michowsky asked. "We got nothing, a big, fat, goddamned nothing."

"We got something," she replied. "We got the creep."

"What? And when were you going to fill me in on that?"

"I just did," Tess replied. "Fradella's running his ID. Sonya's friends picked him out of a photo on our board, a photo with May Lin."

Michowsky whistled. "That's two out of four."

"Yeah, exactly."

She stopped her Suburban in front of the entrance to Drew's condo building and flashed her badge at the doorman. "Leave it here, all right? We won't be long."

Another elevator, this one a little more mundane. Then suite 512, where they rang and banged on the door, but no one answered.

"Want to kick it down?" Michowsky offered.

"What the hell for?" Tess replied, then pulled out her phone and dialed Drew's mobile number. He picked up almost immediately.

"Yes, hello."

"Is this Drew DeVos?" Tess asked, shifting the phone to speaker mode.

"Yes, that's me, who is this?"

"This is Special Agent Winnett, FBI. We need to speak to you immediately regarding the disappearance of—"

"Julie, yes. Sure."

"Where are you?"

"Out there, looking for her," he replied with frustration in his voice, "because no one else is."

"We need a specific address to meet you."

"I'm at the Exhale, talking to employees as they show up for work. Showing her picture around."

"Stay put, Drew. We'll meet you there in 10 minutes."

She ended the call and hopped in the elevator.

"Got to give it to them," Michowsky said, "Drew and Tiffany, they're sharp and willing to go the distance for this girl."

"Yeah, they are. Why aren't the police, though? And don't tell me caseloads, resources, and all that bullshit."

Michowsky shook his head, but remained quiet, probably unwilling to start an argument that wasn't going to end well.

"There he is," Michowsky pointed him out. A tall, skinny, young man leaning against the hood of a yellow Mustang, parked right next to the club's entrance.

"Drew?" Tess asked. "Agent Winnett, we spoke on the phone. This is Detective Michowsky."

They shook hands briefly. She studied him a little. Seeing his pallor and the dark circles under his eyes, he hadn't slept a wink the night before. She checked the time and repressed a groan. Eighteen hours since Julie had vanished. Time flies.

"Good to see you're here," Drew said. "What do you need to know?"

"What happened last night?"

"After we realized Julie was missing, Tiffany and I started looking everywhere for her. We spoke to the bouncers, to club security, no one had seen her and no one took us seriously for a while."

"Then?"

"Then the club closed at 3:00AM, and people started leaving. When they saw her car left behind in the parking lot, they finally listened. They searched everywhere, and at 5:00AM I called the cops again."

"Again? You called before?"

"Yeah, as soon as we searched everywhere and couldn't find her. At about 1:30 or so."

"And?"

"Someone came, a cop, and asked me if she'd left me for some other guy. Yeah... unbelievable, right? He told me there was nothing he could do for 24 hours; he quoted some procedure."

"Then later, at five?"

"The same story, and actually the same cop, but this time he was pissed off because I'd called again. He did look at her car though and took down some information, car plates, stuff like that. But he still didn't take us seriously. He didn't want to open a case."

Tess and Gary exchanged a quick glance.

"That's when we went to her house, to speak with her dad. He pulled some strings, made some calls, and finally got the cops to open a formal case. But that's where it all stops. No one did anything since then, since this morning."

Tess and Gary exchanged a second glance. This time, Michowsky quickly averted his eyes and looked at the pavement.

"I followed up at around noon; no one's really working this case at Miami Dade."

"Well, we're not Miami Dade," Tess said.

"Yeah, I know."

"How do you know?" Michowsky asked, his eyebrows raised with curiosity.

"Because you're actually working the case, that's how I know," Drew replied coldly. "But why the FBI? Has anyone made any ransom demands?"

"Um, no, nothing like that," Tess replied. She and Michowsky looked at each other again, and Tess decided to lie. There was no point putting nightmare images in the young man's mind. "I'm here as part of an interagency best practices exchange program. Look at it this way: nothing to worry about, just upside. More help on your girlfriend's case."

"Uh-huh, I see," he replied, and Tess saw in his eyes he didn't believe her for a second. He turned grim, and his frown deepened.

"How was your relationship?" she asked.

"Great," he replied, still grim. "We're planning to get married, as soon as she passes her bar exam."

Tess bit her lip, pushing away bad memories. Even if Julie survived, their relationship would never be the same. Not ever. Not after what the unsub did to his victims. She took in a deep breath of torrid, humid air.

"Why didn't you meet them last night? What happened?"

"A flat," he replied angrily. "A stupid flat tire... and now she's missing. I should've taken a damn cab."

"Did you notice anything that could mean someone messed with your tire on purpose?"

"What? No... I didn't. Why?"

"We don't know, just asking anything we can think of," Michowsky replied. "Testing all scenarios."

"No, it was just a flat. It took me a long time, because my jack wasn't there; I don't know why. I had to borrow one. That's why I told them to go inside on their own. Oh, my God..."

He grabbed at his dark hair with both his hands, in a gesture of desperation. He was blaming himself; that was obvious. Tess wondered what had really happened to the jack. A young engineer like Drew wouldn't consider driving around without one.

But was the missing jack a lead worth following up on? Or just one of those coincidences, one of life's curveballs, meant to distract, disorient, and delay?

Whether the unsub stalked his prey and set up elaborate traps, or he just snatched on impulse, he still had Julie. They needed to find her, and for that, they needed to find him, Dawn Girl's killer.

30

DARKNESS

She awoke slowly, like emerging from a bottomless pit of silent, petrifying darkness. The first rational, crystallized thought in her groggy brain was that she'd been drugged. She realized that with more and more certainty, feeling a strange numbness controlling her mind, slowing it down, willing her back to sleep.

She resisted the urge to sink back into oblivion and fought to open her eyes. She felt them painfully dry, eyelids stuck to eyeballs. It took effort to get them to open, but once she did, all she could see was still darkness. She felt the same dryness in her mouth, and she went through the motions of swallowing, to ease the feeling of desiccated parchment in her throat.

She tried to rub her eyes, but her hands wouldn't listen. They moved a little, but not enough to touch her face. Dizzy and lightheaded, she tried to get her bearings, but the almost complete darkness wasn't helping. What little light she saw came from the dial pad of an alarm system, mounted on a wall somewhere to her left. The bluish backlight of its screen, a green LED, and a couple of red ones was all she had to work with.

She forced her dry eyes to see, then squeezed them tightly, to get tears to lubricate them. She'd been drugged, and heavily; there was no doubt. Most sedatives dry all mucosae as a side effect, so that explained that. She felt a little better, putting some shred of reasonable explanation to what she felt. But it wasn't nearly enough. She swallowed again, hard, feeling tension clutch her scorched throat. She felt weightless somehow, as if floating in space, and that only made her feel worse, queasy, unable to get her bearings.

She forced herself to flex her arm, at first blaming her inability on the numbness she felt in all her muscles. She focused on her left arm, yearning for her left hand to touch her face. She was able to move it, but only partially, and every move she made got her dizzier, shakier somehow, as if she flew through space, out of control. The sedative she'd been dosed with was still in her system, making it hard for her to figure out what was happening.

She willed her brain into functioning and tensed her arm muscles again, only to fail again. This time, she understood why. Her wrist was bound with soft restraints, so soft she almost didn't feel them, but unyielding nevertheless. She tugged more and more forcefully, gaining nothing more than a rattling noise and increased dizziness.

She tried to move a leg, and the same happened. She could flex her knee a little, even stretch her leg completely, but every move she made shifted her entire body somehow and made her nauseous. Her ankles were bound too, and that realization sent a wave of adrenaline through her entire being, dissipating the remnants of the heavy sedative. She felt her head clear up, her judgment return, and her muscles coming to life. As she regained her bearings, she realized she was hanging from the ceiling in a complicated harness, positioned almost horizontally, face down. Like a puppet dangling on strings, powerless, captive.

She gasped, and, fighting a wave of blinding panic, she focused on what she felt in her body. Her wrists and ankles were cuffed and suspended, yet they still had a little mobility. A wide belt supported her abdomen, and another supported her shoulders. Her head moved freely, and by the stiffness she felt in her neck, it must have been hanging loose while she'd been out, unconscious.

She breathed heavily. Waves of panic rolled in, shooting fresh adrenaline through her body and sharpening her senses. She tried to free herself, tugging desperately against the restraints, no longer feeling the nausea. Nothing budged, and the noise of the rattling restraints was covered by the thumping of heartbeats in her chest, and by the sound of sharp, shattered gasps for air.

As the last remnants of sedative wore off, defeated by adrenaline, panic set in. Fear rose and strangled her mercilessly. It built inside her chest, then came out in an endless shriek that no one heard.

31

FAMILY LIFE

The Suburban's dashboard clock indicated 6:12PM, a little over 19 hours since Julie had vanished. Nineteen hours. Tess didn't want to think what that must have been like for her. Time went by lightning fast for her and Michowsky, but she knew how long each minute lasted for Julie.

She shifted in her seat without taking her foot off the gas pedal. She was restless, second-guessing herself. She believed with all her being that Sonya's killer had taken Julie, but what evidence did she have? The location, Club Exhale, was the same as Sonya's last-seen whereabouts. Maybe a coincidence; could be nothing more than that. There was also the fact that Julie matched the victimology; young, wealthy, overachieving college grad. Probably half the high-end club's female patrons matched that profile. So how was that enough? Was she about to make a huge mistake, one that could cost Julie her life? If Sonya's killer hadn't taken Julie, if she'd been abducted by someone else, she had nothing, absolutely nothing to go on. But that didn't make the scenario more possible; it only made it a last resort, a desperate alternative validated by a lack of options. Something to pursue when nothing else was there.

And yet, in her gut, she knew she was right. She knew she was chasing the right man.

She let her mind wander freely for a while, after giving up the self-doubt and deciding to go with her gut. She found herself reflecting on how silent they were, Michowsky and her, how they avoided talking with each other when they had a choice. It was becoming the norm, their silent drives around town. Little was left to be said between the two of them, each engulfed in thoughts, theories, and their own personal hells. What was Michowsky's hell? She wondered if his back still hurt.

"How's your back?"

"Don't ask," he replied morosely.

That was it for her attempt at small talk. She almost shrugged; at least she'd tried. She checked the GPS; only three minutes left to their destination, the residence of Mr. and Mrs. Reynolds, Julie's family.

Tess took the highway exit and immediately turned into a subdivision of elegant acreage properties. Julie's father, Douglas Reynolds, was one of the wealthiest lawyers in the city, cofounder of Miami's second-largest law firm. He was a divorce lawyer, and apparently marriages didn't last long under the hot Miami sun, especially the ones in the upper-income bracket.

She checked the house numbers and pulled into the Reynolds' curved driveway. She waited patiently for Michowsky to catch up and rang the bell as soon as he'd climbed the last of the five steps to the entrance.

A man opened the door almost immediately. He wore one of those old-style, cardigan sweaters, an undecided shade of brown. His eyes were hollow, and he was pale, a sickly shade of yellowish-gray. His shoulders were hunched forward, and his head bowed. Two deep, vertical ridges marked his forehead, as his eyebrows were glued together in a permanent frown. Not much of the hotshot lawyer's powerful demeanor was left in Reynolds. He was just a desperate father, fearing for the life of his child.

"I've been expecting you for a while," he said, "you sure took your time. Come in."

He led the way to the dining area, where a woman in a white terrycloth bathrobe stood at the table. Her head leaned into her left hand supporting her jaw, manicured fingers fanned on her cheek. In front of her, a glass of white wine had about an inch of liquid left, and the bottle next to it was three-quarters empty.

"This is my wife, Diane," the man made the introductions.

"Special Agent Winnett," Tess said, then pointed at Gary, "and this is Detective Michowsky. Mr. Reynolds, we have a few—"

"Sit," Mr. Reynolds invited them. "Questions?"

Before Tess could answer, a young girl entered the dining area, sauntering about with a defying look on her face.

"Look, the show's on," she said, her amusement genuine as she sized them up.

"Chloe," Mr. Reynolds said, but the girl scoffed loudly and he didn't continue. He seemed resigned, or maybe too tired and sad to put the teenager in her place.

A second of uncomfortable silence filled the room, interrupted by Mrs. Reynolds' glass hitting the table, then it being filled with whatever wine was left in the bottle.

"Um, Mr. Reynolds, what can you tell us about Julie? What w—is she like?" Tess asked, catching herself just in time, before making a horrible mistake. Julie was still alive, and she was going to make sure she stayed that way.

"She's smart and kind, hardworking, everyone loves her," Reynolds replied, his eyes wandering aimlessly.

"Not everyone," Chloe added. A glare from Diane silenced her.

"Do you know of anyone who might have taken her? Does she have any enemies?"

Reynolds glanced quickly toward Chloe, then back to Tess.

Interesting, Tess thought. She wished she'd done better homework. What was the deal with Chloe?

"No, no one. *Everyone* loved her," he said, emphasizing the word, in a preemptive measure to stifle any opposing opinion coming from Chloe.

"How about you, sir?" Michowsky asked. "I'm sure you made quite a few enemies throughout your career. Any clients who lost in court, or husbands who thought the settlement was too high?"

Reynolds rubbed his forehead, thinking.

"No doubt I've made enemies," he eventually said. "But the people I work with sue when they're mad. They're not kidnappers. They're mostly businessmen, musicians, that kind of people."

"Has there been any contact, phone call, or letter, advising of ransom demands?"

"No. Not yet." He paused for a while, then smiled bitterly. "I'm hoping for a ransom call, if you can believe it. Anything would be better than this."

Tess glanced at her watch. They were almost 20 hours into her disappearance. The ransom call would have come by now, or so the bureau stats indicated. But she knew why there was no ransom call; only she couldn't share that information with the Reynolds. She decided to lie, and give the man some hope. It was all she could do at the time.

"They will call, Mr. Reynolds. Sometimes they like to make people wait so they—"

"Pay more," he replied coldly. "I get it, but I don't care. Anything to get my daughter back."

"Ain't karma a bitch, huh?" Chloe said.

Tess turned her attention toward Chloe.

"It's Chloe, right?"

"Yes," she replied, offering an affected hand and swinging her narrow hips as Tess shook it. "Chloe Barr."

"Barr?" Tess asked.

"Not Reynolds, if that's what you mean. I'm sure you heard me the first time, it's Barr. I'm not going to change my name every time my mother decides to fuck another loser."

"Chloe," Diane said, a moderate, almost timid pushback. Not in the least the response Tess would have anticipated. "Don't embarrass me, all right?"

"I can't embarrass you more than you embarrass yourself, Mom. This your second bottle yet? Oh, wait, it's after lunch, so it's your third!"

"Chloe!" Reynolds said, his anger picking up.

"You vicious little bitch!" Diane said, staring her daughter down.

A moment of silence developed, one of those uncomfortable, disturbing scenes quite common for troubled, dysfunctional families.

Tess decided to break the silence. They weren't there for the family; they were there for Julie.

"Chloe, what's crawling up your ass?" Tess suddenly asked.

"What?"

"Yeah, you heard me... You don't like Julie that much, do you?"

Chloe turned to her stepdad, fuming.

"So you let them question me? A minor? What kind of lawyer are you?"

"There's a guardian present," he replied undisturbed, engulfed in his sorrow. "I give them permission."

"She hates Julie, if you wanna know," Diane said, slurring a little.

"And why is that?" Tess asked.

"Because when Mom wanted to get laid with a license, I suddenly have to share everything! And I don't wanna share shit!"

"Huh," Tess blurted. How classy.

"Julie wouldn't buy her booze and smokes," Diane added. "That's if you want to know the real truth."

"Ha! You don't know what you're talking about," Chloe retorted. "If you're a wino, doesn't mean that I am."

"There's more," the mother added. "Chloe's old boyfriend gave Julie some appreciative looks, so Chloe dumped him. But she's still pissed, if you asked me."

"That's what you think!" Chloe fought back. "I hate her 'cause she's so damn perfect! Makes me look bad."

Tess saw Reynolds cringe and squeeze his eyes shut when he heard Chloe's vicious words.

"Cheap," Diane added. "The word you're looking for is cheap, and it's you, not Julie, who makes you look cheap. A bitchy, venomous little slut, that's my daughter."

"You know what they say," Chloe replied almost indifferently, "the apple doesn't fall far from the tree."

"All right," Tess said, decided to interrupt the family drama and get on with their investigation. "Where were you last night after 8:00PM?"

"Here, doing house arrest."

Tess turned her inquisitive glance toward Reynolds.

"That means she was grounded," he replied calmly. "She was here all evening and all night, locked in her room."

"Thank you," Tess replied. "I think this is it for now."

"No, that's not it," Reynolds said, his voice loaded with tears. "Please tell me what to do. I can go on TV and offer a reward. I can make it big, attractive enough for someone to take the risk and tell me where my baby is."

"We'll be in touch, Mr. Reynolds. Give us a few more hours. We're following some leads. We might come to that, but let's exhaust all our other possibilities."

"Why? Why won't you let me try?"

"Julie is safer if whoever took her doesn't see us coming. Typically, if no ransom has been made, and no one has actually seen Julie get taken, these cases are classified as missing persons, and dealt with... differently."

"You mean, not really investigated, right?"

"Right. You see my point."

"Yeah. Then let me ask you, how come you're investigating it?"

"Because of Drew and Tiffany, of how diligent and organized they were, how quick to react, we were able to classify this case as an abduction, not a missing person." Tess was getting more and more comfortable at lying. She didn't want Reynolds to fall apart.

But then there was Chloe.

"No, that's not it. It's because of Dawn Girl. Julie looks just like her, or haven't you noticed, Daddy?"

"No!" Doug Reynolds collapsed on the floor, hugging his knees and sobbing hard. Tess touched his shoulder, trying to comfort him, while she shot Chloe a fierce look.

"You'll make a fine criminal one day," she told Chloe, "unless you change your ways. I don't think you'd last long in jail. Maybe a couple of days, maybe a week. The teeth go first, you know."

Then Tess looked at Diane. Unfazed, the woman was refilling her wine glass.

A few minutes later, Tess let out a long, tense breath, as she started the engine and restored the flow of air conditioning in her overheated Suburban.

"You can say that again," Michowsky said.

"What?"

"You sighed."

"Yeah. I need a shower after visiting with these people," Tess chuckled. "I'd expected more familial bliss out of the best divorce lawyer in town."

"You married, Winnett?"

"Nah... it's not for me."

A silent beat, while Tess noticed Michowsky didn't volunteer any personal information. She didn't press. That kind of silence normally meant there were issues in his relationship. He wore a wedding band though, a simple, narrow gold band. What was it that Cat said? Each wearing their own brand of misery?

"I've seen enough viciousness in that kid tonight to classify her as a viable lead," Michowsky said. "Even if she was home, she has access to money. These people get their stuff done for them."

"What, you think Chloe hired a contract killer?" Tess scoffed. "I don't see that. The parents have the kind of money it takes to get this kind of work done, not her. I don't see her doing it. She's all mouth, no brains."

"The mother is pickled half the time. Do you think she locks her credit cards?"

"All right, I'll give you that. I'll give you one more. Narcissistic teenagers like this one do something else. They sic others onto the target of their hate. Call it contract work for free, but that's what teenagers like Chloe do."

"How the hell do they do that?"

"There are ways," Tess replied. "For example, she could hang out with the wrong crowd of gangbangers, and tell them her sister is this really hot chick who loves gang action, and she's going to be on so and so date, at the club. She even shows them a picture. The idiots then do her dirty work, without even realizing they've been had."

Michowsky whistled.

"Yep, seen it done. Kids today aren't what they used to be."

"So you agree Chloe is a lead in this case?"

"Nope, I don't. I still think the serial killer is our strongest lead."

"He never struck twice in the same spot," Michowsky said, raising the pitch of his voice a little, to match his frustration.

"That you know of," Tess replied. "This conversation is like a bad case of déjà vu. Didn't we talk about this? You don't start your career as a serial killer with this level of skill, knowledge, and boldness. He has killed before, and we don't know about those victims yet."

"Winnett, if you focus on your serial and you're wrong, you're ignoring a lead that could save this girl's life."

32

A Couple of Calls

Tess drove silently for a while, mulling over Michowsky's words. He'd said exactly what had been on her mind, but hearing the words spoken out loud made a difference. Was she wrong in pursuing Sonya's killer to save Julie? Was that wishful thinking, knowing she'd kill two birds with one stone?

Catch, not kill. She still found herself thinking what would happen the day she'd finally track down the unsub. How she hoped he'd resist arrest, or, even better, draw a weapon on her. Suicide by cop would be a nice way to go for such scum, although more deserving would be to rot in jail, countless years, learning what it means to be at someone's mercy, bound and raped. Day after day, with no hope of ever getting out. Yeah, that's what he deserved. Catch, not kill.

Her knuckles hurt, forcing her to relax the grip on the steering wheel. Tense and immersed in thought, she'd white-knuckled the damn thing since they'd left the Reynolds. One hand at a time, she wiped the sweat off her palms against her slacks, discreetly, glad that Michowsky watched the familiar landscape so deeply absorbed in his own thoughts.

Her phone quacked loudly, amplified by the car's audio system. SAC Pearson's name was displayed in large font on the LCD, but she decided to take the call on her handheld, for privacy.

"Hello," she eventually replied, after fumbling with the settings.

"So it's confirmed, you've got a serial killer at large, huh, Winnett?" Pearson went right into the topic, no chitchat.

"It's my strong belief, sir, and I think SSA McKenzie can confirm."

"He just did, in light of Julie Reynolds's kidnapping. He'll wrap up the full profile and send it to you later today."

"Good to know, sir. I appreciate the help."

"Do you now? I want to send you a team."

Her knuckles turned white again, gripping the phone with one hand and the wheel with the other.

"I already have a team, sir. I'm working with Palm Beach."

Michowsky scoffed quietly and tried to hide a sarcastic grin.

"Why was I even thinking you'd suddenly turned into a rational, compliant agent who takes direction well?" SAC Pearson said.

"Sir..." she didn't even know how to respond to his rant, but ventured a reply anyway. "We're handling this case just fine."

"You're in over your head, Winnett. You need help. If you fuck this up, you'll never forgive yourself."

She bit her lip, refraining from yelling at him. That never helped.

"Give me 24 hours," she said quietly, almost subdued. "If I don't have my unsub zeroed in by then, send anyone you want. For now, they'd hinder more than help."

"Give your fellow agents some credit," he said, sounding insulted.

"I will, as of tomorrow evening. Please."

He hung up on her, without a word. She disconnected the call, then mumbled some cuss words.

Gary chuckled lightly.

"Oh, shut it, Michowsky."

"Who was that?"

"SAC Pearson, my boss. He's not my biggest fan lately."

"Gee, I wonder why," he quipped.

She shot him a homicidal glance, quickly interrupted by another call coming in. She didn't recognize the number, but Gary did.

"That's the squad room," he said, and accepted the call via the car's system. "Go for Michowsky and Winnett."

"I got the creep's ID, and it's bad news, guys." Fradella sounded worried, tense.

"How can it be bad?" Tess asked.

"He's as loaded as they can get. His family is very well connected. The governor attends their family events. We can't touch this guy."

"Huh, we'll see about that. What's his name?"

"It's Matthew Feldman Dahler, 33. His record is clean as a whistle."

"*The* Feldman Dahlers?" Michowsky asked. "Oh, shit."

"Hey, why are we freaking out? We're the good guys, for Chrissake," Tess said.

"You can't go near these people, Winnett, trust me. They have lawyers who can eat you alive for breakfast without pickles and without breaking a sweat. You can't touch them."

"Sure, I can. Just watch me."

"We got nothing. No evidence, no motive, no criminal history," Michowsky said.

"We got guts and brains," she said, implacable.

They heard Fradella chuckle over the phone.

"I like your style, Winnett," Fradella said. "Maybe you don't know who these people are."

"I vaguely remember hearing the name."

"John Dahler, Matthew's father, is a real estate developer, third generation. You know the five-stars hotels in Miami Beach, right off Ocean Drive? Yeah, the ones that sell suites at $250 a night and above, and they're still booked solid? He owns the entire area. The resort, several condo high rises, a few restaurants. His family bought that stretch of land when it was dirt cheap, right after the big Depression in 1930."

"We were expecting that. It's in the profile. Our unsub is wealthy, with a flexible work schedule, socially adept."

"Wait, I'm not done. Matthew's mother, Edwina Feldman Dahler, is the CEO and founder of Global Risk Ventures, a multinational insurance conglomerate. She made the top 100 richest people's list before her husband did. She doesn't waste any opportunity to tell people she owned a private jet *before* she met John. Rumor has it she's a vicious bitch, and that *the* John Dahler is under her thumb a lot. That's social media gossip, nothing more, but I've seen one of those short movies online, with Dahler cringing while his wife told people just how powerful she was compared to him. Apparently, she doesn't pull her punches with hubby. Or with anyone, I would say."

"Okay, so?" Tess asked, a little irritated with Fradella's rant. She hated cops who cowered in the presence of affluent suspects, afraid for their jobs. Just because the parents were loaded, didn't mean the son couldn't be a sadistic psychopath. These guys needed to grow some balls.

"So they'll hide behind a barrier of overpriced lawyers, that's what they'll do. We'll spend more time dodging lawsuits and complaints than working the case."

Complaints… how wonderful. SAC Pearson was going to be thrilled if she added a few more of those. Yet her gut told her she was on the right track.

"Let's dig up everything we can about this guy. Facebook accounts, scandals, gossip, yearbooks, the works. Remember the analyst my boss assigned to our case? I gave you his number. Call him and ask him to get it done like it's burning."

"Got it," Fradella said.

Without warning, she flipped a U-turn, in a concert of honks and curses.

"What the hell?" Michowsky asked, frowning and holding on to the door armrest.

"Detective Fradella, get a few printouts of this guy's face and meet us at the club, pronto. Let's do some real police work."

"Got it," he repeated, then hung up.

"Wait a second," Michowsky protested, "you can't go into that club and show his picture to people, like he's a common criminal. He'll hear about it, and it will be a disaster."

"We can't afford not to, Gary. We just can't."

33

THE GLADES

Most people wouldn't be caught dead in the heart of the Florida Everglades at dusk. A treacherous land of myriad insects and predators, it kept visitors away effectively. Blood-seeking insects don't even matter for the accidental visitor, more concerned with the few but deadly poisonous snake species, the huge pythons, and the 10-foot alligators. Here, in the Glades, only the skilled and the irresponsible venture, and the latter don't usually make it out.

Matthew knew his way around the Glades really well. He liked the environment, one of the very few things in life that still challenged him and kept him on his toes. The tropical, hardwood hammock brimmed with life, chirping, hissing, and chittering through the wetlands, slithering in the ferns, or stalking him with narrow, vertical pupils from the surface of the stagnant water. He loved the thrill of the Glades, where one second of carelessness could cost him his life. Like every time he hunted, he needed to be careful, and that was a trained skill more than a native talent.

He hunted for black bear that evening, moving slowly and silently through the thick, hardwood forest, ready to pounce. Black bear hunting season had been suspended, but Matthew didn't care about the regulations. He was a hunter, a true hunter in the way his ancestors were, thousands of years before him. When he wanted fresh blood, he left his cave and went out there, armed with only a bow with arrows and a tactical knife. No firearms. Not ever. They took away the pleasure of the kill. Firearms were noisy and lacked elegance. Any idiot with a gun could pull the trigger and kill a bear. He was different. He wanted to come near the agonizing animal, downed by his arrow, and watch it as it drew its last breath, then snatch the bloody arrow out of its chest.

The forest was losing light as the sun was getting ready to set, and the myriad insects and small critters in the hammock gained enthusiasm, raising their voices in heated dialogues of countless sounds. He walked slowly, breathing shallow in the humid, tropical air, and paying attention to every twig snap, every leaf moving, every jungle scream.

He could feel the bear nearing, although not a single sound stood out from the general racket. Slowly, without making a sound, he grabbed his bow and nocked an arrow, getting ready to extend the string and release. He could feel the animal approaching, unsuspecting, trusting of his environment, just like Matthew had once been.

Flashbacks invaded, superimposed against the hammock's densely forested landscape. Voices, feverishly articulating words over one another, arguing for hours, to no avail. The feeling of powerlessness, the most unbearable feeling he'd ever had to endure, followed by the moment he had to concede the fight, throwing the battle in the hope he'd win the war. Someday.

Not many people held the power to make him suffer; very few did, actually. In truth, just one did, and she'd hurt him so badly it still burned to remember. The wound was deep and still bleeding, his ego unaccustomed to hearing anyone say no to him. Yet she did, and her word overtook his, again and again, and he was forced to comply every single time. The humiliation, the degradation he'd felt, the shame and indignity at the thought that others might have known about his defeat were unbearable. All he could think about was the day he'd make her pay.

Until that day, nearing fast, he had to seek his release by taking other lives, weak compensations for his daily dose of degradation, when he was forced to do what she wanted instead of having his own way. But the day she'd finally pay was near, and nothing she did could stop that from coming. Just thinking of that day, of how it would all play out, brought an adrenaline rush to his body, a wave of anticipation excitement that sent his blood rushing through his veins.

He visualized her begging for his mercy, saying what she'd always said to him, "No." Only this time she'd beg, she'd cry, she'd plead for his benevolence as he'd punish her again, and again, and again. At the end of that day, only he'd be left standing, not her. She'd be kneeled forever, imploring his forgiveness, for the ultimate sin of her existence: having said no to him, her son. There was an almost poetic sense to his vision; the circle of life, where new replaces old, spring defeats winter, and son supersedes mother.

His lips curled upward in an anticipatory smile, thinking of the evening's prize, waiting for him to return from the Glades. She'd be waiting for him, alone and terrified in the darkness, just another test drive, as he liked to call these surrogates. The more she'd wait, the more she'd be ready for him. The fruit isn't tasty until it's ripe, someone had once taught him. Oh, yes, it was his mother, when she'd lectured him about patience, and how better everything was when it's thoroughly planned and executed. Soon, she would have the opportunity to judge him on his ability to wait patiently for his reward, on his aptitude to plan and rehearse before executing to perfection.

A tiny noise got his attention, almost imperceptible against the concert of critters, and he turned to face his unsuspecting prey. It was a large one, that bear, only 20 feet away. He drew back the string, holding the arrow snug against it with his fingers. He leaned his cheek into the string, aligning his line of sight with the arrow. He waited patiently, and the bear didn't disappoint. He turned slowly, then stood on his hind legs, exposing his underbelly. That's when he released his arrow, and immediately loaded another one, ready to shoot it.

There was no need for a second shot. The animal roared as it fell to the ground on its side, and then groaned a couple of times. Matthew approached it, looking straight into the beast's eyes. The initial surprise was soon replaced by agony, then by acceptance. Then they glazed over, as life left that magnificent body.

Matthew kneeled and cut one of the bear's claws. He tucked it into his side pocket and walked away briskly. It was getting late. He had work to do that night.

34

MUGSHOT

The Suburban came to an abrupt stop in the Club Exhale parking lot. The area was starting to fill up, as darkness announced to patrons that it was time to sample Miami's night life. Only a few cars behind theirs, Fradella's cruiser showed up, cutting the flashing lights on his vehicle's lightbar before entering the club's property.

In the distance, the club's music was already in full blast, and the club's exterior lightshow had started, flashing laser spots and searchlights toward the starry sky.

"It's going to be hard to talk to people in this goddamn noise," Tess muttered. "Got the prints?"

Fradella handed her the printed mugshot, and she looked at Matthew's face, studying it. Could he be the one torturing and killing young women all over the country? Pensive, she rubbed the back and the side of her neck, right under her left ear, with vigorous strokes. Her fingers were cold, but didn't bring much relief to the burning sensation that bothered her right there, at the hairline between her ear and her nape. She rubbed it some more, willing it to go away, while staring at Dahler's picture. No matter how hard she scrutinized that face, she didn't see the monster she was looking for; the photo showed a young man, neatly dressed and cleanly shaved, posing for some official purpose, maybe his driver's license. He seemed relaxed, at ease, and sure of himself. He was charismatic, attractive even, and in no way did he seem creepy. Ashely had been right; no red flags went up with this man.

And yet, when she looked at his deep blue eyes, something uncoiled in her gut, tugging at her instincts. She couldn't quite pinpoint what it was. She was sure she hadn't seen him before, not even on TV, so it wasn't that. It was more like her gut was telling her she should run, nesting fear in her belly while it made the hairs on the back of her head turn sensitive, sending shivers down her spine. Which was just as ridiculous, as it felt déjà vu. She never ran; she was one of the good guys. Looking at this man's photo, it didn't seem like there was anything to run from either, from a rational point of view.

She remembered reading somewhere that man's ability to recognize predators instinctively had almost completely vanished, the skill becoming useless in the modern world of safety and comfort. That was the reason why so many unsuspecting victims fell prey to psychopathic killers everywhere. Such instincts had long been deemed unnecessary by our natural evolution, and the victim can't tell anymore if she's in the presence of a predator. In some people, studies had shown, atavism had preserved the ability to identify such danger, allowing them to react instinctively and recognize predators without even seeing them, or by looking at mundane photos. Like the one she was holding. Matthew Dahler didn't *look* like a creep, but he was still worth investigating.

"All right, so how do we do this?" she asked impatiently, shooting a glance at her watch. Twenty-one hours since Julie had vanished; twenty-one hours of terror and pain. *Oh, God...*

"How do you suggest we handle it?" Fradella asked. "We can't control all the people we should be interviewing. If one of them tells Dahler we're asking questions, we'll have lawyers up our asses by tomorrow morning."

"Watch me not give a shit," she replied, already on her way to the club entrance. "Do your damn job, threaten them if you have to, and let's get Julie back. That's what you should be thinking of." She didn't even turn her head to see if he'd heard her. She didn't care. She was perfectly capable of working the case alone if she needed to, and she wasn't willing to waste another second.

There was already a line formed at the club entrance, and Tess bypassed it in a hurry, then flashed her badge at the bouncers.

"Seen this man around here?"

The two bouncers looked at the photo, then at each other quickly.

"Yeah," one of them said, "he's a regular."

"Uh-huh," the other one added.

"Comes here alone? With a woman?"

"Um, sometimes alone, other times with friends. Normally stays a few hours."

"Did you see him leave with women he picked up here?"

The two bouncers looked at each other again.

"Um, no, don't think so."

"Uh-uh," the other one confirmed.

"Is he here tonight?"

"Haven't seen him."

"All right, thanks," Tess added and started toward the entrance, then stopped. "If you share our little conversation, it's obstruction of justice. Keep that in mind for your future health and well-being. You don't want to see me come back here again."

"Yes, ma'am."

She entered the club and felt instantly deafened by the blaring music. It was getting crowded, the proximity of so many strangers making her jumpy and uneasy, almost claustrophobic. With the corner of her eye, she saw Fradella walk to a bartender and show her the mugshot on his phone. She approached the long counter and waved to a bartender for attention.

"I got five orders ahead of you, sweetie, hold your horses," he shouted from the sink.

"Now," she shouted back, lifting her badge up in the air.

"Fine," he replied, turning off the water and dropping the half-rinsed glasses back into the sink. "What do you need?"

"This man, he's a regular here, right?"

"Yeah, his name is Matthew, I think."

"What's his favorite drink?"

"Really? You go around asking that?" A patronizing smirk developed on the man's lips.

"Humor me," she replied coldly, and his grin died.

"He drinks Grey Goose, nothing else. One or two per evening, never more."

"Comes alone? Picks up girls? What does he do?"

"He tips well, that's for one. He sometimes comes alone, but just sits at the bar, watching people dancing. Sometimes he dances too, especially when he comes with friends."

"How about girls? Does he hit on girls?"

"Hmm... you won't believe this, but girls hit on him more than he hits on them. He's not into picking up chicks, you know."

"Does he talk to you? What about?"

"Um, nothing much, just small talk. Cars—he drives a Porsche, you know. I'm more American muscle, myself."

"His Porsche, is it a 911?"

"Nah... Cayenne."

Oh, an SUV, how interesting, Tess thought. That was the first intriguing bit of information she'd gathered so far. The fact that he didn't leave with girls was disappointing. She needed more information; she needed to find out how he operated.

"What else do you guys talk about?"

"I don't know... girls, sometime we comment on girls, and what we see them do, here on the dance floor. You won't believe me if I told you, the things we see. Man..."

Tess gestured impatiently with her hand, shaking her head.

"Yeah, I remember, we talk about hunting sometimes. He hunts. I used to hunt too, back when I lived in the Midwest. I used to hunt deer. He hunts here, in the Glades, which I'd never do. Too scary."

He hunts right here, at your counter, she nearly said out loud. Instead, she collected the photo and moved away, heading for the other end of the bar.

She beckoned the other bartender and didn't have to insist in his case. Either he'd seen her flash her badge before, or he wasn't that busy. She pushed the photo on the counter, right in front of him.

"Tell me everything you can about this guy."

"You know who he is, right? I mean, you *must* know who he is."

"Yeah, I must. So tell me something I don't know."

"He's a regular, comes at least a couple of times a week. Drinks Grey Goose, sometimes lime water or tonic water."

"Does he pick up girls?"

"No, he's not into that kind of action. Although, if they hit on him, he talks to them, sometimes dances with them if they're really hot."

"Takes them home?"

"Not that I've seen, no. I mean, who knows, right? I'm behind this counter all night."

"What do you talk about?"

"Whatever, just causal talk. Music, mostly. I used to dream of being a musician, you know. Dream died a few years back, when I couldn't pay the bills with my singing. He plays the guitar, you know."

A couple of girls landed on the counter right next to Tess, loud, feisty, and most likely drunk.

"Gimme Sex on the Beach, hot rod," one of them, a tall, pretty blonde, shouted over the counter.

The bartender grinned at Tess before grabbing a glass and starting to mix the order. The girl propped herself up on a bar stool and reached for the photo, just as Tess was getting ready to collect it. The girl turned the photo around to take a better look. She tapped on it with perfectly manicured fingernails, encrusted with rhinestones.

"I know this guy, what's he done?"

"Nothing," Tess replied quickly. "Have you ever talked to him?"

"Yeah..." she said, then looked at the floor for a second, apparently embarrassed. "I did, but, well, it didn't work out."

"You hit on him?" Tess asked, frowning.

"You're direct, aren't you, huh?" She took a sip from her drink, just placed in front of her, umbrella, straw, and all on top of a highball glass filled to the brim. "Yeah, I hit on him, but I guess we didn't click."

"What did you talk about?"

"You know, pick-up stuff," she said, smiling. "But he didn't even ask me to dance or buy me a drink, so I got the message and I walked away. Too bad, the guy's superhot. And loaded."

Tess thought for a second. Why did he reject this girl? She was the right age, physiognomy didn't quite matter with this unsub, and she sort of resembled Sonya anyway. Tall, slim, blonde with long, sleek hair. Emerald green eyes. She wore expensive clothing, and, if Tess wasn't mistaken, her high-heeled pink Louboutins went for over a grand. So what went wrong?

"Tell me, what's your major?" Tess ventured a shot in the dark.

"What the hell is wrong with people these days? What, huh? So if a girl doesn't have a major, she can't have a little fun?"

Jackpot.

"Why, what's wrong?" Tess probed, forcing a camaraderie smile she didn't feel.

"He asked me the same thing. He said that's how he made sure I'm not jail bait. I dropped out, I don't have a major. I told him that, and he lost interest on the spot. Asshole."

Tess snatched the photo from the counter, patted the girl on her shoulder, and walked away. That's how he did it. That's how he sifted through all those girls, finding the overachievers easily, without raising any suspicions. Anyone who'd graduated ahead of time would brag about it, if given the opportunity, with plenty of detail. Her one and only lead looked better and better, gaining detail and sharpness like an image coming into focus.

She searched the crowd for Fradella and found him chatting with a couple of servers. She waved at him, gesturing she was going outside.

A few minutes later, he and Michowsky joined her in the heat of the early Miami night.

"He's a regular," Michowsky started to say, but Tess stopped him with a hand gesture.

"I know all that. Todd, I need you to screen last night's CCTV feeds looking for this man. Search around the time codes when Julie disappeared, so any time after 10:15PM. See if he's anywhere on video, and what he does, who he talks with, and where he goes. See when he leaves, and with whom. I got a phone call to make."

"Care to share?" Michowsky asked.

"Yeah. I think it's time to ask the Lin family a couple more questions."

"It's 10:45," Michowsky protested.

"Tell that to Julie," Tess snapped, then tried to make it a little better. "It's only 9:45 in Chicago."

She dialed the Lins' number with cold, sweaty fingers and put the call on speaker.

"Hello," a woman's voice picked up immediately.

"Mrs. Lin? This is Special Agent Tess Winnett with the FBI. We talked yesterday."

"Ah, yes. What can I do for you?" Mrs. Lin asked in a trembling voice.

"Do you know Matthew Feldman Dahler? He is in that picture of your family you shared with me."

"Yes, I know Matthew, what's this about?"

"At that gala, did Matthew interact with your daughter at all?"

There was a brief silence as Mrs. Lin probably tried to remember.

"He danced with May once or twice, I think. He's a courteous, gentle, young man, and May loved speaking and dancing with him."

"Thank you, Mrs. Lin, I appreciate your help."

"What is this about? I'm sure you don't think that Matthew had anything to do—"

"No, Mrs. Lin. We're just covering all bases, that's all."

She ended the call, biting her lower lip with excitement in her eyes. Matthew dancing with May Lin confirmed, at yet another point in time, this unsub's MO. She felt the excitement grow inside her, swelling her chest. She was close and drawing closer with every step. Too bad Dahler wasn't the type of suspect you could easily locate, so you could then bust his door open in the dead of the night with a bunch of SWAT agents. No judge would issue a warrant for *all* the Dahler residences, vacation homes, commercial properties, boats, business real estate, and whatever else they owned, where Matthew could be holding Julie.

She was close and drawing closer, but she wasn't there yet. She didn't even think she had enough grounds to get a search warrant for Matthew Dahler's main residence, especially if the judge would prove to be just as starstruck as everyone else. They didn't have any hard evidence either, not yet. Only coincidental, mundane facts, casual encounters, and tidbits of apparently harmless information, all pieces of a puzzle that promised to come together nicely and draw the complete picture of their serial killer. Promising, but definitely not enough for a search warrant. Dahler fit the profile, but probably so did thousands of other young, affluent, Caucasian males who possessed charisma and the financial freedom to move around unrestricted. Club Exhale must be a common theme for many of them.

Tess knew she only had one shot at doing this right. If she searched the wrong property, warning Dahler they were getting close to finding his lair, he'd kill Julie and cover his tracks. He'd get away with it, with all of it. They'd never catch him. No, she couldn't rush into getting warrants or questioning Matthew Feldman Dahler. She had to be smart about it.

"Let's go back to the precinct. We got work to do."

35

SERUM

A small, hotel-size fridge took a section of the counter, humming quietly at times. He approached it and opened the door, but then hesitated. What should he take? What would be the perfect mix for the night? What was he in a mood for?

Small boxes with vials lined the refrigerator's shelves, and a larger box with IV glucose bags took the bottom. He had a separate drawer for powders and pills, but it was the vials that needed refrigeration to stay potent for longer. They weren't easy to come by, some of those vials. He had to plan ahead and order the precise formulations from smugglers who then brought them from Mexico, or the Dominican Republic, or the Bahamas, using fake medical certificates when accompanying elderly tourists. It was an ingenious method to get the rare stuff he was after, but even with his ingenuity put to work, it took time and lots of money. Even in Mexico or the Bahamas, some of those drugs weren't readily available. They had to be made to order. Sure, 5 percent glucose was an easy job; he could get it from his favorite dealer in about 10 minutes for about 50 bucks. Druggies everywhere needed that to rehydrate after long nights of partying, and that demand put the offer right there, at the local street corner.

Rohypnol was easy too, and so banal he didn't want to use it anymore. What was the challenge, the charm in using the same date rape drug idiots everywhere used to get laid? No, he'd used it in the past, when he was just learning ways to enhance his experience, but not anymore. That particular bottle stood at the back of the shelf, almost half empty, and abandoned, forgotten in favor of new, wonderful applications of modern pharmacology.

He'd been a dedicated student, teaching himself anatomy, physiology, and chemistry. It had taken him effort and commitment, but it was well worth it. He understood how all those formulations worked, and what they could do to the human body, by themselves or in carefully dosed combinations.

He was a fan of natural products; fascinated with nature's endless ability to formulate venoms and poisons with the most spectacular results, he stocked a shelf with such hard-to-come-by, expensive extracts. Among other natural concoctions, there was a powerful, South American frog extract that acted as a potent pain reliever, completely removing the ability to feel pain. A few drops of that, combined with an opioid injected in the thigh muscle, and he could do to her whatever he pleased, and she wouldn't fight him much. Wouldn't scream, wouldn't struggle. Later on, when he'd be done with her, and the drugs would wear off, she'd feel pain again, all of it, coming at her like a freight train. Sometimes he liked to make her feel the pain even more—enhance the pain with a different drug, but he'd save that for later.

He hesitated, staring at the shelves, unsure of what he wanted. Should he try the new serum, fresh out of Australia, or should he stick to known recipes? Did he want feisty? Struggling against his body, begging, pleading, and screaming? Or was he in a mood for endless shrieks of pain only he could hear?

36

MIDNIGHT OIL

Few lights were still on at Palm Beach County Sheriff's Office; most of the county's finest had left for the day. The basement had its light on, where the coroner's office was located, and there was still some activity going on in several offices, on the first and second floors of the main building.

Julie had been gone 23 hours, and Tess wondered how was she preparing for her second night of captivity. How does anyone get ready for endless pain? There was no getting ready for something like that… she knew it better than most. For the helpless victim, terrified of death just as much as of life in the hands of a sadist, there can be no getting ready. Only a faint shred of hope, fragile like the wisp of a cloud on a sunny morning, that someone might come soon and rescue her. That someone might hear her screams and break down the door to set her free.

Tess parked the Suburban right in front of the entrance, and Fradella pulled in alongside. She hopped out and trotted into the building, stopping at the front desk. The night officer, flustered, hopped to his feet, dropped the magazine he was reading, and tugged at the stubborn earbuds that wouldn't leave his ears.

"We'll need pizza, order us some, will you?" she ordered him with an impatient tone. "Pepperoni, double cheese, olives, mushrooms. No onion, and nothing else that stinks. Get sodas too, some soda water."

"Um, for how many?"

Fradella and Michowsky watched her with amazement.

"For eight people. If you want to partake, you'll have to do more than read junk and listen to music. You'll need to actually work. Think you could handle that?"

"Yes, ma'am," the officer said quickly, then shot Michowsky and Fradella an inquisitive glance. Michowsky couldn't contain a grin.

"Who else is invited to this party?" he asked, scratching the roots of his buzz-cut hair.

"I don't know, you tell me," she replied, and turned to face them. "You tell me who's fast, smart, and has decent computer skills in this office. Any names come to mind?"

"Yeah, sure. There's Brad and Harvey, but they've gone home for the night," he replied, his eyebrows raised a little.

"Watch how I don't give a fuck," Tess said, grabbing the front-desk phone and offering him the receiver. "Call them. Dinner's on us, but then they have to hit the streets, pronto. It's rush hour for drug dealers out there. The best of the best of Miami's scum are waiting for us."

Michowsky nodded once, visibly swallowing his frustration, and started dialing.

"What's your name?" Tess asked the front-desk officer.

"Garth, Garth Brooks," he said, smiling shyly.

"Really?" Tess asked, and heard Fradella chuckle.

"Really, and it's just a coincidence," he added, turning a couple of shades redder in the face.

"Are you good with a computer, Officer Brooks?"

"Sure, I'm a computer science major from Florida State."

"So what the hell are you doing at the front desk?"

He shrugged. He probably didn't have an answer to that question, and he most likely wasn't too happy about it.

"Call the detention center and have them send a replacement to read junk and listen to music at the front desk while you work with us upstairs."

"On whose authority?"

"Special Agent Winnett, FBI. Tell them they can bitch about it in the morning, when everyone else will."

Michowsky nodded encouragement in Garth's direction, and the young officer picked up the other phone.

Within minutes, they were set to work upstairs in the conference room. They'd turned the space into a war room of sorts. Brooks and Fradella moved a couple of computers and fumbled with their wiring and Internet access for a few more minutes, while Tess powered up her laptop and logged into her FBI systems. She started by bringing up DIVS, because she had a burning, unanswered question she'd been dying to research.

"Can we project?" she asked.

"Yeah, here you go," Fradella replied from under the table, extending an HDMI cable for her laptop. She plugged it in, and the TV on the wall fired up automatically.

Then a young officer wearing detention center insignia came in, carrying three boxes of pizza and a bag full of soda cans. He put them on the table, firing Tess a disappointed, frustrated glare.

"Thanks, mate," she said, unperturbed. "Grab a slice, if you'd like."

She watched with amusement how his frustration melted away, leaving room for a more relaxed demeanor, and a glint of craving anticipation in his eyes. What was it about food that made people instantly collaborative? More human? Probably the millennia of sharing meals as a sign of trust and closeness had left an imprint in the modern man's DNA.

She grabbed a steaming slice and started wolfing it down. She couldn't even remember if she'd had anything to eat that day. Most likely not, and neither had Fradella or Michowsky. Holding the pizza slice with one hand, she slowly typed DIVS search parameters with the other, until Fradella grabbed the laptop from her.

"Enjoy your pie, I'll do this," he said.

"Thanks," she mumbled with her mouth full.

"What are we looking for?"

She swallowed her pizza half chewed, and washed it with a couple of gulps of soda water.

"We're looking for all missing persons, female, under 30, cases still open, who were last seen at Club Exhale."

"Hmm... interesting," Michowsky said, between pizza mouthfuls. "What's your theory?"

"*Your* theory is he never strikes twice in the same place," Tess replied. "I'm thinking no one put it together before, that's all. If the creep is our unsub, his home base is Miami, and I promise you he didn't start his killing career in Chicago with May Lin, or in any other state. He started killing right here, in Miami."

"Going back how long?" Fradella asked. "The search."

"Since the club opened for business," she replied. "By the way, when was that?"

"Eight years ago." Fradella hit enter and the TV screen showed 11 results. That was a lot.

Michowsky whistled, blowing pizza crumbs over the table's shiny finish.

"Yep, that's a lot," Tess voiced her thoughts. "How come no one's put it together until now?"

No one ventured an answer for a long, loaded minute. Then Tess spoke in a voice tainted with bitterness.

"I'll tell you why. Because a female missing person last seen in a club is considered, inherently, as high risk. Sleazy, cheap, even if the club is high-end. No one normally even files the report into the system for at least 24 hours, per procedure, because we care more about our stats than we do about human lives. The idea is to give these girls enough time to return from their drunken spells or their one-night stands, or whatever law enforcement considers these women to be doing after they vanish. After 24 hours, though, the report is finally being filed, but no one really works it, right?"

No one replied.

"Right?" she insisted, raising her voice, mercilessly. "Eleven women, for Chrissake! I'm not saying our unsub killed them all, but what happened to them? Do you even care? When we're done with this, after we find Julie and nail this son of a bitch, I'll open an investigation into how these cases were worked. Four of these cases were filed right here in this office."

"Hey, that's not fair," Michowsky said, throwing his half-eaten slice of pizza back in the box. "You have no idea how busy we get, how overworked, and how much we wished we could do something, but we can't!"

"I'm not buying it!" Tess replied in a low, threatening tone. "As long as a single goddamn speeding ticket was issued by this office, you have no excuse! None."

"You really don't know how things work around here, do you?" Fradella asked sarcastically.

"I don't, and I don't want to know. So save it. We got work to do."

"Don't piss on our work, Winnett. Don't." Michowsky said. His face was contorted in anger and frustration, and he breathed heavily.

"Tell me that deep in your heart you don't feel the same, Michowsky. Tell me I'm wrong. Look me in the eye, and tell me these 11 girls won't haunt you for years to come."

He lowered his head and sat back on his chair, without a word.

"We'll work together, and we'll save Julie. I promise you that," Tess said, "then we'll see. Let's get to work." She took another slice of pizza and took a big bite. She swallowed it quickly, and gulped some more soda. She'd long lost her appetite, but she knew she needed the energy. She wiped her mouth with a paper tissue, as two men came through the door.

"These are Detectives Brad Spaulding and Harvey Bateman," Michowsky introduced the two.

"Help yourselves," Tess offered, but only Spaulding took a slice. Bateman stood, leaning against the wall, frowning. He was definitely not happy to be pulled back into duty so late at night. Tough shit.

"What do we know?" she said, bringing everyone up to speed. "Four women have been abducted, raped, tortured, and killed over the past two years. Their bodies have been posed on east-facing beaches and discovered at dawn or soon thereafter. Autopsy results indicate that the killer used a complex array of drugs, mostly hard-to-come-by at the street corner. Unusual, hospital-only stuff. This is where you come in," she gestured toward Spaulding and Bateman. "We have identified a suspect, a man who had met the first victim, and who the fourth victim had referred to as 'the creep.' This man, Matthew Feldman Dahler, fits the profile delivered by Quantico. Yeah, yeah, I heard it all before," she replied to the murmurs exchanged by the three officers. "He's rich and powerful, but that was also in the profile. And we're all terribly afraid of the rich and powerful, aren't we?" she scoffed.

They were still commenting in low voice, shooting her angry, frustrated glares.

"I'll take the heat if it comes to that, all right? Now, can we please focus?" Her tone didn't leave room for discussion. "A fifth young woman was abducted 24 hours ago, Julie Reynolds. We need to find her fast. We don't have enough for a warrant, and we need to tie this suspect to the exotic drugs Doc Rizza found in the victims. Drug lists are here, sending them and his mugshot to your phones. Get out there, talk to dealers, to confidential informers, whatever you can do. As soon as you have anything, let me—let us know. Questions?"

Neither of the two spoke; both had deep frowns and clenched jaws.

"That's it, then," she dismissed them. "Let me know what you find."

The two detectives left the conference room without saying anything else.

"Let's work the girlfriend angle," Fradella offered. "He must have had some issues with girlfriends; I think it's worth a shot."

"Yeah, you take the girlfriends. Find anyone who we can talk to. Officer Brooks, do you know how to run property searches?"

"Um, yeah," he answered.

"Nationwide?"

"Yeah, sure."

"Good. Grab a computer and let's find out what this man owns, everything that's in his name. Cars, boats, businesses, anything and everything."

"You got it," he replied, typing fast. Judging only by his keyboarding skills, the man was totally underutilized in his job at the front desk.

"Michowsky, you and I will look at financials together. Let's see if any transactions get our attention."

"You've subpoenaed his bank accounts?"

"No. In kidnapping cases, there's a way our analysts can circumvent that process and get the unsub's financials without delay. We have everything in my inbox already, going back six months."

Michowsky frowned, squinting a little at the documents she displayed on the wall TV. It was going too slow like that. The moment she scrolled down he wanted to go back; it was simply not working out.

"Let's print them out, it will be better. We can divide and conquer." She sent the documents to the printer, and took another slice of pizza, now cold.

Doc Rizza appeared in the doorway. He was visibly tired, grayish pale and drawn.

"I heard you guys were up here," he said. "I got something you might find interesting."

"Shoot," Tess replied, chewing fast.

"Sonya's most recent superficial cuts shows signs of inflammation and had traces of a substance, like the scalpel had been doused in something before cutting her. The lab came back with the result."

"And?"

He pressed his lips together before responding, in the universal gesture of revulsion.

"It was wasp venom," he said eventually. "Undiluted. It must have cost him a fortune."

"Oh, my God," she said, suddenly feeling too sick to eat anymore. She put her unfinished slice of pizza back in the box and took a few gulps of water to settle her nauseated stomach.

"I guess this confirms the behaviorist's theory. He's a pure sadist, looking to inflict as much pain as possible, and keeping his victims alive for as long as they can endure."

She put her hands on her face, hiding the wave of sickening emotion she felt. A familiar feeling rose up inside her, as her heart rate accelerated abruptly and sweat beads formed at the roots of her hair. She made an effort to control the approaching panic attack and breathed slowly, deeply, focusing on the time it took her to breathe in, hold the air in, then breathe out.

"There's a silver lining to it," she heard Doc Rizza say. "The damn thing is so rare, that if we establish a connection, that's enough grounds for whatever warrants you'll need."

"Yeah..." she replied, "there's that. Doc, forgot to ask, is there even the remotest of possibilities that Sonya's bite could have happened on February 28? Three weeks before her death, not two?"

He frowned and stared at his feet, while rubbing his forehead.

"Um, with bite marks it's always hard to say. I'd venture to say yes, but it's a stretch. Why?"

"I'm thinking that's what happened to make Sonya dub him the creep, and dump him in the parking lot. I'm thinking it's all related."

"Hey," Brooks intervened, "this guy's permanent address is at his parents' house. That's funny, considering."

"That's more than funny," Tess replied, invigorated. "That's smart. That's an intrinsic alibi, a smoke screen meant to discourage us. Keep digging."

"Where's that address?"

"Some oceanfront acreage home in Key Biscayne."

"Maybe it's time to visit," Tess replied.

"You're committing career suicide," Michowsky replied, "you know that."

She scoffed in his direction, but frowned a little. She was risking a lot if she went to interview the family before the crack of dawn. She cringed, imagining SAC Pearson's reaction. Yet she couldn't stop thinking about Julie, and what she must have been going through. *Wasp venom. God...*

"Grab a seat, Doc," Michowsky offered, "and have a bite. You look like you need it."

Doc Rizza sat with a long sigh, more like the groan of tired bones and a weary soul.

Gary's phone rang, and he took the call immediately on speaker.

"Go for Michowsky and crew."

"Yeah, this is Bateman. One of our informants said he knows this guy, Matthew Dahler. He said Dahler was looking for something really exotic, and one of his buddies finally got it for him."

"What was it? Wasp venom?"

"Huh? No, but close. It was platypus venom. This gangbanger said the dealer brought it straight from Australia."

Doc Rizza covered his mouth with his hand.

"Can you get to the guy who sold it to Dahler?" Tess asked.

"Don't assume I didn't try, but no. You know how these things work. A guy says he knows a guy who knows a guy, when, in fact, your informant could be the dealer himself, doing you all the favors he's ever going to."

"Turn up the heat on your guy, Harvey, please," Tess insisted. "We need more than hearsay to hold up in court."

"Yeah, I know. One more thing. This guy said he heard the venom was sold for $145,000, and Dahler paid in cash."

"Precisely $145,000? Not 150 grand?" Tess probed.

"Yeah, precisely that, for about two ounces of venom. That could be something, if you guys tie this amount to his accounts somehow."

"Keep looking," Michowsky said. "Maybe there's more."

The call ended, and Tess leaned back in her chair, thinking. The unsub was evolving, further perfecting his sadistic methods, and bringing a new dimension to his knowledge of toxins, venoms, and pharmaceuticals. Who would have that? Who knew that the platypus is venomous? A scientist? No, he couldn't be a scientist. The typical psychopath is not dedicated to science; he can't be. There's no emotional reward for the hard work that goes into becoming a scientist. Psychopaths are like asphalt rollers. They go over anyone and everything to achieve their goals. They level everything in their path, but they don't work hard. They're predators, not builders. Then what? What kind of psychopath would even go that far to gain what, a different flavor of pain? Like trying a different flavor of ice cream?

The new data supported her theory that the unsub was perfecting his methods, in search for the ultimate—what? Revenge? Maybe... punishment? Also possible. Who does that, though? Who spends countless years and endless resources to perfect such a method? When in theory, at least, the sexual sadist gets his release relatively quickly. From that point of view, the unsub was an artist, seeking perfection, while finding pleasure in raping and torturing women along the way. This psychopath had turned sadism into an art form, and he was still working on his masterpiece.

She shuddered, feeling the tickle of fear at the back of her head and a chill down her spine. The burning sensation on the left side of her neck came back with a vengeance, and she rubbed it forcefully, almost angrily.

Silence took over the room for a while, with the exception of keyboard noises.

Then Doc Rizza spoke, in a quiet, loaded tone.

"Do you guys know what the platypus venom does?"

No one replied.

"It's one of the very few hyperalgesics known to man, and it's very effective."

"In English, Doc, please," Michowsky said, not raising his eyes from Dahler's financial statements.

"It's the exact opposite of an analgesic or pain killer. It increases the perception of pain, making it stronger, more acute, excruciating. Platypus venom irritates nerve endings, making them hypersensitive."

"It's not deadly?" Tess answered, her eyebrows raised.

"No. It just makes the victim feel pain hundredfold, whatever that pain might be."

37

EXIT STRATEGY

The sun peeked from behind the trees, shooting sharp orange rays into the conference room, dulling the image displayed on the TV. They worked in silence, occasionally interrupted by the popping of yet another soda can or the rustling of papers. After a long, exhausting night, they still had very little information. Not nearly enough for a blanket warrant.

Tess had retrieved Dahler's financial statements in her analysis software and massaged and filtered them in any way she could think of, but there were no large cash withdrawals. Nothing more than the occasional few hundred dollars any individual needs. So where was Dahler getting hundreds of thousands in cash from? He hadn't liquidated any assets, sold any stock, boats, or vehicles. His paycheck was a hefty, biweekly deposit into his checking account. His financials were clean as a whistle and annoying as hell.

"I'm not getting it," she sighed and stood abruptly, pushing the chair back and trotting in place a little to get the blood flow restored in her numb legs. "I'm not seeing where this man gets his cash from."

"How much does he spend each month? On average?" Fradella asked, his eyes still affixed to a screen loaded with social media profiles.

"Um, about 350 thou," she replied, already intrigued. How the hell didn't she think of it? "You're a genius, Detective Todd Fradella," she said, smiling widely.

"Huh?"

"He spends more than enough to cover that, and more. But everything he spends leaves a paper trail here… it's legit. Nothing even remotely interesting here, except," she said, tapping her palms against the table in an improvised drum roll, "he's apparently a very bad gambler. He loses about $250,000 each month at the same casino."

Her noisy enthusiasm failed to wake Doc Rizza, who'd collapsed a couple of hours earlier, with his head on his folded arms on the table. It was his second night in a row without any rest.

"So?" Michowsky asked. "Do you think he's what, laundering his own money?"

"Exactly," she said, feeling invigorated, but lowering her voice to almost a whisper after giving the doc a quick glance. "I think he's not such a bad gambler after all, but everything he wins he cashes out, instead of returning to the same account. We need to test this theory."

She turned to Officer Brooks, who was scrolling through endless lists of property listings.

"How are you doing on property searches?"

"I'm done with Florida, and it's a lot. Under the family name, they own a gazillion things, but even under Matthew Dahler's name, or his name plus associates, there are more than 10 listings."

"Shit," Tess mumbled. No way they could get warrants for everything and execute them at the same time. Julie could be held anywhere on those properties, or even elsewhere if they were out of luck. "Why don't you park that for a while and do a little field assignment for me?"

He hopped to his feet, excited.

"Awesome! What do you need?"

"I need you to go to Casino Real in Miami Beach and confirm my theory about Dahler's winnings. Does he pull out cash? I'll give you the dates he last gambled there. Ask to see the videos and find out how much he cashed out. Find out how he does it."

"It's almost 9:00AM," he said, "they could be closed."

"Bang on some doors, wake some people up, will you?"

"Sure will," he replied and cantered out the door.

"Speaking of video," Michowsky said, rubbing his tired eyes with his fists, "I forgot to tell you, the guys we sent to Exhale to find Dahler on the videos came back empty. They lost him in the crowds and couldn't determine when he left the club or with whom."

"Why didn't you tell me?" Tess snapped, then calmed herself somewhat. "Yeah, you forgot, okay, you told me. Did they lose him at about the same time Julie vanished?"

"They said they lost him more than once, leading them to think the entire video angle is just unreliable, and that's that. They think they saw Dahler in the club at 11:27PM, which is much later than Julie's last timecode."

"What?" she growled between clenched teeth. "And you forgot to tell me? You know what that does to our theory?"

"Look, I'm sorry... I guess it didn't stick in my mind because they weren't sure it was him. The operating word here is, 'think.' They *think* they saw him, but they're not sure."

She scoffed and rolled her eyes.

"Fantastic. We need to get that video to our analysis lab, to get it cleaned up and enhanced. If that was Dahler on it, more than an hour after Julie vanished, we might be chasing the wrong guy." She clasped and unclasped her hands together, then rubbed them angrily. Her sore neck called for attention, and she rubbed that stretch along her hairline a few times, getting insufficient relief. "Dahler still *feels* right, though. I *know* it's him, damn it. How does he do it?"

"What if he drugs them?" Doc Rizza spoke quietly, lifting his head from the table with a groan. "What if he dances with them or approaches them, then pokes them quickly, they faint in his arms, then he waltzes right out the door, carrying his passed-out girlfriend?"

"You think that could be done?" Tess asked.

"There were trace chemicals in Sonya's bloodstream consistent with a strong, fast-acting sedative, an anesthetic actually. It kept bugging me, because it didn't make any sense."

"Let's walk through this," Tess said, going to the front of the table, where she had room to move. "He approaches the girls, or they approach him. He asks them a couple of benign questions, prequalifying them. If they fit his desired profile, he dances with them, and pokes them while on the floor, where no one sees anything." She stared intently at the ceiling, visualizing the scene. "Brilliant," she whispered. "Then suddenly the girl's in his arms, where he holds her tight until she's out completely, pretending they're dancing. Then he walks out the door with her, but—"

"Why don't we see him carrying Julie on the video, right?" Fradella asked. "We looked at every second of the entrance video and Julie wasn't in any frame of that video."

"He's a regular," Michowsky added, "he knows the place inside and out. What if he—"

"Uses a service door?" Tess interrupted. "Yeah, that fits. Let's see what service doors can be accessed from inside the club and what video feeds cover them."

"Give me a couple of minutes," Fradella asked, and started typing fast.

Tess paced the room anxiously. She felt that excitement she always sensed when she was within reach of catching her man. Like a predator herself, her nostrils flared with excitement, and her heart beat fast and strong, eager to finish the hunt. Soon, she'd be able to put together the final pieces of the puzzle and find Julie. With every fiber in her body she hoped Julie was still alive, and whatever had happened to her could be healed, forgotten somehow.

"Got it," Fradella said, and projected the video feed on the TV screen. "See here? This is the back entrance to the kitchen and bar area. There's no direct camera above that entrance, but this side parking one covers it. Julie vanished from the hallway video feed at 10:16, right? Watch this at 10:22PM."

The grainy, dark video feed showed a man supporting a woman who walked with difficulty. She was closer to the camera than he was, partially covering him, obliterating his face. He supported her with his arm around her shoulders, and, even in the bad quality video, they could see the woman was wobbly and unable to walk on her own. Her legs buckled at every step, and her head leaned on the man's shoulder.

The two silhouettes didn't enter the main parking lot, well-lit and filled with cameras, and Tess mumbled an oath. Instead, the man went across the alley and unlocked a truck using his key, not the remote. He loaded the woman onto the back seat of the truck, then locked it, again using his key. Then he went back into the club, through the same door as before.

"Ah," Tess gasped, "that's his alibi, right there. That's why he shows up on the cameras an hour later. He's cool, this guy. Can you imagine? She was right out there, in the car, for more than an hour. He's gutsy. All right, it's time to visit the Dahlers."

"There's no stopping you," Michowsky asked, "is there?"

"No, but you could stay here, Gary. Knocking on the Dahlers' door could prove to be a career killer. Let's minimize the damage."

Michowsky grabbed his car keys and caught up with her before she got to the staircase.

"In for a dime, in for a dollar," he said with a tired smile. "But you're driving. My back's still killing me."

38

EX-GIRLFRIEND

Tess started the engine and cranked up the air conditioning. Midmorning, and it was already torrid, the humidity making it much worse. She yearned for a shower with every pore of her sweaty skin and wished for a fresh change of clothes. There was no time for that though, not while Julie fought for her life, at the whim of a sadistic serial killer.

"You sure about that?" she asked Michowsky, before pulling out of the parking lot. "Coming with me on this house call?"

"Yeah. We got to do what we got to do in this line of work. You don't get a pass; I shouldn't get one either."

"This is not a pissing contest, you know," she said softly. "It's okay to sit one out when it's lethal, when you can afford it."

"I'll be fine," he said, letting out a long sigh, "as long as you remember we don't have much. Even that video, there's no way to say that was Dahler, and that truck wasn't his car either. There are no trucks registered to him. We still have zilch."

"Yeah, yeah, I know, I'll be gentle." She snickered. "You know, as much as it could surprise you, I also want to keep my job."

"Really?" he quipped. "You could have fooled me."

"Ah, shut it, Michowsky."

They rode in silence for a few seconds, but it was a different silence. The air between them was a little lighter than before.

Michowsky's phone rang, and he recognized Fradella's number.

"What's up?"

"I found an ex-girlfriend of Dahler's, Jennifer Alvarez. I think you should see her before you go to Dahler's house."

Tess frowned.

"Why? Talk to me."

"On her Facebook account, pictures of her and a younger Matthew Dahler stop a few weeks before her financial situation drastically improved."

"As in...? she won the lottery? or some hush-hush money?" Michowsky asked.

"I'm guessing settlement, and a big one."

"Any trace of that info anywhere? Court documents maybe?" Tess probed. "I'd love to have something I can use."

"None of that, no, and I checked. But a lottery winner would post more stuff on Facebook after she got rich, not less. She stopped posting anything altogether for months."

"Did you get her financials? How big a settlement are we talking about?"

"Five million dollars, seven years ago."

Michowsky whistled, then gave Tess the thumbs up, a smile of excitement twitching his lips.

"Send her address to my phone," Tess asked.

"You got it."

Seconds later, a chime and Michowsky grabbed Tess's phone.

"Turn around," he said, "she lives in Coral Gables."

It took Tess 20 minutes to cross through the dense traffic, using her flashers and horn without hesitation. Sunday mornings were the worst. Rush hour was no longer contained to two time frames, one in the morning and one in the afternoon. Flooded with tourists, the coastal traffic turned into a bumper-to-bumper exercise in frustration.

Finally, on South Bayshore, Tess pulled to an abrupt stop in front of the covered entrance to a high-rise, oceanfront condominium. It seemed like déjà vu: the building, the lifestyle, the entrance lobby, even the smooth elevator ride.

"You notice?" she asked.

"Yeah, Julie lives like this, her girlfriend too," Michowsky replied.

"But this is Jennifer's lifestyle *after* the settlement," Tess thought out loud.

"Yeah," he said, and rang the doorbell at apartment 1704.

Tess pulled her badge and positioned it in front of the peephole, as soon as she heard footsteps behind the door. Then she heard the deadbolt unlocking and the door chain being removed.

The woman who opened the door was dark-haired, tall, and slender, with the sun-kissed skin tone Latinas have, only somewhat pale. Her face held an internal sadness, and her eyes were sunken, as if they'd seen images and witnessed things that couldn't be unseen, couldn't be undone. One look at Jennifer Alvarez, and Tess knew she'd found one of Dahler's earlier victims.

Jennifer let them in without a word, and they took seats on deep, leather armchairs.

"What can I do for you?" she asked softly, after the introductions.

"We need your help with some information," Tess asked, as gently as she could. "What can you tell us about your relationship with Matthew Feldman Dahler?"

Jennifer flinched as she heard his name, and her pupils dilated. It was an infinitesimal move, but Tess caught it, knowing to look for it, to expect it.

"There's nothing to say," she replied, averting her eyes. "We used to date, then we broke up. Years ago."

"How was your relationship with him?"

"Um, really, there's nothing I can say. Just a relationship, I guess."

Her shoulders were hunched and her head lowered, under the burden of an unspoken shame, a terrible secret.

Tess watched her turmoil and decided to take a different approach, instead of threatening her with obstruction of justice.

"Did you sign an NDA?" Tess asked gently. Settlements always came with paperwork.

She nodded quietly.

"You know, no one can come after you if you speak with the authorities, Ms. Alvarez," Tess explained. "Those NDAs are meant to prevent you from speaking with the media. They're meant to prevent gossip, slander, and stuff like that. You *can* talk to us, and you should."

Jennifer's chin trembled, and a tear rolled on her cheek. Tess waited quietly for her to be ready to speak.

"He was doing drugs," she finally said, "when we were together. Not the usual stuff, like everyone does. Not cocaine, or meth, no. He was into exotic stuff that he prepared himself. Dealers brought those drugs to him on order. Stimulants, enhancers of all sorts. He… experimented."

"What did that look like?"

She didn't answer for a while.

"He was sweet, and kind, and smart when I met him, or so I thought he was. But he hated himself, and he hated his mother. Oh, my goodness, how he hated her."

"Why? Do you remember?"

"I'm not sure if she'd done something to him, but he kept saying she was limiting him, holding him prisoner, humiliating him, and that she was going to pay for it, one day." Jennifer paused for a little while. "When he was on those drugs, you didn't know what to expect. At times, he wanted me to try some of that stuff, but I was scared. I wanted to leave him… I got more and more scared of him, until…"

She trailed off, and didn't continue.

"How about your sex life with Matthew? What was he like?"

She pursed her lips and another tear fell, staining her light blouse.

"I know it's hard to talk about this," Tess said, "but a girl is missing."

Jennifer's eyes locked with hers, wide open. Somewhere inside, Jennifer must have known this day would come.

"Please help us find her. Any information you could give us is critical."

She sighed, then cleared her throat quietly.

"It got rough at times," she said, turning her head away from them. "Especially when he was high. He liked to tie me up. He experimented with that too, at first, but then it got rough."

"How rough?" Tess asked in a whispered tone. "Hospital visits?"

She hesitated, staring at her feet.

"No... private doctor house calls. Portable X-ray machines at his house. Private clinic surgery, at night. Then one day, the NDA and the settlement. That day was... rough. Really bad."

Tess exchanged a quick glance with Michowsky, and stood, getting ready to leave.

"Thank you, Jennifer," she said, touching her arm gently. "I know how hard this can be. One more question, if I may. Who paid you off? Who had you sign the NDA?"

"His mother."

39

THE CLEANSE

He took his time shaving, making it an elaborate ritual. First, he gave his face a gentle massage, savoring the scent of lime extract, the signature essential oil in Castle Forbes Shaving Cream. Then he gently shaved every inch, making sure not a single undesired stubble survived the process. He rinsed the remaining foam thoroughly, and then patted his skin dry. The final touch was a few sprinkles of Serge Lutens aftershave.

Satisfied, he took a step back and looked into the wall-sized mirror. He liked what he saw. A lean, fit, muscular body, a strong, almost intimidating appearance, a fierce, unforgiving look in his eyes. He was getting close... he could feel it.

He'd cleared his mind and had groomed his visage. One more step remained in his ritual, before he could go downstairs for another serving of his special treat: a cleansing shower. Already naked, he entered the impressive shower cabin and closed the patterned glass door. He turned a knob, and water started falling from an intricate showerhead that emulated rainfall. He let the hot water fall on his head, as he leaned forward, his hands pressed against the marble-tiled wall. He closed his eyes, and let his visions take control.

In his mind, he saw the girl downstairs, tied up, suspended, getting ready for him. If he listened hard enough, beyond the water falling on the marble tiles, he could hear her cries, fueling his fantasies. Without opening his eyes, he squeezed shower gel in the palms of his hands and started washing his body, gently, thoroughly, feeling his erection growing stronger.

She'd scream as he'd touch her, writhing against her restraints, begging, pleading, crying. He loved the way she struggled against him, trying to get away when there was no escape.

A ghost inserted itself into his vision, and he grunted angrily. He pounded his palm against the wall, then pounded again, with another grunt. Jennifer... the last one who lived. The one he couldn't finish, because some stupid concierge doctor had expressed his concerns. Unbelievable. He was paid a fortune to keep his pie hole shut, patch Jennifer up quickly, then get lost. Instead, from there he went straight to his parents, to squeeze more money out of them. That was his first bitter lesson. He couldn't let them live, not ever again. Not after being with him, not after knowing what he was like.

He would have finished Jennifer; he knew he had it in him even back then. He just wanted the pleasure to last longer, so he'd kept delaying the moment he'd let her blood spill. But he made a mistake; he hadn't thought of everything back then, he didn't know how to extend his pleasure without damaging her too soon. People are messy when they're broken... he'd learned that too. Sometimes he fantasized about going back to Jennifer and finishing what he started, but the risk was too big. It wasn't worth it. There were others out there he could get.

Keeping his eyes still closed, he pounded on the wall once more, angrier than before. His blissful anticipation was gone, leaving him stymied and resentful, while his erection vanished, defeated. Whenever Jennifer's face appeared in his visions, his mother's image wasn't far. Yes, he'd made a mistake letting Jennifer live, but he'd learned his lesson. Since then, it hadn't happened again. Yet remembering his mother, and the day she came in to clean up his mess, that hurt him still, humiliating him at a level he didn't think possible.

Her terms had been awful. She dictated everything, in a manner that left no room for any negotiation. What he'd do, where he'd live, how much money he'd have, who he was allowed to date. She'd been cruel, merciless, taking pleasure in twisting his life around her fingers like it was a twig she snapped out of boredom. Maybe she did enjoy punishing him; there was something awry about her he couldn't understand. She'd demanded that he bring his dates home for sex, not hotels or anywhere else, but home, where she had installed cameras, "to make sure he stayed true to their agreement." Yes, their so-called agreement demanded that he lived the life of a saint, without so much as a parking ticket. That his sexual partners would leave the premises without so much as a broken fingernail. Or else he'd lose everything, the entire family fortune, worth more than a billion dollars. And that's how the bitch won. That's how she owned him.

For now.

Little did she know.

Good thing she'd still let him gamble and didn't care much about how much he lost. Her stupid shrink must have fed her some bullshit, that he was getting back at her by losing her money at the green table or some other crap like that. He was a decent, cool-headed poker player. He'd easily siphoned cash the following months after she'd pinned his balls to the wall. That cash, elegantly invested in the local drug scene, turned into millions of dollars no one was surprised he had, given his heritage. It turned into his secret home, bought and paid for in cash, that the bitch didn't know about. Then he'd stopped messing around with the drug networks; it wasn't worth risking jail over something he no longer needed. He had his secret lair, and, for the rest of his unofficial needs, there was always gambling.

Water still rained on his head, relaxing, yet strengthening. He opened his eyes, not bothered by the falling water, and, against the cream-colored marble, a vision started to form. It was the girl downstairs, strapped in her harness, screaming for mercy, fighting desperately to free herself as he circled her, getting ready to possess her body. As he moved around her in the almost complete darkness, he noticed her hair was no longer brown, but blonde and short. When she looked at him and pleaded for his mercy, her deep blue eyes pierced his, jolting him. He touched himself again, and he was strong and ready. He found his release, as the woman in his vision was no longer the girl downstairs. It was his mother, begging for his forgiveness.

40

FAMILY

Tess drove north on the Interstate, her lightbar flashing and horn blaring, weaving through traffic whenever she didn't drive on the shoulder. It was late. It was close to noon, and they still had no idea where Dahler held Julie. But Dahler looked better and better as the unsub, not just a twist in her gut, but a strong, viable lead, supported by evidence. He was seen buying exotic drugs, pain enhancers no less. He had developed a method to syphon untraceable cash from his bank account; Officer Brooks had already confirmed he cashed out over two hundred grand in the past three months. He had a history of severely abusing his girlfriend; finally, there was someone who could testify in court. Now they could probably get a ballsy judge to sign a search warrant. But for what address?

Driving as fast as she could to Key Biscayne, Tess didn't know what to expect from her visit with the Dahler family. Would they even be home? She hoped so. Was Matthew Dahler living with his parents? Or did he just forget to change his address on his driver's license? How come a rich kid in his 30s still lived with his mom and dad? That didn't fly. Especially him. He needed privacy to torture his victims. He couldn't have done any of that in the family mansion, surrounded by countless staff and always risking to get caught. Then where? Officer Brooks was back at the precinct, doing property searches, and he'd come back with several choices. Too many. Irritated with her own powerlessness, she bit her lip angrily.

"Gary, can you please call our very own Garth Brooks?"

"What's up?"

"I got an idea. Dahler suspends his victims, that's what Doc Rizza said."

"Yeah, but I'm not following."

"I'm thinking he might have needed modifications to his property. Dial him."

A few seconds later, Officer Brooks picked up.

"Garth, here's the second field assignment of your career. Harness suspension requires some modifications to the home. Typically, athletes request such installations for their home gyms, those who do inverted ab crunches and stuff. It could be a long shot, but I don't think there are a lot of companies who install suspension bars or any type of ceiling equipment. Run Dahler's photo by all of them. Maybe we'll hit the jackpot."

"On it, ma'am," he replied, with a smile in his voice.

"Is Fradella there?" she asked.

"Where else?" Fradella replied.

"We haven't found out where he kept the victims when he was killing out of state. Let's say here, in Miami, he has a place. How about Chicago? Where did he keep May Lin?"

"We've been digging for that, but—"

"Because we were looking for straight-up transactions, like home rentals and stuff. Now we know he doesn't like paper trails. Dig deeper. Pull financials for all his businesses and correlate with the geographical locations and his air travel. He must have traveled there, eaten there, stayed in hotels there. Then see what else he bought."

"That will take a while," Fradella replied.

"No, it won't. Call the FBI analyst, Donovan, I told you about. He'll turn that around in minutes. Call me when you got something."

"You got it," Fradella replied. "Hey, here's another thought. I want to check the properties he owns, to see if any of them were purchased in cash or if taxes are being paid in cash."

"That's brilliant, Fradella. Get it done."

She ended the call and immersed herself back in her thoughts. They were close, so close.

"I should have thought of that, you know," Michowsky said.

She glanced at him quickly and saw the deep frown on his face, the tension around his mouth, the bitterness.

"Give yourself a break, Michowsky, you're sick. You're on pain killers. That does stuff to your brain."

"No. Maybe I'm just too old for this job."

"Hang in there. You'll feel much better after we nail this sick son of a bitch. I promise you that."

He was silent for a while, then changed the subject.

"I've never been to Key Biscayne before. On official duty, I mean."

"I knocked on a few of those doors before," Tess said with a crooked smile. "Went badly every single time, and lawyers were the least of it. By the way, my offer still stands. You can wait in the car."

He kept his eyes focused on the road ahead, and his face immobile.

"You lied to her," he eventually said.

"To whom?"

"To Jennifer Alvarez. Only if subpoenaed she can break the NDA. You knew that."

"Oh, come on. It wasn't really a lie, just a time-saving maneuver."

"Just a timesaving lie. Own it, Winnett."

She bit her lip again, but managed to contain the biting answer that was fighting to fly off her lips. Seconds later, they pulled in at the Dahler residence.

"Wow," she whispered.

She stopped in front of the covered porch done in modern marble columns, worthy of a high-end hotel. From there, a flight of marble steps flanked by the same type of columns led to a recessed double-door entrance.

A man dressed in uniform opened the door before they had a chance to announce themselves.

"We're here to see Matthew Dahler," Tess said, pulling her badge.

"He is not available at this time," the man replied, unimpressed with Tess's badge. "You can leave your business card, and he'll be in touch."

"How about Mr. Dahler? Or Mrs. Feldman Dahler?" Michowsky insisted.

The man hesitated a bit, then stepped aside, inviting them in.

The interior was just as impressive, and marble remained the common theme, covering floors, walls, even some ceilings. They waited in the vaulted ceiling atrium for a while, then they were invited to the living room. The entire oceanfront wall was glass, welcoming the morning sun. The wall-to-wall windows incorporated several French doors, overlooking a patio, a pool, and a stretch of ocean beach. In the distance, on the beach, Tess saw a woman in a yoga pose, facing the sun.

"Yes, how can I help you?"

She recognized John Dahler from the news; he had at least one weekly appearance in the local media. She'd never met him before, and she hated to admit that in person he was even more imposing. Tall and bulky, with reddish-blond hair that only showed beyond a seriously receding hairline, and with features carved in stone, Mr. Feldman was not displaying even a hint of helpfulness. Just determination to get the issue over with.

"We'd like to speak with Matthew Dahler," Tess asked, after clearing her throat.

"He's out at the moment," he replied dryly. "What is this about?"

"We need to speak with him regarding an old friend of his who was killed."

"Who?" Dahler seemed genuinely surprised.

"May Lin from Chicago," Tess replied.

He softened a little bit.

"Yes, Hank's daughter. What a tragedy. I didn't know Matthew knew her though. He should be home soon; he's at work."

"On a weekend?"

"My son is ambitious, driven."

"Where does he work?" Michowsky asked.

"With his mother," he replied frowning, then broke eye contact and looked outside for a second, a shade of concern clouding his eyes.

He seemed uncomfortable, almost embarrassed, and Tess was dying to learn why. She waited patiently, and he didn't disappoint.

"Like most affluent young men, our Matthew drifted without purpose for a while, after he finished school. We asked him to make a choice of careers, and he chose to work with her, not me." He scoffed quietly, and the ridges lining his mouth deepened. "He doesn't have an inkling of interest in real estate, although everything I own will be his one day. It broke my heart. He's my only son."

A French door whooshed open behind them, and they turned. Edwina Feldman Dahler walked in, barefooted, wearing a black swimsuit, with a white beach towel around her neck. She looked familiar somehow, but Tess couldn't place her. When their eyes met, she noticed Edwina's irises had a stunning shade of ultramarine blue, giving her the same unsettling sensation in her gut she'd felt when she'd first seen Matthew's mugshot: fear and the unexplainable urge to run. They had the same eyes, mother and son. Same color, same expression in them. As Tess recalled details about Matthew's appearance, she realized Edwina seemed familiar simply because she looked just like her son. She was a more feminine, older version of Matthew. Same tousled, short, blonde hair, same square jaw, same powerful, proud demeanor.

Tess presented her badge without a word. Although polite when she spoke, Edwina Feldman Dahler made them feel small, insignificant.

"What is this about?"

"Poor May Lin, Hank's daughter," John replied quickly. "They're looking to talk to Matthew."

"Ah… I see. Well, Matthew's not here right now." She turned around, opened a drawer, and then offered each of them a business card. "This is our attorney. Please call him to set up a meeting with Matthew, sometime next week." Edwina's eyes were ice cold, and the intelligence in them, the determination Tess saw in her jaw as she spoke, told her she had little hope of getting more information out of the Dahlers. The conversation was over.

She pulled out her own business card and handed it to Edwina.

"Please hand this to Matthew when he returns. He might want to give us a call before next week. We'd appreciate a call today, if possible."

She took it reluctantly, barely touching it, and dropped it on the side table. Then she showed them the door with a definitive gesture.

Tess turned to leave, but then stopped in her tracks.

"How come he still lives with his parents?" she asked serenely, like they were chitchatting over coffee.

"My son was—" John Dahler started to say.

"Our attorney will be happy to answer any pertinent questions," Edwina replied. "Please make an appointment."

"All right," Tess replied. "One more thing. How did you get that scar on your lower lip?"

Edwina's steel gaze flickered, and her pupils dilated a little.

"Matthew bit me when he was three years old," she replied reluctantly. "It's a phase some kids have. I'm trusting this will be all?"

They didn't bother to answer, and the massive doors soon closed behind them.

41

AGONY

It was dark, the absence of light almost complete. Darkness changes things; it alters realities. In darkness, even the tiniest sounds gain the destructive force of an explosion— terrifying, paralyzing, weakening the scared, the lame, the dying.

Noises, amplified by visual sensory deprivation, gave Julie an acute perception of where he was and what he was doing. Earlier, he'd pulled some strings, rearranging that abhorrent harness, and now she was positioned at an angle, her head higher than her body, but not fully upright. It was better, if the simple notion of better could exist in hell's darkest corner.

She breathed shallow and fast, afraid of the sounds her breath made, afraid she'd get his attention. She watched him move around the room, calm, precise, unhurried. He was comfortable in the darkness, unhesitant. When he was absent from the room, Julie struggled to regain a shred of hope, forcing herself to believe her hell would come to an end. Surely someone must be looking for her, out there, and they would find her soon. Maybe in the next five minutes, she prayed, maybe in the next ten. *Oh, God, please don't abandon me...*

She hadn't prayed in years, since her grandmother's funeral, and even then she'd done it for her sake, not because she believed. In here, in the hands of her tormentor, prayer came naturally, and belief was the only alternative left to undiluted despair. She prayed, instead of thinking about what had happened to her or what was about to happen again. She needed to believe she'd be safe again soon, safe in a world where pain didn't exist anymore.

Her throat was sore from screams that no one heard, and her eyes, swollen, impaired what little night vision she had. She was exhausted, lack of sleep taking a toll and feeding her fears. Most of all, she wasn't ready for him to come near her again, although he was preparing to. Fear choked her with a desperation to break free. Forcing herself to be rational, she didn't try to break free anymore; she'd tried before, when she was rested and strong and had failed. She still hung from the ceiling in that horrible harness, naked and vulnerable, a marionette in the hands of a skilled torturer, primed to be preyed on. Her heart beat fast, fear fueling the adrenaline that kept her conscious, despite the endless hours of torment she'd endured. The same adrenaline probably fueled that last remaining shred of hope, the waning belief that someone would find her soon. *Please, God, please, let them find me... Let them find me before he...*

A noise caught her attention. He was approaching her, calm, naked, and smiling. He reached for her, gently touching her face, caressing her. Unable to control herself, she sobbed hard, desperately.

"No, no, please," she managed to say between sobs. "Please, let me go."

He stopped touching her and stood in front of her, feigning offense.

"My dear," he said, "I want to hear you say yes. I don't like hearing you say no."

She let out a convulsive cry, gasping. "No, please... I'll do anything."

"Yes, darling, *yes*," he said calmly, like teaching a child. He touched her swollen cheek again, caressing it, playing with her hair. "Say yes, please, and we can be friends."

She tried to stifle her sobs and do as he'd told her. "Y—yes," she uttered between gasps.

"Excellent," he replied.

Then he went to the counter, barely visible in the darkness. A flip of a switch, and the room flooded with light, powerful, fluorescent light coming from the ceiling.

She gasped, knowing what was coming.

"No, please," she whimpered, before she could stop herself.

He turned to face her, and she saw the scalpel in his hand.

"No, no," she screamed, fighting against her restraints.

"Don't you dare say no to me," he whispered, so close to her face she felt his breath against her skin.

Then he went back to the counter, where he prepared another syringe with expert dexterity, pulling fluid from two vials. He tapped against the syringe body with his fingernail, and pressed the piston gently, eliminating air bubbles until the liquid was clear and all the trapped air gone. He took a cotton ball and doused it with alcohol. Then he approached her, under her terrified, rounded eyes.

"Do you know why paper cuts are so painful?" he asked.

She couldn't bring herself to answer, her eyes fixed on the hand that held the syringe. She whimpered weakly.

"It's because the paper only cuts the nerve endings, where they're the most sensitive," he explained patiently, as if he were teaching a class. "It's a unique experience, I'm sure you agree."

She whimpered again, trying to keep her mind from giving in to panic. *Please let them find me.*

"This will hurt a bit," he added, "but don't worry. It's nothing compared to what's coming."

Scared out of her mind, she screamed and fought desperately as he came near her, syringe in hand. She must have kicked him while flailing hysterically, because she felt her foot hit something and heard him cuss under his breath.

"Bitch," he growled, then slapped her so hard that her lip started bleeding. She froze, as he leaned forward and grabbed her torn lip between his teeth, clasping her chin with his fingers. Then he bit hard, and her mouth filled with blood, its metallic taste fueling her panic. She screamed again, and he let go of her lip and moved to her side. With a steeled grip, he grabbed her thigh and pushed the needle deep into the muscle, then thrusted the plunger forcefully.

She screamed in agony. No one was coming to save her.

42

CONSIDERATIONS

Tess started the engine without a word, and, as soon as Michowsky closed his door, she floored it. She couldn't breathe, and no amount of air conditioning relieved the pressure she felt in her head or the pounding in her chest.

At the corner of the street, she missed a stop sign and honked angrily at the oncoming traffic, although her flashers were off. All she'd had so far were roadblocks, obstacles of all sorts, keeping her from catching the unsub. With Julie gone more than a day and a half, and with the Dahlers fiercely protective of Matthew, what could she do? Shortlist a few properties, in the hope they'd nail the place where Matthew Dahler kept Julie? What if they were wrong? What if Edwina Dahler was about to tell Matthew the cops were looking for him? The moment he heard, he'd kill Julie and clean up the mess. They'd never find her body, not ever, not with the Glades a quick drive away.

"Son of a bitch," she shouted, pounding her fist against the steering wheel.

Michowsky turned and stared at her.

"Mind telling me where we're going?"

"I need to think, that's all," she replied. "Should I drop you off somewhere?"

"I'll tag along," he replied, and crossed his arms at his chest. "We're supposed to be a team. At least in principle."

She turned on the flashers and stepped on it, mumbling oaths under her breath. The traffic was still bad, clogged to a standstill on the Interstate, but she took the shoulder and didn't slow down until she reached her exit.

"Did you notice?" Michowsky asked. "About the house."

"Huh? What?"

"It faces east, and it has sand, its own beach."

"Goddamn… no, I completely missed that."

"Did you see Edwina out there?"

"N—no, I kept my eyes on Dahler. He was a little too forthcoming, in my opinion. Why?" She frowned, angry at herself. How the hell did she miss that?

"She was doing yoga poses facing the sun. All kinds of poses. This can't be a coincidence. I think he's—"

"And he bit her too," Tess interjected. "Bit her lip, just like with some of the victims. Just like with Sonya."

"What do you think he's doing? Sending her a message?"

She didn't reply for a while, frowning and white-knuckling the steering wheel, as she maneuvered through busy streets cluttered with bad drivers in rental cars. Tourists paid more attention to the ocean and the sites, than to incoming traffic. Distracted and holding phone cameras in their hands, tourist drivers made the worst of Miami's asphalt woes.

"He could be," she eventually replied. "He could be reliving some trauma that has something to do with his mother, that beach, and the sunrise. Or something. But he's also experimenting, perfecting his method. That's what Doc Rizza said, that's what SSA McKenzie, the profiler, said, and that's what makes the most sense to me."

"So you're saying he's planning to—"

"Kill his mother, yes."

He nodded, scratching his head.

"Family fortune aside, when do we put an APB on this scumbag? What if we can't talk to him until next week?"

She glanced quickly in his direction and scoffed quietly.

"We don't. The moment we do that, the family will find out, and that means Matthew will too. Someone on the force will give the Dahlers a call, either because they're acquainted somehow, or because they want to score a quick payday. And that's the moment Julie dies." She bit her lip and slammed her hand into the steering wheel. "I might have killed her already."

She didn't say anything else, regardless of how intently Michowsky gazed at her. Eventually, he turned his head away, staring out his window, quiet. He saw it too, the possibility that their visit with the Dahlers might have spooked Matthew, and there was nothing left to say.

She pulled into Media Luna's parking lot, close to the entrance. The lot was almost completely empty at that early afternoon hour. She recognized Catman's Jeep Wrangler, dressed up with bull bar, winch, and roof projectors, and painted in a military camouflage pattern. A few things made Catman who he was, and that Jeep was one of them.

"You need a fix, Agent Winnett?" Michowsky asked, disappointment tinting his voice.

She smirked in his direction and went straight inside. He followed closely, his frown deep, and the corners of his mouth edging downward.

She hopped on a stool and tilted her head in response to Catman's grin. He wiped his hands on a rag and approached them.

"Burgers and fries?" he asked.

Tess nodded once. Cat turned to Michowsky, and his grin died.

"Bud Light, was it?"

"Yeah, sure, why not," he replied, still frowning. "If it's a party…"

She buried her face in her hands, relishing the coolness of her fingers against her tired eyes. What the hell could they do? Maybe the guys could find something in the financials. A location, an address, another hint. For now, they were stonewalled, and she kept going over the options they still had in an obsessive, repetitive cycle, the way a computer does when it can't process a set of data.

She hoped that through some miracle Matthew didn't get spooked and didn't decide to kill Julie sooner to cover up his tracks. She hoped they still had a chance. Lately though, hoping had done her little good. She hoped she'd find Matthew at his parents' home, and from there they could tail him and find out where he's going. She hoped she could see, beyond any doubt, that he was the killer, just by talking to him.

"Do we still have doubts that Matthew Dahler is the unsub?" Michowsky asked.

She almost flinched when she heard her thoughts spoken out loud. Sometimes Michowsky was uncanny like that. He was a good cop, who got lost a little, or got roughed up by life, and had temporarily misplaced his edge.

"Do you?"

"He fits," Michowsky replied, thanking Cat with a hand gesture for the beer in front of him. "As much as I hate to admit it, he fits. We could probably get a warrant at this point. There's a judge in Palm Beach County who's not intimidated much by money. He might go for it."

"We need an address, Michowsky. We can't ask for a blanket warrant, covering all his property. He owns too much, and the judge will never go for it. Not to mention he could be using some business space or some property that belongs to his parents. Who knows. We ain't got it, not yet." She gulped her drink thirstily, stopping only when she was about to choke on the mint leaves.

"Whoa, easy there," Michowsky muttered. "We got time. Assuming he didn't freak out, we got time. It's only the second day."

She slammed her hands against the bar counter so hard that their drinks clattered, and Cat turned his head, watching her carefully.

"You think we got time, Michowsky?" she shouted, ignoring the few other customers. "That's what you think, huh? That she's at a spa somewhere, getting her fucking nails done? Have you even seen the other victims? What the hell is wrong with you?"

Catman quietly replaced her empty glass with a full one, sweaty and murky, filled to the brim. Then he disappeared without a word.

Michowsky glared at her with his jaw dropped. "I didn't mean—"

"People never recover from this, Gary, they almost never do. There's no time. There never was. Not since he grabbed her."

She closed her eyes, and memories of her own nightmare invaded her. She remembered trying to run, to free herself from her attacker's grip. Squirming under his heavy body, trying to claw and bite and kick. Feeling overpowered, defeated, just before the pain came. She shuddered and discreetly wiped a tear from the corner of her eye. She took another mouthful of icy, soothing liquid, feeling its coolness dissipate the ghosts and restore normalcy.

Michowsky's phone rang, in time to save her from having to apologize for her outburst. He put the phone on the counter between them and took the call on speaker.

"Fradella and Brooks here. We have info on his locations."

"Shoot," Tess replied, invigorated.

"We've narrowed the list of possible locations in Florida. Seven years ago, he bought a villa on the north end of Palm Beach Island. He paid for the whole thing in cash, and he's been paying its taxes in cash too. It's a wonder it's under his legal name," Fradella said. "We got lucky."

"Address?"

"In your inbox. But there's more. The only thing he's done in all the states where he's killed was rent cargo containers on shipping docks. That's the only common denominator we could find."

"Why did we miss that before?" Michowsky asked.

"Because he didn't pay for them with his own credit cards. He used various business subsidiaries to pay for the containers.

Invoices, checks, everything to make them look legit. By the way, your man Donovan is one hell of an analyst."

"He is… please give him my thanks," Tess replied.

A moment of silence, then quiet snickering from either Fradella or Brooks; Tess couldn't tell.

"Umm… we did, and he said to tell you to go screw yourself too."

She cringed, remembering the coffee disaster only two days before.

"It's an internal joke we have," she managed to say. "Anything else?"

"Yeah, there's a cargo container in Florida too. We assumed he'd use his home if he's killing here, locally, but there's a 30-foot container on a long-term storage lease, parked at the Port of Palm Beach."

"Isn't that across from—" Tess started, hesitantly.

"Yeah, it's right across the water from his paid-in-cash home."

"Brooks, any installations of gym equipment?"

"It's the weekend, so it's been hard to find people. We're still waiting on two companies, but nothing so far."

She gritted her teeth.

"All right, call me as soon as you know, and Brooks? Pound on some damn doors, don't wait. I need that info now."

She grabbed a handful of fries and shoved them in her mouth, the first she'd touched since Catman brought her the plate.

"Ready for that warrant now?" Michowsky asked.

"Nope, I'm ready to go," she said, hopping off her stool and grabbing a few more fries. "That's it, we got him."

"Where? Where do you think you're going?"

"To the Port of Palm Beach. I'll visit that container first, then go to the house."

"The hell you are!" Michowsky said, grabbing her arm. "Maybe after you sleep it off."

"Huh? Take your fucking hand off me," she growled, frozen by his touch. "Before I break it."

Michowsky let go of her arm, like it was burning his skin, and raised his hands in a pacifying gesture.

Cat approached silently, his eyes dead serious, and his hands shoved deep in his pockets. He got near Michowsky, his eyes drilling into him, and put his hands on the counter.

"At least down some coffee, Winnett, what the hell?" Michowsky insisted.

"I'm about to break the law in many ways, Michowsky. Trust me when I tell you to back off. Sit this one out."

"What happened to getting a warrant?"

She didn't bother to answer, just left, car keys jiggling in her hand.

Michowsky shook his head, getting ready to chase after her, but turned to Cat.

"Why don't you stop her from driving?"

"Now why the hell would I do that?" Cat asked calmly, not a hint of humor on his face.

"That's why," Gary pointed at Tess's empty glasses. "Three mojitos are reason enough in my book."

"They're just virgin mojitos," Cat laughed.

"Huh?"

"Mint lemonades," he explained, continuing to laugh. "You're the only one who had any alcohol here. You shouldn't drive, buddy, all right?"

"Ah, hell…" Gary said, as he burst out the door. He ran to the corner of the parking lot, just in time to see Tess speeding by, flashing lights on. He waved behind her with both his arms high up in the air.

"Hey! Hey! Wait, for Chrissake," he shouted.

She hit the brakes, raising a cloud of dust, then put it in reverse and floored it until she was close enough. Then she put it in drive and floored it again, before he even got to close his door.

43

DUE PROCESS

"Listen to me," Gary asked, raising his tone. "Just listen, will you?"

She shot him a quick, angry glance, then returned her full attention to the road. She honked whenever cars didn't make room for her fast enough. Scoffing in frustration, she made a mental note to get a damn siren installed on her vehicle. Some stupid procedure... that the FBI agents didn't really have emergencies to justify it? She would've liked to have the bureaucrat who'd coughed up that particular procedure tied up and tortured, instead of Julie, while waiting for Tess to crawl through stupid traffic without a siren. That would serve him well. He'd probably rewrite the damn thing pronto.

"We can get a warrant, Winnett, why risk it?"

"It takes too damn long. I'm not letting that girl endure a minute more than we absolutely have to."

There was no arguing with that point, and Gary's silence confirmed it.

"Listen," she said, "I'm betting my career on two things right now. That Matthew Dahler is our unsub, and I'm 99 percent sure about that, and that we're going to find Julie at one of these addresses. But it's my career I'm betting, and I'm not willing to bet yours. Stay in the damn car when we get there. Have my back if I screw up."

He didn't say a word for a while. He sat there, resentful, eyes forward, scrunching his face, and scratching his head.

"All right, Winnett, have it your way." He sounded almost tired, resigned.

"Do you think we're going to find her?"

"I hope so. If we don't, I—we don't have any more leads, nothing. We're finished, and the consequences will be major, for all of us."

"Yeah," she replied quietly. He was right. If they made a mistake, there was no coming back from it. Entering someone's property without visible cause and without a warrant meant breaking the law. With the Dahlers in play, they'd never let any of them get away with it.

Tess slowed down as she approached the port entrance. The gates were open, and she didn't have to stop, but she did anyway, to get directions to the storage containers area from a marina employee. Then she killed her flashers and drove on, slowly, following the indications she'd received.

A chime, and Gary grabbed her phone to read her text message.

"Pull a 180," he said. "Suspension equipment was installed at the house, in the basement. It's confirmed."

Her tires squealed hard on the overheated asphalt, and Gary had to hold on to the door handle, groaning. She drove out of the marina at full speed, heading toward Highway 1, and took a left turn, heading south. It was a safer bet than any other route, but it crawled through countless busy intersections.

Gary pulled out his Glock and checked the ammo, then holstered it.

"Oh, no," Tess said coldly, "you're staying in the car. We agreed."

"*We* didn't agree. *You* dictated, and I gave up fighting you. I'm just too tired to argue with you, Winnett."

"We can't both go in there, Detective. Think straight for a second. What if he shoots us both, then what?"

"This is bullshit, and you know it. But hey, whatever. I'll stay here," he conceded, not concerned with hiding his crabbiness.

She turned on Dahler's street and killed the flashers. She pulled over two numbers shy of his address and cut the engine. There was no pedestrian traffic on the small street, typical for a late afternoon on a quiet weekend. She checked her weapon in a hurry, then got out of the car and closed the door slowly.

She walked as inconspicuously as she could toward Dahler's house, decided to attempt entry through the back. She checked her surroundings one more time, then entered the backyard, weapon drawn.

~~~~~

Watching her from a distance, Gary fidgeted for a few seconds, then grabbed his phone and dialed the FBI switchboard.

"Is there a Special Agent in Charge by the name Pearson? Could you please patch me through? This is an emergency."

As soon as he got off the phone, he drew his weapon and followed Tess into Dahler's backyard.

44

THE LAIR

It was getting dark, and that helped her remain invisible, covered in part by bushes and a six-foot-tall fence. Tess crouched and advanced slowly, looking out for floodlight sensors she could trip. Above the side entrance there was one, but if she dragged herself against the wall she could avoid triggering it.

She reached the door and tried the handle gently. It was locked. She reached out to her back pocket and extracted a credit card from her wallet. A few seconds later, the door was unlocked.

She opened it slowly, carefully, listening intently for any sounds coming from the house. She could hear the TV on the upper floor, and flickers of bluish light reached into the staircase. The side entrance, on the ground level, was half a story lower than the upper level, and half a story above the basement. Matthew's unofficial home was a split level.

She closed the door behind her without making a sound, and decided to start with the basement. She descended the stairs quietly, helped by the thick carpeting covering the wide steps. Once she reached the basement level, she cleared the laundry room first, holding her gun in her right hand. Her left held a tactical flashlight in the icepick grip, thumb on its pressure switch, and crossing underneath her right forearm, for added stability. Then she checked a couple of closets and an empty storage space built under the stairs.

Only one door left, and she opened it slowly, careful not to make a sound. The space she entered was large, probably extending underneath most of the living area in the house. She closed the door quietly, focusing on checking every corner.

Then she saw it, at the center of the room, the complicated harness sustaining the inert, naked body of a young woman. Her head hung, and her brown hair covered her face almost completely. Her back was covered in narrow lines drawn in dried blood. Tess gasped. She'd thought she was prepared for what she was going to find, after Doc Rizza's report, but there was no preparing for what she saw. The harness hung from the ceiling, and intricate lines and pulleys made it easy to control the position of the woman bound in it. A few feet in front of it, on a tile-covered counter, medical instruments, drugs, and sexual paraphernalia were lined neatly in trays and on the wall, the entire array of accessories for the sexual sadist they had profiled. Her eyes, fixed in horror on what she was seeing, missed the silent alarm on the wall. The LEDs under its display turned red and blinking.

She approached the harness quickly, focused on the young woman, trying to find out if she was still alive. She holstered her gun and checked her pulse, supporting her head gently. She was alive and barely conscious; she flinched under her touch and whimpered weakly.

"Shh… it's okay," she whispered. "I'm with the FBI. I'll get you home."

Julie whimpered weakly and tried to open her eyes but failed. She was heavily drugged. Tess searched for the light switch again, even if turning on the light meant getting Dahler's attention. She finally located it, right above the counter in front of her. She flipped the switch, and powerful fluorescent lights came on.

She rushed back to Julie and checked her pupils. The poor girl struggled, but couldn't keep her eyes open. She moaned quietly and tried to say something, but Tess couldn't make out what she said. Her face was swollen badly and her lower lip was distended and broken, covered in dried blood.

"It's okay, it's okay," Tess whispered, "you're going to be okay."

She gave up trying to revive her, and moved on to undoing her ties. She started with her right wrist, and fumbled with the leather cuff, her fingers trembling, scrambling to get the cuff undone, growingly ignorant of her environment.

She didn't see him coming, didn't hear a sound. She just found herself flying across the room and slammed against the wall, then she fell to the ground. Confused, her heart pounding in her chest, she lifted her head just in time to see Matthew Dahler coming at her with both fists. She evaded one of his blows and managed to grab his arm and use it as leverage to pick herself up, while she tried to reach for her gun. She didn't make it. Dahler clenched her, holding both her arms along her body, and dragged her kicking air next to the counter. He slammed her back hard against the counter edge and she gasped, pain shooting through her back bone. He grabbed a syringe that still held some fluid in it. As in a dream, Tess heard Julie whimpering louder, more desperate.

She watched with terror as the syringe needle approached her neck, and summoned all her strength to get free. He was powerful, his arms like steel pinning her in place. She managed to squeeze her knee up and hit him in the groin, not nearly as hard as she'd wanted, but it destabilized him and threw him off a bit. She seized the opportunity and sent an elbow into his stomach, then, as he crouched in reflex, hit him in the jaw with the same left elbow, supported with her right hand wrapped around her left fist. She heard his teeth clatter, and he groaned angrily, his deep blue eyes drilling into hers, glinting with rage. Suddenly he grunted and closed his fists so hard she heard his knuckles crack.

He came at her with both hands, grabbed her by the arms and threw her against the wall. She flailed and grabbed at him blindly, her left hand grasping a handful of his T-shirt. It tore as she slammed against the wall, leaving his upper arm exposed, where well-developed biceps moved under his skin. She gasped and froze, paralyzed, her eyes affixed on the tattoo she'd uncovered. A snake, entwined on a stick. The snake of her dark memories, of her nightmares. The same one, the unforgettable witness to her darkest hour. The image that had been haunting her for more than 10 years, but couldn't see clearly until now. A wave of nausea crippled her, and she whimpered weakly, crouching down, unable to pick herself up and fight back.

He frowned, prepared for her counterattack that didn't come. He grabbed her by the lapels with one strong grip and lifted her up, her back snug against the wall. Then he studied her carefully, up close, and smirked.

"Well, hello there," he said, "isn't life full of surprises today."

Frozen, she stared at his face, paralyzed by fear, by the wave of brutal memories that came rushing in from years of silence and darkness. She stared at the face she'd been looking for everywhere, in databases as well as on the streets, in stores, on TV. She'd finally found him, but his presence stunned her, turning her into a weak, trembling bundle of nerves and nausea.

Still holding her against the wall with one hand, he took her weapon with the other and threw it on the counter. Then he hit her across her face with his right fist, sending her to the floor, seeing stars. Her right cheek hit the tiles hard, and she saw a flash of light when her head bumped against the cold surface. She tried to lift her head, but his elbow held it in place, and his knee crushed her ribs. He pulled her hair toward the back and exposed her neck.

"There it is," he laughed, running a finger along her hairline, between her ear and her nape. "My mark. I recognize my earlier work."

She whimpered weakly, hating herself for her lameness. She stared into his eyes, so close to hers, remembering that flicker. That night long ago it had been dark, and he'd worn a mask, but that glint, that flash of savage, sadistic cruelty had been there then, and it was there now.

"You recognize me, don't you?" Dahler asked, squeezing the grip on her left shoulder.

By the way it hurt, and by the lack of strength and coordination in her left hand, that shoulder was broken, maybe dislocated. She cried, as pain shot through her bone.

"I knew you would," he added, laughing. "I tried to make our encounter as memorable as possible."

Her eyes moved back to the tattoo. The snake on a rod, the symbol of healing and medicine. The Rod of Asclepius it was called; she'd learned that reviewing thousands of tattoos in the federal database, looking for him, looking for Matthew Dahler, before she'd known his name.

"Unfortunately, you ran away, before I could finish my first masterpiece. Well, there's no time like the present, is there?"

She heard Julie whimper louder and louder, her whimpers turning into desperate cries. Somehow, Julie's cries fueled her courage, infusing strength in her veins, and she started to come out of her paralysis, thinking and planning her next move.

"Get up," he said, taking his weight off her. He took a few steps back and grabbed her gun from the counter, pointing it at her. "Move it."

It hurt to get up, her left arm hanging limp and her head throbbing in pain. She managed to stand, not taking her eyes off his.

"Yes, I ran away," she said, finding the strength to smile. "You know why? Scumbags like you were lined up for me to catch, that's why. I couldn't keep them waiting."

He approached her a step more, grinding his teeth and bringing the weapon one foot closer to her chest. She didn't budge.

"You know why I couldn't keep the scum of this earth waiting?" she continued, forcing the smile to stay on her lips.

"Because I had to clear the floor for you. You're going down next. You're going to learn all about rape in prison. It'll be a blast."

He took one more step forward, twitching his lips in anger.

"Shut the fuck up, bitch. You're at the wrong end of the gun."

She searched his eyes one more time, no matter how disturbing that felt, still making her sick. He wasn't the shooting type. He'd never shot anyone. He wanted her to suffer, to hang right there, where Julie did, screaming in pain. She repressed a shudder.

"I have to wonder," she continued, painting her voice with as much sarcasm as she could muster, "what was it like for you to realize I'd gone, and you're left there with your dick in your hand? Some rapist, huh?"

He took one more step, leaving less than a foot of distance between the gun's barrel and her chest. Her left arm was useless, or almost, and the throbs in her left shoulder almost unbearable, but she had to make a move for it, and that was the perfect chance.

"Safety's on, dumbass," she said coldly.

He diverted his eyes for a split second, looking for the safety, but that was enough for her. The heel of her right hand hit him in the chin with an upward motion, while she took a step to the right, and deflected the hand holding the gun with whatever strength she could summon. He dropped the gun and flailed, trying to maintain his balance, but she shot a knee to his groin hard, as hard as she could. He coiled forward, holding his abdomen with both hands, and bringing his head within range for a strong kick. A second kick to the groin sent him wobbling toward the counter, and she caught the opportunity to pick up her gun. She pointed it at him with cold eyes.

"Sigs don't have safeties, motherfucker." She pulled the trigger, sending a bullet ripping through his thigh. He screamed in pain and crouched near the wall, trying to stop the blood loss with both his hands.

Then she slapped him across the head with the butt of her gun and put his lights out.

"Now we're set, asshole," she muttered, and holstered her gun.

Julie was awake, her eyes badly glazed over and out of focus. She'd stopped whimpering when Tess shot Dahler and tried to say something, but Tess still couldn't understand what she said. Tess resumed undoing her cuffs, this time starting with the ankle cuffs, so she could stand on her own legs as soon as possible.

"We're almost ready now, just a second more," Tess said gently. "I promise you no one will see you like this."

Julie whimpered quietly, and a fresh tear rolled on her cheek.

Tess finished with the ankle cuffs and guided her feet to the ground gently, as gently as she could, but Julie still jolted and fidgeted each time she touched her. She was weak still, and couldn't support her own weight. Although her feet could touch the ground freely, her knees buckled and she hung in the harness, shaky and frail.

Then Tess moved to her waist, undoing the three buckles of the main support belt. Julie started whimpering again and struggled to say something.

"Just a few seconds more, I promise."

Julie whimpered louder, a note of panic in her weak voice, her glassy eyes staring somewhere behind Tess.

"Look," she muttered.

Tess turned to see just as the blow came. Something heavy hit the side of her head and sent her to the floor, seeing stars, confused. She crawled backward until she hit the wall, looking for the source of the attack.

"That's my son, you fucking bitch," the man said.

Then she saw him, Matthew Dahler's father, his back turned to her as he reached for a baseball bat at the end of the counter. She pulled her gun and shot him, just as he turned toward her. Her bullet put a hole in his temple. He landed on the floor with a heavy thump, blood pooling around his head, just a few feet away from his son.

Matthew grunted and opened his eyes. He stared at his father's body and smirked.

"Poor old Dad," he said, "always on my side, no matter what I did. I think deep inside he liked it. He liked the thought of getting back at Mom."

She trained her weapon on him and took a firing stance, crooked and weary, with no strength in her left shoulder.

"Here. Arrest me," Dahler continued, extending his hands, wrists joined together, ready to be cuffed. "I'll get out by tomorrow, as soon as I tell everyone about the good times we had in college, you and I."

Julie moaned quietly.

"This was personal, a vendetta, a setup. Everyone will see it."

"Get on the ground, face down, hands behind your head. Now," Tess said. She wasn't going to let this son of a bitch play games with her head.

"My mistake... My one and only mistake, staring me in the face," he laughed. "Can you see the headlines? We're going to have so much fun, you and I. Just like old times."

He winked, and Tess felt a wave of rage boiling her blood.

"On the ground. Now." Tess repeated.

"Or what? You can't shoot me; I'm unarmed and wounded. And I'll get out. She won't say a word," he said, tilting his head toward Julie. "She won't testify. She'll say it was consensual, and this was a setup. An old, vengeful girlfriend with separation issues turned federal agent. Silence can be purchased, you see. Freedom too."

Tess looked at Julie, keeping her gun trained on Dahler. She whimpered and closed her eyes.

"Please, make it stop," Julie whispered, barely audible.

Dahler laughed.

"It's never going to stop, not for her, and not for you, Theresa Winnett."

Tess couldn't hide her reaction, hearing her name spoken by that despicable man.

"Yes, I remember you," he continued, "the one who got away. The one who ran, and then became a fed. The one who never saw my face... Oh, how that must have pissed you off, huh, Theresa?"

She looked at Julie and nodded once. Julie nodded too, after holding her gaze for a long, loaded second.

"Please," Julie whispered.

"On the ground, now," Tess shouted, her gun trained on Dahler's chest. "This is your last warning."

Then she pulled the trigger, twice, double-tapping him in the chest, before he had a chance to react. Dahler froze in death, his eyes still open, conveying surprise as life left his body. She let out a long breath and holstered her gun.

"Come on," she said, freeing Julie from the last cuff. "Time to go now." She searched the room quickly and found a light blue, flat sheet. She wrapped Julie in it and helped her lie down on a couch, gently.

"I'll get us some help, okay? Now it's really over."

"Don't leave me," she mumbled, panic seeping in her voice.

"I won't. I'm right here." She pulled out her phone and speed dialed Gary's mobile number. She heard his phone ring close by, too close, right outside the window.

"Oh, no," she gasped, and ran outside.

There he was, lying on the grass, immobile, blood dripping slowly from a head wound. She checked for bullet holes and found none. His pulse was stable, but weak. As she called for help, she heard sirens closing in, and a SWAT truck pulled up, followed by SAC Pearson's SUV.

She waited for them just long enough to make sure Gary was taken care of. She rushed back inside and sat next to Julie, holding her hand. She listened closely as SWAT cleared the rest of the house, then some of the agents came downstairs.

One of the men offered to carry Julie to the ambulance. She whimpered and turned her head away.

"Don't touch her," Tess replied, squeezing her hand. "Let's have EMS in here with a stretcher. No one touches her, you hear me?"

45

AN INVITE

Tess sat on the rear bumper of an emergency rescue vehicle, while an EMT fussed over her. Her adrenaline was vanishing, and, in its absence, a wave of pain kicked in. Her left shoulder was in bad shape, her head pounded, and her ribs had caught too many of Dahler's direct hits. But none of that mattered, because Julie was alive and safe.

The EMT unpacked a blood pressure cuff, and she offered her right arm, absently. She still reeled from facing her own monsters, from finding herself inches away from the man who had permanently altered the course of her life, more than 10 years ago. She still reeled after killing him. Now, with him wiped off the face of the earth, maybe she could hope to live again.

"Winnett," SAC Pearson said, almost startling her.

"Sir," she said, turning her roughed-up face toward him.

"I have a slew of complaints to deal with. Palm Beach Sheriff's Office called twice about your condescension and disregard for procedure. Apparently, you reassigned workforce without an approved overtime budget. Then the governor called right after your visit with the Dahlers, citing your name, and saying you had inappropriate questions for one of the most respectable families in the area. Mrs. Feldman Dahler is over there, threatening hell because you entered without a warrant."

"Sir, I—"

"Don't interrupt, Winnett. We had this conversation already, about you letting people finish what they have to say." He ran his hand across his shiny scalp, then across his face. "It hurts me to say, but here goes. Great job," he said, letting out a long sigh. "For God's sake, I hope whatever method you used on this case never makes it in the Quantico manuals. What a bloody mess."

She smiled, a tiny twitch at the corners of her lips.

"I'm willing to bet your report will be a mess, just like this is," he continued, gesturing vaguely toward the street, blocked by emergency vehicles and flooded in red and blue flashing lights. "Don't make me wait too long."

"Yes, sir."

"And Winnett? When you come back from whatever R&R these guys prescribe, you'll get your new partner."

"All right," she replied, no longer feeling apprehensive. Maybe she was too tired, or maybe things could begin to be different.

"All right?" Pearson reacted. "What, you hit your head, or something?" He didn't wait for her answer. As usual, he just turned and walked away, ending the conversation Pearson-style.

She smiled for a while after he left, absentminded again, while the EMT removed her vest and cut her T-shirt to evaluate her shoulder. His fingers danced on her skin, and she no longer cringed inside. She took out her phone and retrieved SSA McKenzie's number from memory. She gave his name a long look, but then decided to call him later, from a more private setting. It was time for her healing to begin.

"This will need X-rays and probably surgery to set it," the EMT said. He was a young man, not even 30, with steady, cool fingers and a calming demeanor. "Some ligaments and nerves might be torn. Then you'll need other X-rays too. We'll take you in."

"Oh," she reacted, not thrilled with the perspective. She wanted a hot shower and one of Cat's burgers and fries. Make that a double, with cheese and bacon and pickles. Artery-popping, soul-mending, Cat therapy. Then she remembered something, and her blood froze in her veins again, and a feeling of revulsion hit her hard.

"Hey, do you mind checking here, on the hairline?" she asked, exposing the left side of her neck to the EMT. "I can't see… what's there? Something like a scar, maybe?"

"This is nothing; it's not even bleeding," the EMT said. "It looks old."

"Yeah, but what is it?"

He touched her skin with his gloved finger.

"There are three parallel lines, very thin. Like shallow cuts or something. You don't remember getting these?"

"No," she shuddered. "I don't. But it was years ago, so it doesn't matter. How's my partner, Gary Michowsky?"

"He's fine. He has a concussion; he's going in too."

"Is he conscious?"

"Yeah, he's over there, giving us trouble. Cops, what can you expect?" The EMT scoffed and pointed at Gary, who sat on his stretcher instead of lying down, while two EMTs were struggling to keep him in place.

"Give me a minute, will you?" She hopped off the ambulance bumper, instantly regretting it, as the abrupt move sent waves of throbbing pain to her shoulder and her head. She went over to Michowsky's stretcher and put her hand on his shoulder.

"Lie down. It's over," she said. "You can afford to relax."

"I'm fine. I don't want to be carried around like a baby. It makes me dizzy."

She leaned closer and whispered in his ear.

"Lie down, or I'll tell everyone about your midlife crisis." Then she winked at him, and watched him lie down, letting the EMTs secure him on the stretcher. "We're going to the same X-ray party, you and me. So relax. Maybe someday you'll tell me what the hell you were doing in Dahler's backyard, when you were supposed to stay in the damn car." She hesitated, and smiled at the ground. "Thanks for having my back," she added.

He waved her away, and she turned to leave.

"Winnett?"

"Yeah."

"Maybe we can grab a mojito after we're done with this mess, huh? A real one."

She grinned and continued to walk away.

"Hey, Winnett?" he called again.

She turned *on* her heels, feigning frustration, but smiling still.

"What now?"

"You know, for a stuck-up fed bitch, you ain't that bad."

~~ The End ~~

If *Dawn Girl* had you totally enthralled and gasping at the twists, then you have to read more captivating page-turners by Leslie Wolfe!

Read on for a preview from:

THE WATSON GIRL

She's young, she's beautiful, and she's a serial killer's loose end.

~~~~~~~~

THANK YOU!

A big, heartfelt thank you for choosing to read my book. If you enjoyed it, please take a moment to leave me a four or five-star review; I would be very grateful. It doesn't need to be more than a couple of words, and it makes a huge difference. This is your shortcut: http://bit.ly/DawnGirlReview

Join my mailing list to receive special offers, exclusive bonus content, and news about upcoming new releases. Use the button below, visit www.LeslieWolfe.com to sign up, or email me at LW@WolfeNovels.com.

Did you enjoy Tess Winnett and her team? Would you like to see her return in another story? Your thoughts and feedback are very valuable to me. Please contact me directly through one of the channels listed below. Email works best: LW@WolfeNovels.com.

If you haven't already, check out *The Watson Girl*, a gripping, heart stopping crime thriller and the second book in the Tess Winnett series. If you enjoyed *Criminal Minds*, you'll enjoy *The Watson Girl*. Or, if you're in a mood for something lighter, try ***Las Vegas Girl***; you'll love it!

CONNECT WITH ME

Email: LW@WolfeNovels.com
Facebook: https://www.facebook.com/wolfenovels
Follow Leslie on Amazon: http://bit.ly/WolfeAuthor
Follow Leslie on BookBub: http://bit.ly/wolfebb
Website: www.LeslieWolfe.com
Visit Leslie's Amazon store: http://bit.ly/WolfeAll

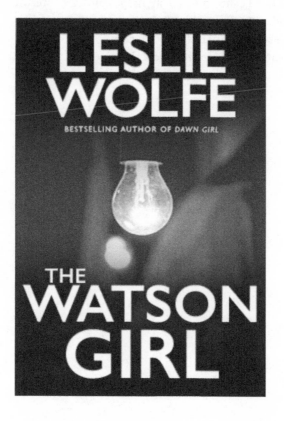

1

Cold-Blooded Beginning

Fifteen Years Ago

He knocked on the door with the barrel of his gun, then screwed on a silencer while waiting for someone to welcome him in. He checked the surroundings one more time. In the heavy dusk, shadows were long, and sounds were too muted to disturb the suburban peacefulness. A dog barked in the neighborhood somewhere, and the distant rumbling of remote highway traffic were so distant he could barely register them.

The two-story house had warmly illuminated windows on both floors, with white sheers that made the soft lights shimmer, and gave the massive, Colonial Revival home a fairy-tale look. The distant sound of a cartoon made it all the way to the dimly lit porch. He recognized the guttural voice of Daffy Duck.

Only one car was parked on the wide, three-car garage driveway, the silver minivan Rachel Watson liked to use while performing the functions of modern-day motherhood, with one or more of her three children loaded in the back seats. Allen Watson's car was nowhere in sight. But Watson always garaged his Benz, careful not to get a speck of dust on the custom paint that must have set him back a small fortune.

Even if he couldn't see his car, he knew Watson was home.

He knew it because he never left anything to chance. He'd waited patiently in his own car, parked discreetly around the corner and almost entirely hidden by the generous foliage of a thriving palmetto. He kept his eyes glued to the street, watching, stalking his target. Now he was ready.

He heard footsteps approaching the door, and he tightened the grip on his gun, hidden behind his back. The door swung open, and Allen Watson stepped quietly to the side, a tentative smile on his lips, and a hint of an intrigued frown creasing his brow. He waved him in, and he obliged, his gun firmly in hand. Watson closed the door, then looked at him inquisitively.

"What are y—" Watson's question faltered mid-word, as he registered the weapon in the now-visible hand and froze, taking wavering steps back until he hit the wall behind him. Watson's eyes, rounded in surprise, drilled into his, while words failed to come out of his gaping mouth.

"No... No..." he finally managed in a hoarse voice, weak and choked.

He hesitated a little and took his time to raise the gun higher, aiming for Allen's chest from only a few feet away. Then the sound of tiny feet pattering on the hardwood upstairs preceded a high-pitched voice, resounding loudly above their heads.

"Who is it, Daddy?"

He looked up briefly and saw two of Watson's kids staring down at them, dressed in colorful pajamas, their hands gripping the balusters supporting the balcony banister above the main living room.

"No..." Watson whispered. "Please..."

He couldn't delay anymore.

He pulled the trigger twice, in rapid sequence, and Watson fell to the ground in a motionless heap as the terrified shrieks of the two children pierced his ears. He lunged up the stairs, climbing three steps at a time, then ran toward the bedrooms. Within a few leaps, he caught up with the two screaming children. Then silence engulfed the home once more, as he searched the house room by room, looking for the third kid.

The light was off in the last bedroom, and the pajama-clad offspring was lying on her belly, arms folded under her chin, facing away from the door and watching cartoons on a tablet. The sound coming from the small device was unexpectedly loud, shrieking and grating like only cartoons can sound. Why she couldn't watch them on TV with the other two was of no concern to him. The bluish light emanating from the tiny screen contoured the kid's head like a surreal halo, drawing a bullseye for his weapon.

Soon he was finished upstairs and ready to go back downstairs, when a knock on the front door made him freeze mid-step. He pulled back, closer to the wall, and held his breath. Worried, he checked the windows next to the main door, only partly covered by curtains, then he shifted his gaze to Watson's body, collapsed just a few feet from that door.

The visitor might see his body through the open curtains. All he had to do is want to peek inside, and lean to the side a little. Damn!

The knocks repeated, a little louder and longer this time, followed by the doorbell chime. Then he heard a man's voice, suppressed by the massive door.

"Hey, it's Ben from next door. I have your cordless drill." The man stopped talking, knocked a couple of times more, then continued, "I'll leave it here, on the porch. Thanks, buddy!"

The unwanted visitor went away, his footsteps loud and heavy, but almost indistinguishable against the animal voices on TV. He breathed slowly, calm, calculated.

A moment later, he made his way through the sprawling first floor cautiously, looking for Rachel Watson. He listened intently, and somewhere beyond Daffy Duck's nasal voice, he heard clattering noises coming from the distant kitchen. A hint of a smile stretched the corner of his lip and curled it upward as he headed there with silent, feline steps.

He didn't know how long everything had taken, but it was time to go. The sound of sirens in the distance brought an urgency to his departure, and he left the home quietly and hurriedly, after checking the undisturbed, peaceful surroundings once more, paying thorough attention to every detail. The home across the street had its main floor flooded with light, with all the curtains pulled aside, allowing the yellowish shimmer to overflow into the street. The family there was on display while they went about their business. He frowned. People should be more concerned with their privacy. With people like him.

He decided to sneak behind Rachel's minivan and screen the surroundings once more before heading back to his car. He crouched a little, and within a few steps, he was hidden behind the minivan, careful not to touch it. He looked at nearby homes and listened for any sounds that didn't belong. His frown deepened with the nearing sound of police sirens, but then he looked up and froze, feeling his blood turn to ice.

There was a decal on the back window of the minivan, the stick-figure caricatures of a happy family, showing a man, a woman, a boy, two girls, and a cat, all exhibiting anatomically impossible smiles.

A sickening stab of uneasiness pierced his gut. The two kids he'd downed on the hallway were Allen's oldest two, a boy and a girl. Now, staring at that ominous decal, he realized he'd barely given the third kid a decent look before he'd pulled the trigger and returned downstairs. The room was dark. The kid's chin rested on her folded arms, near the floor. Her hair... he didn't remember. Allen's youngest had long, blonde curls. But now, no matter how hard he tried, he couldn't remember seeing the kid's hair. Just the stupid blue pajama with the Cars themed design. The bluish halo. No curls.

That was a big problem. Or was it?

He crouched closer to the ground and groaned, rubbing the deepening frown on his forehead furiously, as if that friction would solve any problems or hold any answers.

"Think, think!" he whispered angrily, staring at the offending decal.

It had to have been Allen's youngest. Everyone else was accounted for, including the cat, whose threatening, phosphorescent eyes had followed his moves from the top of the kitchen cupboard as he'd dealt with Rachel. He'd let the cat live; it wasn't worth a bullet, because cats can't talk.

But this? This made no sense, he kept thinking, his eyes still glued to the decal. It clearly depicted two girls about the same age, because the respective stick figures were almost identical, down to the double pigtails with bows. The boy figure was a little larger than the girls' sizes. What was Rachel doing? Replacing the damn stickers every year? Probably.

Then, what was going on there?

Something was terribly wrong. He could feel it.

He listened some more, trying to pinpoint the location of the approaching police cars. Had someone called the police on him? He was sure the gunshots had been quiet enough, but maybe someone had seen the flickers of light through the windows. Maybe the neighbor returning the cordless drill had seen Watson's body through the open curtains. Maybe.

But perhaps there was still time to set things right.

He stared for a second at the back of his hand, slightly shaky in the dim light of dusk, then he decided to do what he had to do. He sneaked back inside the house, closing the door gently, quietly. He went straight upstairs and into the last bedroom. Then he started searching the house, moving quickly, room by room, gun held tightly in his sweating hand.

2

Back to Work

Present Day

Special Agent Tess Winnett leaned forward, closer to the mirror, studying the circles under her eyes with a critical, disappointed glare. Unforgiving and dark-hued, the subject of her disdain circled her eyes generously, tinting her eyelids and making the blue of her irises appear hollow and lifeless. She looked pale and her face drawn, her skin taut and almost translucent against the high cheekbones.

Makeup wouldn't hurt. Too bad she wasn't into that stuff.

It was her first day back at the office, after taking three endless weeks to recuperate after injuries suffered in the line of duty. A dislocated shoulder. Torn ligaments. A couple of broken ribs that still stabbed her side with every breath. But she was back, unwilling to spend another single day bored out of her mind, counting the hours, and pacing the floor between the 300 channels of crap television and the stack of novels she just didn't have the patience for.

It wasn't the physical injuries she thought to be the source of her pallor; it was the monsters that lurked inside, in the deepest recesses of her weary brain. The memories she wanted gone forever, but which refused to fade, the raw memories of that one terrible night, more than ten years before, when her life took an abrupt turn for the nightmare. A night when she was the powerless victim fighting for her life, not the fearless FBI agent she had become.

Those wounds were still painful, still making her go through life in a constant state of hypervigilance, although her assailant couldn't hurt her anymore. Those wounds hurt much worse than a bunch of cracked ribs could ever hurt.

Focused on her physical fitness and most likely oblivious to the rest of her baggage, her doctor had prescribed six weeks off, with the last two spent in daily physiotherapy sessions, strength building, and mobility exercises. She had pleaded and threatened, but he'd already spoken with her supervisor, FBI Special Agent in Charge, or SAC Pearson, as she liked to shorten his title, advising him she couldn't return to duty for medical reasons. When she'd heard that, she'd flipped, turning on the doctor with the full force of her irrational anger, and accused him of everything she could think of, from violating patient confidentiality to simply being an inconsiderate, selfish, cover-your-ass kind of jerk, the type who shouldn't be allowed to wear a doctor's badge at any time in his life.

That didn't get her too far. The doctor scoffed hearing about patient confidentiality violations, and reassured her he'd only shared the six weeks' rest order with SAC Pearson, and none of the details. Yet, miraculously, later that same day, he agreed to let her off with three weeks, if she were to perform only light duties, as in sitting behind a desk and doing paperwork.

Hell, no.

But at least she could set foot inside the federal building again; the FBI had restored her credentials. The rest was up to her, right? A crooked smile appeared shyly in that bathroom mirror, then extended to a full-blown grin, engulfing her eyes and making her dark circles almost disappear.

She was back. That was all that mattered.

"Welcome back, Winnett," a woman greeted in passing, then slammed the door of the last stall behind her.

Tess jumped out of her skin. She hadn't heard the woman come into the bathroom; she just heard the voice behind her, too damn close when she thought she was alone and safe. Her heart raced and her hands shook a little. She focused for a few seconds on her breathing. In. Out. In. Out.

"Thanks," she finally replied, a little hesitant, then let out a long breath, steadying herself some more.

Was she really ready to be back? She'd better be. *Wake the hell up, Winnett.*

She stared at herself a little more, building confidence for the meeting with SAC Pearson. She'd come in that morning to find a sticky note on her desk, with a quick message, "See me first thing." The message was signed by Pearson, his scribbled name evolving from block letters to a pseudo-signature, overall illegible. But she knew who it was, anyway.

SAC Pearson. Ugh. Her boss, who'd put her on notice a few times already, and who wasn't going to take any more crap from her. A man who'd completed twelve years of service as a profiler with an enviable case record, a case record only she exceeded. He scored 98 percent; she scored 100 percent. Tiny difference, great meaning. She was sure the two percentage points were front and central on her boss's mind, at least some of the time. But, most of all, Pearson was an experienced profiler who would take one look at those black circles under her eyes and send her packing, out for three more weeks of going nuts in her apartment.

She pursed her lips, considering her options, then cleared her throat quietly.

"Hey, Colston, would you happen to have any makeup on you?"

"Uh-huh, here you go," the woman replied, offering her purse under the stall door. "Knock yourself out."

"Thanks," she replied.

She took the offered purse and put it on the counter, but hesitated a little before unzipping it. She struggled invading someone's privacy like that, despite being invited to. How different other people were. How... unsuspicious, and trusting, and open. Calm. Caring. Unassuming. As she unzipped the purse, she felt a pang of envy. She just wished she could be like that, like everyone else out there who shared, trusted, and let their guard down every now and then.

Colston's purse held a treasure trove of makeup items, and she stared, puzzled at the pile of little objects, unsure what to use.

"This is what you'll need," Colston said, picking up a concealer from the pile. Her hand dripped water into the open purse, but she didn't seem to care.

Tess's breath caught, but she swallowed and managed to thank her. How come she hadn't heard Colston flush, or seen her wash her hands? She'd definitely washed them, seeing as she was now drying them thoroughly with a paper towel. What kind of field agent lets people creep up on them like that? She needed to get a grip.

She hid her frown and applied the concealer quickly, with her finger, and smiled with gratitude.

"I'd also put on a little bit of blush. You're too pale. Here, let me," Colston offered, and quickly touched up Tess's cheeks with a thick brush, bringing color to her alabaster skin. "Perfect, there you go. Much better."

They walked out of the restroom together, but then parted ways, as Tess swung by her desk to grab her notepad before heading toward Pearson's office.

There he was, sitting at his desk, with his completely bald head lowered, as he read through the pages of a dossier, flipping through it impatiently and pressing his lips together, a definite sign of annoyance. He'd taken off his jacket and rolled up his shirtsleeves, which meant he was going to be in the office for at least a few hours.

She knocked on the doorjamb and waited silently. He waved her in, without lifting his eyes from the pile of paperwork. She stood and let her eyes wander on the few items adorning Pearson's office. Behind him, taking a shelf in a half-empty bookcase, a cluster of three framed pictures showcased Pearson's family. His wife, a little overweight, was a warm, affectionate woman who held his hand with confidence in a family picture that included their two children.

The other two images were college graduation portraits of his sons, the professional type that higher-end colleges offer on the day of the ceremony. Both boys had their mother's kindness in their eyes; they were younger, milder versions of their father. She wondered if the harshness in Pearson's features was genetic or acquired. She studied the two vertical ridges that flanked his puckered lips, the permanent frown lines on his tall forehead, and the tension in his jaw. Probably his nature.

Finally, Pearson looked up and frowned a little deeper.

"Sit down, Winnett."

She obliged.

"So, you're back. Early."

"Sir."

"Welcome back. Are you up for it?"

"Thank you, sir. Yes, I am."

He rubbed his forehead and pinched the bridge of his nose where glasses had left reddish marks on his skin. Then he leaned back in his chair, deep in his thoughts.

"I have a few things for you," he finally said. The tone of his voice didn't promise anything good.

She nodded, but didn't say a word. She shifted in her chair nervously, but then willed herself to sit still.

"First, there's the issue of your latest case. There will be a formal review of that entire development. It's scheduled to start in two weeks."

"A formal review? May I ask why?"

"My question is, do you really need to ask why?" He drilled his eyes into hers until she lowered her gaze and stared at the floor. "Yes, you've closed the case. Yes, you added one more notable notch to your belt. But the review committee has become aware that some of your stats are not that good."

"Which stats?" She knew she had an impeccable case record, so it couldn't be that. Then what?

"Your kill ratio's higher than everyone else's. You have been cleared in every shooting, but there was something about your last case that got their attention."

"Sir, I—"

"Let me finish, Winnett. I suggest you let the committee finalize the formal review and make their recommendations. Like I said, you've already been cleared in each shooting, so you're fine."

She waited for a full second before speaking.

"Sir, with all due respect, I'm not fine. A formal review can be a career killer."

He stood abruptly, started pacing the floor, and buried his hands deep inside his pockets.

"There's nothing you *can* do, Winnett. There's nothing anyone can do. Let things happen, and don't rock the boat. But it wouldn't hurt you to arrest a suspect for a change, instead of shooting them."

She stared quietly at the floor, feeling the sting of frustration.

"Understood," she eventually replied, managing to refrain from disputing everything that was wrong with the system.

Pearson sat back at his desk, and his frown deepened.

"Second item on the list is definitely not helping you with the upcoming review." He cleared his throat, then continued. "I would like you to work with a partner for a while."

"Oh?" she said, looking at Pearson with poorly hidden annoyance. She didn't want a partner, but she knew it was bound to happen, sooner or later. Pearson had been clear about it. But still. "We're not required to have permanent partners in the FBI, so I was—"

"Don't quote statute on me, Winnett. I still get to decide who does what here, and with whom. That clear?"

"Yes, sir. But that means you actually want me supervised, rather than—"

"Winnett!"

She froze. She didn't want to push him too far, but she didn't feel she deserved it either. Where could she draw that line, between taking direction from her boss and standing up for herself?

"For now, there isn't anyone available to work with you," he said, then glared at her as her relief must have been too obvious. "But I want you to consider having a partner as a next step in your career. It will help you a great deal, and it will help with people's perceptions about you."

"What perceptions?"

"That you're not a team player. That you don't care about how others feel, or about their results; just about getting case after case solved, as fast and as good as possible."

"Umm… and what's wrong with solving cases fast? That's my job!"

"The perception is that you don't care who you hurt in the process. You have to fix this perception, Winnett. You have to, and I'm not kidding. Regain the trust and respect of your colleagues, and make sure you can demonstrate you belong on this team. There's no room for solo artists here, Winnett, regardless of your case record. We're all part of a team, and we have to act like it."

She bit her lip. How the hell was she supposed to do that? Interactions like she'd just had in the bathroom with Colston were so rare, they only proved the rule by being the exceptions. They were enjoyable though, she had to admit.

"I worked just fine with Mike. I think I demonstrated that. But Mike's gone. He's dead."

"Listen, Winnett," Pearson continued, loosening his tie with a frustrated sigh. "No matter what you, or I, or anyone else would be willing to do, Mike's not coming back. No matter how much you blame yourself, or how much you decide you can't work with anyone else. It's time to move on, Winnett. Don't let it destroy your career." He fell silent for a second, letting his loaded gaze say the words he didn't speak.

She lowered her eyes again, not sure what more she could say.

"Then, there's the problem with the governor," he continued.

Tess sighed quietly and refrained from visibly rolling her eyes.

"He called with your name, twice, while you were working your latest case. Twice!"

"He gets calls from all the ritzy people I happen to bother during my—"

"Winnett!" he snapped. "Don't you think I know how the wheels turn? But you have to be smart about it! At some point, he could call and ask me formally to make you another governor's problem! No other agent in this branch has your kind of track record. They all solve cases, maybe not with your record of achievement, but definitely with less noise and disruption. With fewer complaints." He paused for a little while, as if trying to figure out what to do with her. "Be smart about these things, Winnett," he eventually continued. "Don't allow your behavior to cast a shadow on the reputation of this team, internal and external. Do you understand?"

"Perfectly," Tess managed. She was going to have to figure out how to get people to like her, to accept her. She had to change, and that was never easy. She needed to soften around the edges a little, but somehow still be able to do her job, maintain her edge. She had no idea how to do that, or where to start.

"I'm giving you an assignment," Pearson moved on.

She lit up, feeling anticipation and excitement elevate her gloomy spirits.

"There's a serial killer on death row at Raiford; Kenneth Garza."

"Ah, The Family Man," she added.

"Yes, The Family Man," Pearson confirmed. "His execution date is set and it's approaching. It's in three weeks or so, on the twenty-second. I'd like you to study his file, and go there for an interview. Make sure everything rings right, that we've crossed every T and dotted every I, and we're not going to have any surprises in his final hour. Are you familiar with his case?"

"No, just with his reputation. It was before my time."

"Jeez, Winnett, you're something else. Before Winnett and After Winnett, is that it? How arrogant can you get?" The irritation in Pearson's voice was discernible, almost physical in the unusually elevated pitch.

"No, sir. I meant I am familiar with all the serial killer cases closed during my tenure."

"Of course, you are," he scoffed, "because you closed them!"

"No, sir. I meant I'm familiar with all serial killer cases closed by the Bureau, regardless of who closed them, since the day I joined the FBI ten years ago."

Pearson's jaw dropped a little, but then he regained his composure, apparently unperturbed. She felt the urge to smile, but knew better and didn't.

He continued, "Okay, so get familiar with Garza's file, and go have a chat with him before he fries."

"Yes, sir," she said and stood, ready to leave.

He pointed at a stack of boxes, already loaded on a dolly and parked in the corner of his office, near the door. She raised her eyebrows.

"Garza's file," he said, then resumed reading the documents he was studying before her arrival.

She grabbed the dolly's handle and winced. Sharp pain stabbed her side. She shifted the handle to her other hand and managed to roll out of there without hitting the walls or denting any furniture.

Relieved, she focused on pulling the dolly awkwardly on the thick carpet, looking behind her at each step to make sure the stack of boxes still held on. Then she ran into someone, head-butting into a muscular chest, white shirt clad, and

boasting a colorful necktie. She gasped, as the impact sent a wave of pain into her shoulder.

"What the hell, Winnett, watch it," Donovan said. He was the best and brightest on their analysis team. An analyst, not a field agent, despite his numerous applications, and his solid, unwavering enthusiasm.

She tightened her lips and swallowed a long, detailed curse.

"Sorry, Donovan. Are you okay?" A hint of sarcasm seeped in her voice. He shook his head.

"And to think you wield a weapon for a living. Huh... I wonder who approved that," he replied with biting humor.

That stung, and, within that angry split second, she felt the urge to tell Donovan it was the same people who'd denied him *his* application to become a field agent. But then she remembered her commitment to herself and Pearson and swallowed that angry comeback.

"Um, once again, sorry," she said softly, then turned to leave.

Donovan's face dropped, seemingly unsure how to react. The Tess Winnett he and everyone else knew would have ripped him to shreds for far less. He stood there, riveted in place, watching her wince while she struggled to pull the loaded dolly.

"By the way, in case you want to know: you push the dolly; you don't pull it with loads that high," he offered, then turned away and resumed his course toward the elevators.

Gah... She closed her eyes for a second, trying to envision a space where she could let the angry cuss words she felt like shouting at Donovan's broad shoulders actually be articulated, to let off some of the pressure she felt. No such place.

She turned the dolly around and started pushing it, suddenly seeing how easy it was to make it across the wide floor to her desk. She smiled, almost forgetting about the review committee and the weight of the thousands of pages detailing the many gruesome murders perpetrated by The Family Man.

She was back. That was all that mattered.

~~~End Preview~~~

Like *The Watson Girl*?

Buy It Now!

ABOUT THE AUTHOR

Meet Leslie Wolfe, bestselling author and mastermind behind gripping thrillers that have won the hearts of over a million readers worldwide. She brings a fresh and invigorating touch to the thriller genre, crafting compelling narratives around unforgettable, powerhouse women.

Her books are not only an adrenaline-packed ride, but they're also sprinkled with psychological insights, offering readers an immersive, authentic experience that goes beyond conventional suspense.

You might know her from the Detective Kay Sharp series or have been hooked by Tess Winnett's relentless pursuit of justice. Maybe you've followed the dynamic duo Baxter & Holt through the gritty streets of Las Vegas or plunged into political intrigue with Alex Hoffmann.

Recently, Leslie published *The Girl You Killed*, a psychological thriller that's pure, unputdownable suspense. This standalone novel will have fans of *The Undoing, The Silent Patient,* and *Little Fires Everywhere* on the edge of their seats.

Whether you're into the mind games of Criminal Minds, love crime thrillers like James Patterson's, or enjoy the heart-pounding tension in Kendra Elliot and Robert Dugoni's mysteries, Leslie's got a thriller series for you. Fans of action-packed writers like Tom Clancy or Lee Child will find plenty to love in her Alex Hoffmann series.

Wolfe's latest psychological thriller, *The Surgeon*, will have you racing through the pages gasping for breath until the final jaw-dropping twist, delighting fans of *Gone Girl* and *The Girl on the Train.*

Discover all of Leslie's works on her Amazon store, at Amazon.com/LeslieWolfe. Want a sneak peek at what's next? Become an insider for early access to previews of her new novels, each a thrilling ride you won't want to miss.

- Email: LW@WolfeNovels.com
- Facebook: https://www.facebook.com/wolfenovels
- Follow Leslie on Amazon: http://bit.ly/WolfeAuthor
- Follow Leslie on BookBub: http://bit.ly/wolfebb
- Website: www.LeslieWolfe.com
- Visit Leslie's Amazon store: https://Amazon.com/LeslieWolfe

BOOKS BY LESLIE WOLFE

TESS WINNETT SERIES

Dawn Girl
The Watson Girl
Glimpse of Death
Taker of Lives
Not Really Dead
Girl With A Rose
Mile High Death
The Girl They Took
The Girl Hunter

STANDALONE TITLES

The Surgeon
The Girl You Killed
Stories Untold
Love, Lies and Murder

DETECTIVE KAY SHARP SERIES

The Girl From Silent Lake
Beneath Blackwater River
The Angel Creek Girls
The Girl on Wildfire Ridge
Missing Girl at Frozen Falls

BAXTER & HOLT SERIES

Las Vegas Girl
Casino Girl
Las Vegas Crime

For the complete list of books in all available formats, visit:

Amazon.com/LeslieWolfe

Made in United States
North Haven, CT
08 August 2023

40064023R00178